DEADLY
EDITIONS

DEADLY EDITIONS

A Scottish Bookshop Mystery

Paige Shelton

MINOTAUR BOOKS
NEW YORK

First published in the United States by Minotaur Books, an imprint of St. Martin's Publishing Group

DEADLY EDITIONS. Copyright © 2021 by Paige Shelton-Ferrell. All rights reserved. Printed in the United States of America. For information, address St. Martin's Publishing Group, 120 Broadway, New York, NY 10271.

www.minotaurbooks.com

Library of Congress Cataloging-in-Publication Data

Title: Deadly editions / Paige Shelton.
Description: First edition. | New York : Minotaur Books, 2021. | Series: A Scottish bookshop mystery ; 6
Identifiers: LCCN 2020047434 | ISBN 9781250203908 (hardcover) | ISBN 9781250203915 (ebook)
Classification: LCC PS3619.H45345 D43 2021 | DDC 813/.6—dc23
LC record available at https://lccn.loc.gov/2020047434

Our books may be purchased in bulk for promotional, educational, or business use. Please contact your local bookseller or the Macmillan Corporate and Premium Sales Department at 1-800-221-7945, extension 5442, or by email at MacmillanSpecialMarkets@macmillan.com.

First Edition: 2021

10 9 8 7 6 5 4 3 2 1

For Beverly

DEADLY EDITIONS

ONE

The bell above the bookshop's front door jingled. I scooted my chair and stood from where I'd been working at the back table and peered around the dividing half wall. I saw Rosie at her desk. She'd been so quiet that I wasn't sure, but there she was, standing to help the customer who had entered. I could get back to my project. However, when I caught sight of who'd come in, I paused again, curious enough to join Rosie and Hector—the cutest dog in the world—up front.

A young man had come through the door. He stomped snow from his boots and swiped some off the top of his pillbox-like cap before standing at attention. "Ms. Delaney Nichols, please," he said.

"Can I help ye?" Rosie asked as I made my way to the front.

Suited in black from head to toe and wearing that unexpected cap, the young man squinted at her. "Are you Ms. Nichols?"

"I'm Delaney," I said as I put my hand on Rosie's arm. He seemed harmless enough.

"Aye?" He smiled. "I have a note for you."

He and I met halfway, and he handed me the folded note.

"Thank you," I said automatically.

The messenger nodded, smiled again, and then left as if in a big hurry to get out of there. I blinked at his exit, shared some raised eyebrows with Rosie, and then read the note aloud:

Ms. Delaney Nichols,
Your presence is requested this afternoon at 2:00 at Deacon Brodie's Tavern to discuss Ms. Shelagh O'Conner's vast collection of rare and valuable books. Please don't be tardy.
Sincerely and with gratitude,
Ms. O'Conner's representative, Mr. Louis Chantrell.

"Well, isn't that strange?" I said. "What about the collection would we be discussing?"

"Aye." Rosie moved closer to me and peered down at the note.

"Do you think it's . . . for real? Maybe the books are for sale?" I asked.

"I dinnae ken."

I laughed once and glanced at the time. It was slightly after noon. "Do you think I should just go and find out?"

Hector, a miniature Yorkie who lived with Rosie but took care of us all, trotted to my feet and put his paws on my boot. I lifted him to the crook of my arm.

"Do ye ken who she is?" Rosie asked.

"I do, but only because of an article I read recently. It was about her and her books, not to mention her mansion and all her money. Brigid wrote it."

"Aye. I ken who she is and I read that too."

"You're reading Brigid's articles now?" I said with a small smile.

Rosie's mouth quirked. "Sometimes."

"She's really good, huh?"

"Not as good as you."

"I'm not a journalist."

"Och, that's not what I meant."

I laughed. "Well, thank you, but she *is* a fine journalist."

Rosie, my grandmotherly coworker, was protective of me and my recent marriage to Tom Shannon, handsome pub owner—who had also, at one time, been boyfriend to Brigid McBride, pretty blonde newspaper journalist. Brigid and I had become friends, sort of, but that hadn't stopped her from barely reining in snarky comments regarding Tom's previous commitment issues. To his credit he was ashamed of his behavior regarding their breakup, and he'd apologized to Brigid. She wasn't ready to let it go.

Rosie was the most loyal person I'd ever known, and she would always have a suspicious side-eye for Brigid. That was okay.

"Anyway," Rosie continued, "what do ye think? Are ye intrigued by the inveet?"

I looked at the note and then out the front window. I hadn't paid attention to where the messenger had gone. Grassmarket Square's first-of-the-season snowfall had turned the world into a winter wonderland.

"I wish I could ask someone more questions first. Maybe I could find"—I looked at the note—"Louis Chantrell."

Rosie shrugged. "I doubt it. It all seems purposefully mysterious and delivered with little time tae spare."

Briefly, I listened for a bookish voice. My intuition sometimes spoke to me, lent some guidance, using the voices of characters from books I'd read. But all was silent; there wasn't even enough information for my intuition to have an opinion.

"Yes, mysterious. Weird," I said.

"A wee bit. Are ye going?"

"I'm interested in any book collection, of course, but something about it feels manipulative."

"Aye, it does, but if ye want tae go, I dinnae think there'd be any harm done."

"It *is* a public place."

"Aye," she said with a distinctly doubtful tone.

"What?" I prodded, wondering what was bothering her.

Rosie looked at me a long moment. "I think ye should go, but I think ye should call Edwin first. Not because ye need permission from him but because he's met Shelagh a few times I think, and he can give you some insight as tae her personality." She nodded toward the note. "I doubt you'll be able to reach Mr. Chantrell."

"Good plan." I glanced at the time again. "Have you ever met Shelagh O'Conner?"

"Aye, a long time ago, she came into the shop. She didnae stay long but searched for some books. When she didnae find what she was looking for, she left and never came back in, as far as I ken."

"How does she know me?" I asked.

"Ye've been here a while. Ye have a reputation."

"Really? Well, I hope it's a good one."

"I believe it is." Rosie smiled, but only briefly. "Except with the local police—they might be a wee bit worrit about ye."

Inspector Winters, local police inspector and friend, had an esteemed place on my phone's favorite-numbers list, but it wasn't necessarily because I'd been in trouble. I'd just found myself in places where a variety of troubles had occurred, and I'd helped a little to clean up the messes. Inspector Winters and I got along just fine.

Still holding Hector, I made my way to the table in the back.

My younger coworker, Hamlet, usually worked in this space, but he wasn't in yet. I'd been the first one to the bookshop today and had been briefly worried that Rosie hadn't arrived before me as she usually did—it was cold and wintry out there—so I'd stayed on this side of the shop instead of moving to the other side, where my desk was located. By the time Rosie came in, fifteen minutes later, I was enjoying the snowy view and my cozy comfort too much to move.

The Cracked Spine, the Edinburgh bookshop that had called to me from over the sea—*Leave your safe Kansas world and come live an adventure*—was made of two separate buildings that had, many years earlier, been remodeled and connected by a short hallway up a flight of stairs on each side. I'd named the two sides the light side and the dark side, but simply because the light just wasn't quite as good over there—until you went inside my workspace, the warehouse, at the very back of the building. The warehouse was behind a locked door and topped off by a line of windows that, even when it was cloudy outside, let through plenty of natural light. With the help of a bright desk lamp or two, it was easy for me to work, day and night.

The small bookshop's light side, the side where the customers came in to browse and buy, had been homey today . . . well, once I'd turned up the old radiator. Even if I hadn't wanted to wait for Rosie, I might have stayed. The falling snow out the front windows made a beautiful backdrop for the pedestrian traffic moving through Grassmarket Square. I'd seen it snow in Edinburgh the year before, but it was always hard to resist a season's first fall.

The book-filled old wooden shelves were in decent shape, and anything newer would have seemed misplaced atop the scuffed marble floor. The shelves were more organized than I'd imagined I could make them. But I had worked hard, and my system was pretty good. My current project was to create a master list of the location of each and every book, not just the sections they were shelved in. It was a huge process, but I was ready to tackle it, and I'd been jotting down some spreadsheet ideas when the messenger came in.

Rosie had an office on the dark side too, but mostly she sat at her desk on this side. She preferred talking to customers, welcoming them in with her innate warmth. I'd recently learned that she'd even sold a book to the queen a few years back. Yes, *that* queen.

Though Edwin MacAlister owned The Cracked Spine, and it seemed almost everyone knew who he was, it was Rosie who brought people back in time and time again.

I would be honored if my reputation at the bookshop were anywhere near hers, but I knew it wasn't. As I thought about the note, I decided that it must have been Edwin who'd told someone—Mr. Chantrell or Ms. O'Conner—that I was the person to work with if a large book collection were being discussed, perhaps put up for sale.

I was thrilled that Edwin trusted me with such tasks and not surprised that he might have forgotten to mention this one. Lately he'd been stepping away more and more from the bookshop. In his mid-seventies, he'd found a new romance with an Irishwoman who owned and operated a local restaurant. When he wasn't there, they were together somewhere else, enjoying everything from mundane everyday tasks to traveling the world. They'd recently returned from Australia.

It's why he'd hired me—so he could work as minimally as possible and have more fun in his older years. I was happy to accommodate, and his lady love had been a perfectly timed surprise.

Settling Hector on my lap, I grabbed my phone and rang Edwin.

"Lass, hello, how are you this beautiful snowy morning?" he answered.

"I'm well. You sound cheery."

"It's a lovely wintry day."

I smiled. "Yes, it is. Are you heading into the shop this morning?"

"I can if you need me."

"No, no, it's all right." I unfolded the note again. "A messenger just stopped by the shop and delivered a letter, but I'm wondering if you might know about it."

"Tell me more."

"It's from a representative of Shelagh O'Conner. It's signed by a man named Louis Chantrell. They've asked me to meet them this afternoon at Deacon Brodie's pub to discuss Shelagh's book collection."

"Aye? Of course, I know Shelagh some, and her love of books is legendary, but I don't know Mr. Chantrell. The invitation is completely fascinating."

"I thought so too, but I wondered if they'd heard about me because of you."

"No, not at all. Are you going to go?"

"Do you think I should?"

"Seems safe enough. Aye. If her collection is being put up for sale, I would most definitely be interested in it. No budget. Pay what you think they're worth."

I laughed. "I have the best job ever."

"No, lass. *I* do."

I laughed again. "All right. I'll keep you up to date."

"Have fun." Edwin disconnected the call before I could ask

another question. I was going to do as Rosie'd suggested and inquire about Shelagh's personality, but I put the phone down and looked at Hector. "I think I remember reading that there was something unusual about her collection. Do you suppose Hamlet still has a copy of that paper?"

Hector panted up at me as Rosie came around the corner. "What did Edwin say?"

"That I could buy the books no matter the budget. That sounds extreme, Rosie, but I appreciate the leeway. I didn't get a chance to ask about Shelagh's personality, but Edwin said he's aware of her love of books. He didn't even hesitate."

I turned in the chair and reached for the stack of newspapers Hamlet kept on top of a file cabinet. Brigid worked for one of Edinburgh's alternative papers, the *Renegade Scot*. Despite the fate of many of them, this one was defying all odds and doing very well, much of the credit belonging to Brigid herself. She could be highly irritating, but she was quite good at getting and writing a story, and that skill brought in lots of paying advertisers.

I found the edition from a couple weeks earlier and spread it open on the table. Hector stood up and put his front paws on the table so he could better read too. Rosie sat in a chair across from us.

"Here it is, the article about Shelagh O'Conner," I said. I read aloud, relearning that Ms. O'Conner was fond of all literature but most particularly anything written by Scottish native Robert Louis Stevenson. And though Ms. O'Conner enjoyed books like Stevenson's *Treasure Island* and others, it was his *Strange Case of Dr. Jekyll and Mr. Hyde* that she loved the most.

Ms. O'Conner had multiple shelves filled with copies of the short horror novel from the late 1800s, many of her copies considered priceless.

I looked at Rosie. "Is that what you meant about her personality?"

Rosie had fallen into thought. I didn't want to interrupt, but she was silent a long time.

"Oh, lass, it's a wee bit more than that. Ye might not want tae go after all," she finally said.

"Why?"

"Maybe Brigid simply isnae auld enough tae ken some things, things that happened a long time ago. It wasnae in the article, and I didnae even think aboot it until right this minute. Michty me."

Hamlet usually translated the Scots that my older friends spoke, but he wasn't here. "Michty me?"

Rosie looked at me. "It means I'm *surprised*. I should have remembered something sooner."

"Remembered what?"

"There's a story from back in the 1960s, I believe, back when Ms. O'Conner herself was caught imitating a beggar on the street; just like in that book, she dressed as a Mr. Hyde. She was even suspected of murder but was never officially arrested. I wish I could remember all the details."

"What? Really?" I looked at the article and then back at Rosie. "How does Brigid not know something so juicy?"

Rosie shrugged. "Maybe she's not as good as ye think."

Hector barked. I closed the paper.

"What else do you remember?" I asked.

"It was strange. Shelagh was strange. Oh, it's been such a long time, and she was young enough tae do strange things without being held too accountable, I suppose. When she was released, it all blew over. At least that's what I remember. Once that happened, the story disappeared. It was much more interesting to think that a young, rich woman who had everything was misbehaving, committing *murder*, rather than just dressing up and playing a part, roaming the streets."

"Did they catch the killer? Who was killed?"

"I cannae remember, Delaney. I'm sorry, but it's been a long time, and we all came tae know Shelagh as a lovely, philan-thropic woman who gives when it's most needed. She's very charitable."

This new information solidified my plans. "I'm going to that meeting. Want to come with me? Hamlet will be here soon, so he can watch the shop."

"No, lass, ye go and report back." She squinted. "It occurs to me, though, that ye might not know something else ye should. Deacon Brodie's Tavern—it's said that *Dr. Jekyll and Mr. Hyde* was at least partially inspired by the real Master Brodie."

"Who was Master Brodie?"

"A man who built cabinets, for Mr. Stevenson's family and others. He led a double life and stole from his clients. He went sae far as tae have duplicate house keys made so he could later sneak back in where he'd worked tae take the valuables."

"What happened to him?"

"He was hanged before he was an old man. A big crowd showed up to watch his execution, his posture proud and his clothing regal. He was quite the character. We learned about him in school. Now, that part I remember."

"Goodness," I said as the bell above the front door jingled again. Hector seemed to shrug as Rosie stood to greet whoever had come in.

I was still lost in the stories of Deacon Brodie, Dr. Jekyll, and Mr. Hyde—as well as Shelagh's strange behavior and the murder that Brigid McBride, fierce reporter, had forgotten to add to her story. What was going on here? Two o'clock couldn't come fast enough.

TWO

I wrapped the scarf around my head and was glad for the boots my new husband had recently gifted me when we heard that snow was on the way.

"Didn't you have snow in Kansas?"

"Of course we did. Lots of it. I just didn't think there was as much in Scotland, so I didn't bring my boots."

"You need boots."

Too anxious to sit still, I left the bookshop early and decided to first stop by Tom's pub, "The Smallest Pub in Scotland." Well, it was mine too now. We'd gone through all the legal things you were supposed to go through to ensure that it became mine and mine alone if something happened to Tom. He'd insisted, and I hadn't argued. I wasn't made for running a pub, and I really hoped Tom and I would never have to face a tragedy that would bring such a thing to fruition, but I understood the need to be prepared.

"Delaney, hello," Rodger said from behind the bar as I stepped inside. It wasn't busy—probably because of the snow and the fact that there wasn't any soccer (football) showing on the television secured to the ceiling in the front corner. There was only one customer in the place, and after he sent me a friendly smile, he turned his attention out the front window. I smiled back, but as I made my way to the bar, I wondered if I should have stopped to say hello. He didn't seem familiar, but there was something about the smile that made me wonder if I'd forgotten meeting him. Maybe I'd remember by the time I left.

"Hello, Rodger," I said.

"How are you today, Mrs. Shannon?" Rodger said with a nod.

I wasn't legally Mrs. Shannon. I'd kept my name, but I'd still answer to Tom's.

"Great. How are you?"

"Right as rain," Rodger said. "Tom's in the back, filling the mop bucket. He'll be out soon."

"Thanks."

"Can I get you something?"

"No thanks." I sidled up to a barstool just as Tom rolled the mop and bucket out from the back. He made even a mop and a bucket look good.

"Ah, my lovely wife," he said, though more reserved than usual, when he saw me. He directed the bucket on wheels my way and kissed me quickly. "What are you up to?"

"I'm off to be unfaithful, I'm afraid."

"Aye? That was quick. We've not been married even six months yet."

"I'm visiting another pub."

"I can live with that. Which one?"

I told Tom and Rodger about the messenger and showed them the note. The customer couldn't help but hear some of the conversation, but I noticed he tried hard not to look like he was eavesdropping. I noticed something else too: Tom glanced at the man with scrutiny, not curiosity. I took it as a cue to keep my voice low, but still, the pub was pretty small.

"Deacon Brodie's is a lovely pub," Rodger said. "Not as wonderful as this one, of course, but it's fun, particularly with the story attached to it."

"Aye, leave it to the Scots to honor a bad man because his story was intriguing." The customer rose from his chair.

I was so surprised by his interjection that I started slightly. He walked directly toward me, smiled, and extended his hand. "Name's Findlay Sweet. I'm a long-ago friend of your husband's. It's a pleasure to meet the lass who tamed him."

We shook, and I inspected him. He was much older than Tom, but probably not as old as Tom's father, Artair. Findlay's hair was dark steely gray; his eyes matched in color and were pleasantly framed by thick laugh lines. Three deep creases also rode across his forehead. His face held a serious expression, even when he smiled.

"You know each other?" I looked back and forth between them.

"We're buddies from our fishing days," Findlay said.

I looked at Tom. I didn't know he'd had fishing days.

Tom lifted an eyebrow and didn't smile. "Aye, for a while Findlay and I fished on a boat together. I worked for Mr. Sweet but didn't take to the life as much as he might have hoped."

"Aye." Findlay nodded slowly. "I did have hope." He cleared his throat and looked at me. "I've moved on from the lifestyle too. I'm a driver now."

"Oh. A good friend of mine drives a taxi."

"I'm not that kind of a driver." Findlay paused and seemed to look at Tom with something unfriendly in his eyes.

I was so perplexed I might have said aloud, *Huh?* I cleared my throat just in case.

"Always good to see you, Sweet," Tom said. But he didn't mean it. It was rare that he said something he didn't mean, but this time it was clearly his way of asking the man to leave.

A long, uncomfortable moment passed before Findlay nodded again and smiled only at me. "You are lovely. I wish you both the best, but you need to keep your eyes on this one. He can be shifty."

"Excuse me?" I said.

"Delaney." Tom put his hand on my arm. "It's okay."

"Is it?" Findlay said. "Time will tell, I suppose." He turned and walked out of the pub.

"What in the world was that?" I asked.

"Aye, boss, what was that?" Rodger echoed. "That man's been staring out the window nursing one wee drink for a couple hours. When you two spoke earlier, I didn't pick up on anything like . . . whatever that was."

"He wanted to make sure my new wife was aware I might not have been her best choice." Tom shrugged. "I wonder if he was just waiting for her to come in."

"That was a risk," I said. "How would he know I'd be in? What happened between the two of you? Did you steal his girlfriend or wife or something?"

Tom shook his head. "A story for another time. You've got to be on your way. Do you want to take my car?"

"No, I have boots, and it's not far," I stuck out one red-boot-clad foot and smiled. Deacon Brodie's pub wasn't far at all. It was kind of a shame I hadn't visited it—and all the other nearby pubs. I'd been to a couple in Edinburgh, but I'd neglected so many others. I would always choose Tom's over trying anything new. "I can walk there just fine."

"Those are lovely boots," Tom said.

Rodger whistled. "Nice."

We were all trying much too hard to move past the uncomfortable atmosphere Findlay Sweet had left behind. I hopped off the chair and kissed Tom. Rodger whistled again. As I made my way to the door, I glanced back. Tom was mopping the floor, not looking up, but Rodger was. He sent me a comforting smile and a wink. I wondered if he'd get the story from Tom, and I wondered if either of them would share it with me.

THREE

The façade of Deacon Brodie's Tavern did not disappoint. Snow-sprinkled plants hung in flower boxes above three gold entryway arches. Three windows above the arches made me think the pub had a second floor. And three more stone-walled stories above that told me the tavern was topped off by apartments—flats.

My first impression of the inside was "rich." An ornate carved ceiling capped a wooden bar, chocolate wood-paneled walls, a plaid carpet, and jam-packed liquor shelves. The inside wasn't huge, yet big enough for ten or so tables with chairs. It was bigger and busier than Tom's pub, but that wasn't a surprise.

A man appeared from a hallway on the other side of the bar and walked toward me, smiling as he made his way. He was built like Edwin, tall and thin. His legs moved almost as quickly and smoothly as Edwin's too. He wasn't young, but his bald head made it difficult to guess his age.

"Ms. Nichols?" he said as he stopped in front of me.

"Mr. Chantrell?" I guessed as I shook his outstretched hand.

"Aye. Louis, please. I'm so happy you are joining us."

"Frankly, I couldn't resist, and it's Delaney, please."

Louis laughed and nodded. "We like to do things with a certain flair. Ms. O'Conner insists."

"Thank you for including me."

Louis nodded and turned. "Come along," he said over his shoulder.

I followed, but we stopped in front of the bar.

"Can I offer you a drink?" Louis faced me. "We're not going up to the second-floor restaurant, but we can have whatever we want in the room we've booked."

"Water will be fine."

Louis looked at the bartender, who nodded. I thought we would resume walking again, but Louis did a double take and studied the bartender a moment longer.

"Do I know you?" Louis asked him.

The bartender was probably in his sixties, with short brown hair and pale skin. When he smiled, his ordinary face transformed into a handsome one.

"I'm not sure," he said, his accent as strong as Rosie's or that of my friends Elias and Aggie. "Do ye come into the pub a fair amoot?"

I knew "amoot" was amount and was silently thrilled that I could handle the translation, even as easy as it was.

"No, in fact I don't," Louis said. "What's your name?"

For a moment I thought the bartender wouldn't answer. But he did, carefully enunciating the syllables of his name, exaggerating them. "Ritchie John."

Louis studied him a moment more. I felt like nudging my escort to move along, but I didn't.

"Very well. If you would please bring waters back, plus a bottle of the house's best whisky and six glasses."

"I'd be happy tae . . . the very best?" Ritchie asked.

"Aye, no matter the cost," Louis confirmed.

"Absolutely. I'll be by in a moment."

As Louis resumed walking, Ritchie sent me some raised eyebrows and a mysterious frown. I sent him a quick smile and a nod.

Louis led me down a short hallway past the bar and the stairs leading up to the second floor and in through a doorway framing a green-painted door.

The room was richly furnished like the rest of the pub, but it was also small, making it very crowded.

A rumble of conversation quieted as Louis shut the door, and everyone looked expectantly toward us.

"We are all here, how grand!" an older woman I recognized as Shelagh O'Conner said.

She sat on the far side of the table, in the only chair that was padded. Her gold dress and sparkling earrings gave her a regal appearance against the burgundy upholstery of the chair. She smiled under reading glasses perched on the end of her nose. Her gray hair was pulled back into a neat bun, and there were no flyaways in sight.

Brigid had included many pictures in the article she wrote about Ms. O'Conner's library. In the pictures of Shelagh, I'd noticed a rare vivaciousness in her eyes. In person it was even more noticeable.

"You are Delaney?" Shelagh's accent was lighter even than Edwin's, closer to Hamlet's.

"I am. Nice to meet you, Ms. O'Conner," I said.

It would have been too awkward to shake hands over the table, so we just nodded at each other.

"You too. I've looked forward to it," Shelagh said. "Louis, show Delaney her seat, and please introduce everyone."

I spied one person I already knew. He and I smiled at each other across the table.

Birk Blackburn, a good friend. I wasn't surprised he was there, but that was because finding Birk anywhere wouldn't surprise me. As part of the secret auction group that Edwin belonged to, the Fleshmarket Batch, Birk bought and sold things in a world where money was no object. I was happy to see him because I was fond of him, but I was also somewhat disappointed that he was in on this too. He would be formidable competition if we had to somehow win Shelagh O'Conner's approval to purchase her books. He thought the same; I could see the challenge along with the friendly twinkle in his eyes.

Birk was, as usual, dressed impeccably, and I noticed how nice he looked in the suit he wore. I hadn't even thought about running home to dress up. A quick look around confirmed that Shelagh, Louis, and Birk were all dressed to the nines, or at least the eight and a halves. The other three of us looked to have chosen comfort over fashion.

The other two people in the room were introduced as Tricia Lawson and Jacques Underwood.

Tricia might have been forty. She wore very little makeup, and her hair was back in a short, simple, brown ponytail. She wore a blue sweater over a crisp white blouse, and her large round glasses surprisingly didn't overpower her face. She was petite all over, except for those glasses. A frown tugged at her mouth, which made her look suspicious.

Jacques Underwood didn't seem to share her skepticism. He kept his arms crossed in front of his rounded chest, however, even as he flashed a quick, small smile. His dark hair was swept back from his forehead, and his dark eyes shone with curiosity.

Tricia was a librarian at a local secondary school, and

Jacques had come to Edinburgh just that morning from Paris. When he spoke I noticed that his French accent was strong, though his English was perfect.

Louis did the introductions, but Shelagh added a small comment with each person. With me she said, "Works at the loveliest bookshop." With Birk, "He has done so much good for the city." With Tricia, "A true librarian who has instilled the love of reading in children who might never have picked up a book for pleasure." With Jacques there seemed to be a small apologetic tone to her words. "Jacques is one of my closest possible relations. I have no children of my own, but Jacques is . . . I call him my nephew, but he's more like a second cousin, and he calls me his aunt."

"Dearest Auntie." Jacques said genuinely as he and Shelagh smiled at each other.

A knock sounded on the door.

"Enter," Louis said.

The bartender, Ritchie, came in carrying a tray filled with a whisky bottle, glasses of water, and shot glasses for each of us.

After Ritchie handed out the waters, he asked Louis if he could "have the honor of pouring" the shots.

"Aye, please," Louis said.

Ritchie had put the tray down on the table in a space in between Tricia and Jacques. In seemingly smooth, practiced moves, he removed the lid from the whisky bottle and then began to fill the shot glasses. He extended the first glass to Shelagh, who smiled and nodded as she took it. Then he handed a glass to Louis; Ritchie held the glass just out of Louis's reach and kept eye contact with him for what seemed a moment too long. Finally Louis cleared his throat, and Ritchie smiled and handed him the glass.

The rest of the filled glasses were delivered quickly, without incident, until the final shot. Tricia pushed up her spectacles just as Ritchie was scooting the whisky toward her. Something happened—I wasn't sure if it was because of how the shot was being scooted across the table or if Tricia's arm might have hit Ritchie's, but the glass tipped over and fell directly onto Tricia's lap.

Tricia scooted her chair back and stood. "Oh!"

Since there was so little space, the chair couldn't move far and Tricia couldn't have escaped the whisky even if she'd been faster.

"Lass, I'm so sorry," Ritchie said as he grabbed a dishcloth from the tray.

"Damn!" Jacques said as he looked at Ritchie. "Very careless of you."

"I'm so sorry," Ritchie said as he looked at Jacques.

To his credit, Ritchie *did* sound sorry, but he *didn't* back away from Jacques's condescending tone.

"It's okay," Tricia said as she looked at Jacques. "It's just a wee dram, not much to it."

The whisky had spilled onto her shirt and jeans, but the splashes were small.

"Lass, I'll get ye a wet cloth," Ritchie said.

"No, no need. Please just repour the shot. I can wash these things easily." She sat and scooted her chair back into place.

"Aye." Ritchie poured the whisky back into the glass again.

"Thank you, kind sir," Shelagh said, smiling at Ritchie as if to let him know that no harm had truly been done.

Ritchie smiled back at her and then excused himself, apologizing again to Tricia and telling us he would be available if we needed anything else.

"Well, everyone, thank you for coming," Shelagh said as she lifted her glass once Ritchie was gone. "You are the four specific people I wanted here today. I'll cut right to the chase. You see, I'm ready to part with my library, and it shall surely go to one of you in this room."

It wasn't a large enough crowd for a buzz to travel through, but we all had a reaction to her words. Small noises, shifts in our chairs. What did she mean? We waited for what she would say next.

Once her pause had gone on a tiny beat too long, she continued. "My reasons are varied and personal, so don't ask me why you're here, just know that I wanted you. If at any moment you would like to leave, I won't hold it against you in the least. This might be overwhelming, but that's not what I mean for it to be."

We nodded, and when no one jumped up and rushed away, Shelagh lifted her glass, now filled with scotch, and held it high.

"To the written word, the most beautiful creation in the universe," she said.

We all saluted and downed the shot. One would do me just fine, so I was relieved when Louis didn't pour another.

"All right," Shelagh said. "Louis is here in an advisory capacity. He is a longtime friend and my *closest* advisor. He is also well aware of the fact that sometimes I listen to him and sometimes I don't. I haven't shared all the details of my plan with him, so if you have questions, please direct them to me."

Louis nodded again, but I sensed he didn't like being left in the dark.

The air in the room grew charged. The game was about to be on, whatever that meant.

"Down to it, then." Shelagh paused, and her face became very serious. "Here's what's going to happen. You will all search for a treasure. The person who finds the treasure will be the winner and will receive my entire library, upon my death."

Silently we looked at each other. Perhaps a treasure hunt was a bit cliché, but I felt a thread of excitement at the idea of it. Did everyone else feel the same?

"Are you sick, Auntie?" Jacques spoke first.

"No, I'm sixty, though. I wish I could live forever, but alas, that's not going to happen, and since my birthday I've felt much more aware of my mortality. It's time to take care of some things. My books, many of which came before me, will live much longer than I will. They will need a home after I'm gone. But please understand, the four of you were chosen because I am one hundred percent certain that none of you will simply tuck the books inside boxes, hide them away. You will all do something appropriate, loving, with them." She held up her hand as it seemed Tricia wanted to ask a question. "No, I'm not going to ask what your plans for the books might be. I'm not going to require that information. I am certain that whatever any of you choose will be perfect."

I took a drink of water.

"What's the treasure we will be hunting for?" Jacques asked.

"What do you think it is?"

Birk leaned over the table toward Shelagh. "A book, of course."

Shelagh smiled. "Of course."

"Auntie, is it one of your Jekyll-Hyde books?" Jacques asked with such a tiresome tone that I suddenly wanted anyone but him to win his aunt's books.

"That's *The Strange Case of Dr. Jekyll and Mr. Hyde,* if we're being technically correct, Jacques. And yes, that's exactly it."

Jacques sighed.

Shelagh continued. "I have . . . hidden my most prized copy of my most favorite book of all time. Louis and I have taken great pains to put together the hunt."

Louis nodded solemnly. I noted to myself that he was in on at least that much of the plan. What more could there be?

Shelagh continued. "Now, please let me finish, and then I will answer questions. I believe, and I hope, that none of you is capable of hurting anyone, which is part of the reason you were all chosen. This will be a fair hunt with no threat of violence. And if one of you becomes harmed in the search, I will go to the police immediately about the other three."

I opened my mouth to say something, but nothing came out.

"Also," Shelagh went on, "once the book is found, you each will receive a large sum of money. You will all receive the same amount, and it is substantial, but I'm not going to share the number with you—not today at least."

"Why are you giving us money?" Birk asked.

"Because I have to do *something* with it, Birk. I think that using some of it to pay you for your efforts is only fair. Also, if you all receive money when this is over, you might cheer each other on rather than compete in any dangerous way. Does that make sense?"

I could see Birk's answer in his eyes. Lots of this didn't make sense. The whole thing seemed oddly frivolous, but also fun and exciting. Birk only nodded.

"This is how it will begin. I want to give each of you an individual tour of my library. I don't want to do this part as a group, and that's probably unfair. But that is my rule." Shelagh glanced briefly at Jacques. I thought I saw some sort of challenge there, but it was over too quickly for me to be sure. "We will draw straws to see who gets to visit first, and it is during the tours that I will give you each the first clue. We'll do the tours tomorrow.

"Now, a wee bit more about the book. It's a first-edition copy, signed by the author. I realize most of you have seen such things before, and you know they are the most valuable of all editions, particularly if they are in pristine condition. This one is. This one has been long hidden in my library, away from the elements as well as any human touch. It is a precious book, although it isn't perfect, and that's why I love it so. I love imperfection so much more than perfection. This book, my book, has a pen mark. By hand, someone changed the year of issue inside from 1885 to 1886."

"Why would anyone do such a thing?" Tricia asked, appalled.

"The original publication date on the books was supposed to be 1885, but there was a delay in shipping, and because of Christmas most people didn't get their copy until 1886. A helpful bookseller made the change. I think it's a charming anecdote, don't you?" Shelagh smiled and then closed her eyes. "I can see it. The diligent bookman, working late in his lovely shop one evening, and the box of books he ordered arrives. He locks his shop door against the dark and snowy post-holiday night, gathers his jumper around himself as he adjusts his glasses and sets down his pipe. He opens the box and sees the contents inside. He becomes gleeful. He takes it upon himself to fix the date, because, gracious, he can't let his faithful patrons think he had the books in the back, keeping them to himself until after the season." She opened her eyes and gave a satisfied nod.

"You should be a writer, Auntie," Jacques said.

"Oh, not at all. Doesn't everyone have such an imagination?"

The four of us looked around at one another.

Again Birk spoke up. "No, Shelagh, they don't."

"Well, they should. Grab the straws, Louis. Now, who's in?" Shelagh looked around expectantly.

"I . . . uh, don't know," Tricia said.

"What's on your mind, dear?" Shelagh asked.

"I wonder about all of it, and I'm not sure I'm able to do what might be needed to hunt down a book."

"You are one of the cleverest librarians in all of Edinburgh." Shelagh leaned forward on the table. "I have no doubt that you can figure out anything at all."

Tricia pushed up her glasses, and her eyes got big behind the lenses. "Ms. O'Conner, Shelagh, I wonder if you would share with us what happened to you back when . . . you were in trouble. I think it's only fair for us to know as much as we can about the person sending us on a treasure hunt."

I wanted to hear that story too, but I waited silently as Birk cringed and Jacques turned his gaze downward. Louis didn't seem fazed in the least.

Shelagh's mouth pinched tight. She took a deep breath. "I hoped it wouldn't come up. Gracious, it has been over fifty years since all that silliness, the late sixties, for goodness' sake. Hasn't everyone heard the story? With the internet and everything."

"No," Tricia said. "I did some research before coming here today and found some mention of the trouble, but there were no details, no copies of any articles that ran back then. I wanted to stop by the *Scotsman* and ask to peruse their archives, but I didn't have time. Would you mind sharing what happened, from your point of view?"

Shelagh tsked. "Well, ultimately it was tragic, of course, and my inclusion was all very silly, really. I was young and bored—I was seventeen. I first read about Jekyll and Hyde when I was sixteen, and my passion for the story was immediately ignited. Anyway, because of my obsession with the story—I'm willing to call it that—I decided I wanted to try to live a double life and see if I could fool anyone, see if I could give myself something *interesting* to do. Life is so dull when you're rich, young, and dramatic, you know.

"Anyway, I lived as a beggar during the night, going so far as to wear old clothes and dirty up my face. My own version of Mr. Hyde, though without the voilence. It was an act at first, just something fun. Then I enjoyed observing people's reaction to my beggar's behavior. I was treated so differently than in my real life. Truly, it was a real study of human behavior, even if I didn't quite understand that then. It became fun, interesting." Shelagh shrugged.

"Were you treated better or worse as a beggar?" I interjected.

Shelagh smiled knowingly. "Excellent question, Delaney. In fact, I think I was treated more *honestly* as a beggar. Some people were disgusted by me, some wanted to help. When I was the rich me, people catered to me, but I doubt much of it was genuine. As a beggar I felt the need to 'trust the kindness of strangers,' if you will. If someone helped, they truly wanted to. In my real life, people just thought they should—they were being paid or wanted something from me. No one behaved as if they were disgusted by the rich girl, though I'm sure some were."

"Interesting," I said.

"So it was fun until you were accused of killing someone?" Tricia said.

"Yes." Shelagh frowned. "I didn't kill anyone, and I was never arrested. It all came from rumors and speculations, the press wanting to make me into the rich girl who'd gone bad."

Birk made a small noise. "Some people enjoy those sorts of stories."

"Who was killed?" I asked. I hadn't done even as much re-search as Tricia had.

It didn't appear that Shelagh was going to answer.

Birk and Shelagh looked at each other then, and I sensed the years falling away. I saw something there in that small moment of time travel. They'd known each other before this meeting, perhaps well.

Shelagh blinked and then looked away from Birk and down at her lap. "A secret beau. Oliver McCabe. A potential beau. We never . . . it never really developed into a relationship."

I sat up straighter.

Birk cleared his throat. "He and Shelagh were close."

"And then he was killed." Shelagh looked up at Birk, her eyes keeping a level gaze.

"He was." Birk nodded.

"Who killed him?" Jacques asked, looking at Birk.

"The killer was never found, as far as I know," Birk said.

"No, never." Shelagh sat up straighter too. "That's the part that people forget. Though at first our relationship was a se-cret because my parents wouldn't have approved, it later be-came clear that I'd lost someone I cared about, and there has never been any resolution. My crime was lying, maybe pre-tending to be someone I wasn't. When I was recognized in the crowd in the picture near . . . Ollie's body." She paused. "Well, I was young, I didn't know how to handle all of these things.

"We didn't have cameras everywhere back then, but some-one managed to snap a picture and I was there, yes. I saw the man I loved, now dead. Whoever took the picture then took the film in to be developed and then discovered the photo two months after the murder. Instead of taking it to the police, they took it to the newspaper. It was embarrassing, for me and my family. But ultimately no evidence was found against me. Still, though, imagine what was thought of me when our relation-ship became public knowledge. My family was unfairly and fur-ther shamed. It was horrible, and Ollie was gone." Shelagh shook her head. "No one cared that my heart had been irreparably broken. My possible involvement became even more important than the fact that a good man was now dead."

"I read that it looked in the picture like you had blood on your jumper." Tricia wasn't sympathetic to Shelagh's broken heart.

"It wasn't blood."

"The jumper was never tested, though," Tricia said.

"Dear, it seems you've read more than you mentioned. But no, I'd thrown it away. I'd thrown away all those clothes."

"They found suspicious remains of a fire in your back garden."

"There were no remnants of clothes in the fire."

"It was indeterminable."

"All I can do, Tricia, is tell you that I did nothing wrong and I was dismissed by the police." She looked around.

Tricia pursed her lips and then nodded at Shelagh.

"Do you want to stay, dear girl?" Shelagh asked, her tone less friendly than her words.

Tricia thought a long moment. "I do. Thank you."

"Very well. I would ask if anyone has any further questions, but I simply don't feel like answering them now. We will begin the library tours tomorrow. Let's draw straws to see who gets to go first."

I wasn't disappointed that she'd ended the questions, but I was certainly looking forward to asking her some during my tour the next day.

Louis seemed to enjoy his role as the holder of the straws. "Ladies first," he said, and then moved around the table to Tricia, then me, followed by Birk, and finally Jacques.

Birk drew the longest straw, Tricia second, Jacques, and then me. I was happy with where I landed but tried not to show it too much. I would love to find Shelagh's lost book, and I knew that Edwin would do something spectacular with her library, but I wanted to be the last to view it so our meeting wouldn't be rushed.

I was excited, caught up with the idea of the hunt, the story of the long-ago murder. What happened next, though, made me think that perhaps I should be more concerned.

Once library tour times were determined, Louis stood and went to the door. He opened it and said, "Ah, there you are. Yes, I believe that Ms. O'Conner is ready to go."

The person he spoke to entered the cramped room and made his way around the table to Shelagh. He was there, it seemed, to escort her out of the pub. He didn't miss the opportunity to look pointedly at me, sending me a wry and far-too-knowing smile. So that was what Findlay Sweet, Tom's former fishing buddy, meant by being a driver. He was Shelagh O'Conner's chauffeur.

I blinked at him openmouthed for a beat, then scowled. What was going on?

I had so many questions, but I wasn't sure whom to ask what. For now I'd continue to think on things, formulate a list. Tomorrow I'd get some answers.

FOUR

"Findlay?" Tom's eyes opened wide.

"Yes!" I reached for one of his fries—chips, that is.

I'd walked into our favorite takeaway a little later than I expected to. I'd gotten stuck on my spreadsheet project at work and texted Tom that he should start without me. As soon as I got there, I plunked myself down on a stool next to him—one of three seats in the entire place—and told him about my running into Findlay at the meeting with Shelagh.

"Oh, I don't like this one bit, Delaney." Tom put down the piece of fish he'd been holding.

"I don't either, but I don't know why. What's the story between the two of you?"

Tom thought a moment. "Order your dinner and I'll put the story together in my head, so I don't look like a foolish child."

I smiled. I was still learning about Tom's past, which included some less-than-gentlemanly behavior. Even if he told me a story that did in fact make him look foolish, it would not diminish my love for him. He knew this by now. He caught my smile and quirked a quick one back.

"You love these stories, don't you?" he said.

"I love that you're human."

"Too human for my own good."

"Tom, nothing is that bad," I said.

"Findlay might think so, and that worries me. Go ahead and order."

I scooted off the stool and walked the two steps to the counter, where I ordered quickly and then moved back to Tom as Mica, the shop owner, dropped my fish into the fryer.

"Are you okay?" I asked Tom.

"I'm fine, lass. I just wish I'd grown up a wee bit sooner."

"Then you might not have waited for me."

Tom smiled all the way now. "I would have waited, but you do have a point—things are meant to be and such. Anyway, I suppose it wasn't that I did the wrong thing. I did the right thing, but I just went about it the wrong way."

"Okay."

Tom and I both appreciated how Mica pretended not to overhear the conversations that took place in his small restaurant, but he wasn't far from us as he attended to my dinner.

"I was sixteen, and Da was tired of me hanging around the house. I got myself in enough trouble back then—small stuff like skipping class—that he wanted me to have a job during the school year as well as the summer. I spent a year working as a floor sweeper in the university's library, somewhat under Da's watchful eye. Surprising him, I took school seriously that year. Da was proud, but I was tired. I quit my job at the library and thought I'd just have some fun over the summer. Da disagreed." Tom smiled as the memory transformed from contentious to fond. "He told me that if I didn't get a job, he would get one for me and I wouldn't like it. I didn't believe him, but that's exactly what he did."

"He knew Findlay?" I asked as Mica handed me my paper boat full of food.

"No, he knew me. I was always fond of looking at the water, but I didn't like being on it back then. I get a wee bit seasick, aye, but open water was a real fear for me when I was young. Not manly, I know, but Da thought I could get over it, face my fear and all. I knew how to swim. He went to the docks and found a fisherman who needed help." Tom smiled again. "You saw Findlay—he was old and grizzled back then too."

"Findlay was the fisherman your dad found?"

"Aye. Findlay." Tom nodded.

I took a bite and waited as he fell into thought again.

"It started off well enough." Tom pushed his food away. "Except for the seasickness. At first Findlay was upset that neither Da nor I had told him I suffered such an affliction. He wanted to fire me, but I was just stubborn enough—and didn't want to disappoint my father—to tell Findlay I could stick it out. And in truth it did get better. Or I just learned to better live with it. Either way, it became bearable. I could work full days for Findlay and not have to take one extra break. I didn't ever feel great on the boat, but I could do it."

I'd come to know his stubborn focus, and it was one of the many things I loved about him.

Tom continued. "Anyway, after I worked for him for a month or so, we began to get along as friends. I enjoyed his raucous sense of humor, and his gruffness became endearing. In the afternoons he'd take off a couple of hours while I processed the morning's catch. He claimed that that was his time to rest, that I'd been hired mostly so he could take a nap in the afternoons. I didn't mind working alone. It was messy but fun, until the day things went south.

"I was working on the fish, cleaning and filleting, when

another man stopped by looking for Findlay. I'd thought Findlay was the most life-worn man I'd ever seen until this man showed up. I couldn't tell you his name, but he was rough around all his edges, snockered and angry too, looking for my boss, not willing to let me tell him I didn't know where Findlay was or when he'd return." Tom shook his head. "He grabbed my ear—just like in the old movies—he grabbed my ear and demanded I take him to Findlay."

"He assaulted you," I said.

"That's not how it was looked at. And I knew Findlay wasn't far away. He lived near the docks. I'd been to his flat, though only briefly. I became scared enough to take this man directly to Findlay's place. I tried to make noise as we approached the building so Findlay could be prepared or run out the back or something, but it didn't work.

"When we got to the front door, the man just broke through. He kicked it open. Inside, there was Findlay and a young woman in a . . . compromising position."

"That's unfortunate."

"Aye, particularly since I'd met Findlay's wife, and that wasn't the young woman with him. Apparently Mrs. Sweet did her shopping and errands every afternoon when Findlay took his naps, if you know what I mean."

"I do. So Findlay was angry at you for bringing the man to his flat?"

"No. Though he wasn't happy about that, it was something else that angered him. I told his wife on him. A week later a sense of propriety came over me, and I told on my boss. Ironic, considering, aye?"

"Considering your reputation?"

"Aye. At the time I was young enough not to have much of a reputation, but it did come later."

"You didn't cheat on anyone. You just never ended things well. You broke hearts, Tom. You didn't smash them because of infidelity. There's a difference."

"Well, nevertheless, Mrs. Sweet left her husband and I was sacked. Da wasn't even unhappy about it."

"I bet not."

Tom shrugged. "I haven't seen Findlay in . . . what, fourteen or fifteen years. He came into the pub today for the first time ever as far as I know."

"He works for Shelagh now, and the messenger with the note stopped by the bookshop probably about the same time Findlay came into the pub. I wonder if he was with the messenger. Maybe the timing was all coincidental, but I doubt it."

"When he came into the pub, he didn't even say hello at first. I recognized him. He got a pint from Rodger and went up to the front window. He watched out the window, looking toward the direction of the bookshop. He stayed there a long time, until you came in."

"He couldn't have known I would come in."

"He might have thought it was possible. Maybe he knew about us—Shelagh might have researched everyone she invited to the gathering. He might have put it together. Whatever the reason he was there, I want you to be aware around him."

"I will be."

"I'm sure we'll understand it at some point, but I'd rather you didn't have to see him. He was angry at me all those years ago, and it was an anger I was sure would never be forgiven."

"I think it will be fine," I said. And at that moment I did think so. "Let me tell you about the rest of the meeting."

"I'm listening."

I told Tom about my time at Deacon Brodie's pub. He was fascinated and had some of the same questions I did, many that would presumably be answered the next day at Shelagh's house. At the same time, I could see him working to hide his concern. I appreciated that, but again, I really did think everything would be okay.

"Do *you* know anything about Shelagh's past and the man named Oliver McCabe?" I asked.

"No, it was all before our time, but Da might. I'll ask him."

I nodded. "Shelagh took the role she'd created seriously. Today she said she was too young to realize that what she was doing was a real study in human behavior, but I can see how it was. She was treated differently as a beggar than she was a rich girl."

"Better or worse?" Tom asked.

"Differently. More honestly as a beggar. I tried to find more on the internet, but there really is very little. Since she wasn't arrested for murder, it probably just went away. Tricia certainly knew about it, though, and Rosie had mentioned it to me, though her memory was foggy. I'm curious enough to keep asking Shelagh about it tomorrow."

We finished our dinners and wiped our fingers on some paper napkins. With a friendly farewell from Mica, we walked out into the cold, clear night. It had stopped snowing, the roads slushy now. I would have enjoyed walking home. I had my boots, after all. But Tom's car wasn't far away.

We crossed Grassmarket, through the slush and around to Tom's parking spot. It was in between the two long buildings bordering the market—Tom's pub was at the far end of one. The parking spot was set back out of the way of all traffic, which meant it was also somewhat hidden.

Just as we came around to it, a noise sounded from across the parking space. It was like the crash of an old aluminum garbage can and some breaking glass.

I gasped, and Tom pulled me behind him.

"Who's there?" he said.

The silence was so loud I was sure someone was watching us.

We took another step back, and Tom lit the flashlight app on his phone. He directed it toward the back corner just as a figure started moving out of it, from around a couple of old garbage bins. The figure was moving too quickly for us to get a good look, but there was no doubt it was a person, clad in a tattered coat and with a hat pulled down over their face.

Tom and I kept our distance and watched for the few seconds it took for the person to scurry away and out of our sight. No harm done.

"Someone trying to get warm, most likely," Tom said, doubt lining his words.

"Yeah," I said, just as doubtfully.

It was the day's events, of course it was. My imagination might not be as grand as Shelagh's, but it had certainly been sparked. So had Tom's. He was probably correct, though—it was just someone looking for a place to warm up or maybe to sleep undisturbed.

I was pretty sure neither of us really, truly believed it was something that simple, something that safe, because even less-than-grand imaginations could turn almost anything into a monster, particularly when the right seeds had been planted.

FIVE

Despite the bothersome events of the day, I was able to find calm inside the beautiful blue house by the sea where Tom and I lived. This previously landlocked Kansas girl never thought she'd live by the ocean.

Though it was small, the two-story house had the bedrooms upstairs and the living and dining room and kitchen on the bottom floor. The appliances were old, "from the best era of appliances" according to my good friend and former landlord, Aggie McKenna. Elias, her husband, a taxi driver I'd met on my first day in Scotland, just liked the way the table and chairs inside the dining area were surrounded by windows that looked out over a back garden.

The view from the living room displayed the ocean and all its many different personalities. I could watch it for hours, see it transform from beautiful to menacing, cheery to foaming at the mouth and hungry. It was hypnotic.

When Tom and I returned from our honeymoon, we had to stay in the cottage behind the McKennas' cottage and guest-houses because there'd been a problem with the blue house's old electrical system. That was the story Tom had told me, but

I'd found out a little later that there was a different reason we couldn't move right in.

Tom had been building a library. My very own personal library. If I hadn't been head over heels for him before, I would have fallen hard when he brought me into the house and directed me upstairs, where he pulled on a rope attached to a door in the second-floor ceiling. Stairs unfolded as the door opened, and we climbed into the attic—he had transformed the place by furnishing it with bookshelves, new floors, good lights, and comfy chairs. He'd made sure the space could be heated in the cold winters and had even picked out cute curtains for the alcove windows.

Fortunately, Tom liked to read too, and he'd put enough comfortable seating in my library that we could invite guests if we were so inclined.

Our current houseguests weren't much for climbing the attic ladder, but they knew they were always welcome.

Elias and Aggie were spending a couple of weeks with us because their cottages were, in fact, being rewired for modern electrical and their guesthouses had been booked out for months.

Ours wasn't a big place, but it wasn't tiny either. We might have been cramped if we didn't all like each other so much and if Elias and Aggie weren't such thoughtful guests. They'd cleaned everything to spotless, and when we didn't have dinner out somewhere, Aggie always had something ready to warm up quickly.

Whenever we came home tired from the day, they gave us hot chocolate and cookies. We'd entertained the idea of sabotaging the workers fixing their electrical.

"Your new husband is going to be fat," Tom said as he leaned over toward me.

"Your new wife will be right there with you."

"That works." Tom smiled and then bit into a chocolate chip cookie that was better than any cookie I'd ever eaten, except for all the other cookies Aggie had made for us during the week they'd been in the blue house.

Tonight we sat on the couch enjoying our evening snacks. Elias and Aggie were cleaning up the kitchen and would join us shortly. Tom and I had offered to at least clean, but they'd scooted us out of there without a real chance to argue. I told them we had an interesting story to share, and they were intrigued, but Aggie simply couldn't sit still if the kitchen wasn't tidy first.

Tom and I had tried to tell them they shouldn't do so much—they were constantly cleaning, cooking, looking for something to repair—but our efforts were in vain. They couldn't be stopped, so we decided just to enjoy them and hope we could return the favors one day.

"We're ready, lass," Elias said as he and Aggie finally hurried into the living room with their own mugs.

They sat in two chairs that faced the couch; a coffee table perched in the middle of everything. I noticed a new quilt on the back of Aggie's chair and wondered if she'd just stitched it up today. I'd ask later.

"Tell us aboot yer day, lass," Aggie said with a smile as she sat and leaned into the quilt.

I wanted to tell her it looked too nice to be leaned into, but that seemed somehow rude.

In between bites of another cookie, I told them about the day's turn of events. They listened with the same rapt attention as Tom had, but they weren't as concerned as he had been. Though I mentioned Findlay, I downplayed his anger with Tom from all those years ago.

"I ken Ms. O'Conner," Aggie said when I was done. "Och, weel, I used tae. I've ken all aboot the lass all these years."

"You knew her personally?" I asked.

"Aye, she and I were actively involved in the children's hospital fund-raising many years ago. She was always lovely, but a wee bit strange too."

"How?" Tom asked.

"A very vivid imagination," Aggie said.

"That's still obvious. I actually wondered if she knew the difference between reality and her imagination. She's a daydreamer, I bet. But she seems smart, savvy," I added.

"Aggie and she were freends when Shelagh was in all that tribble," Elias said.

"Tribble is *trouble*?" I said.

"Aye," Elias responded.

I looked at Aggie. "Did you think she committed murder?"

Aggie shook her head. "First of all, we wernae close friends, but more than acquaintances, I would say. I wasnae so sure back then if she was a killer. I ken she was up tae something. I caught her in the middle of one of her transformations."

I sat forward on the couch, cradling the warm mug with both hands. "Really?"

Aggie shrugged. "I walked into the loo, and she was putting on the auld clothes. A brown coat, riddled with holes, a men's fancy but moth-eaten hat, and some charcoal rubbed over her cheeks. She was in full costume and knew she was caught." Aggie lowered her voice. "I promised I wouldnae say anything tae anyone, and I didnae, even after she was suspected of murder. I felt bad about that until she was cleared, but I still wonder."

"You wonder if she was a killer?" Tom asked.

"Mostly I just thought she was up tae something she should-nae been. I didnae expose her then, but it's been bothersome for me over the years, even after everyone ken what she'd done."

"The dress-up, the act?" I said.

"Aye, it was strange, but what I couldnae let go of was that though she took the idea from the book, she wasnae a violent lass, not a t'all. Hyde was more than a simple beggar, he was a killer. I just couldnae make her into that, no matter how I tried tae think aboot it. She was so young. We all do stupid things when we're young. I'm a wee bit older than Shelagh and I just saw a lass with too much energy and too much imagination, who needed tae grow up some."

Elias put his hand over his wife's arm. "Love, ye did right. Ye promised her, and ye kept yer promise."

A person's word would be one of the most important things to Elias McKenna. He was cut from the same cloth that many of the older men in my life were, and keeping one's word would be important no matter what else was involved—probably even murder.

"Weel," Aggie continued, "anyway, I didnae tell anyone. She was always kind to me, but again, that was many years ago. I dinnae ken what kind of person she really is now, but her library and books have been popular topics of conversation for many."

"I guess I'll have a front-row view tomorrow."

"Why do ye think she made a hunt?" Elias asked.

I shrugged. "She's a bit over the top and probably likes to have fun. I wouldn't be surprised to find bigger challenges along the way. The book collection is quite valuable. It won't be a simple hunt."

"I dinnae like Findlay Sweet's involvement," Elias added.

"Me either," Tom said.

"I'll be careful."

Truth be told, I didn't like it either, but I still didn't think it was any big deal. For now I was willing to think that his working for Shelagh and then stopping by Tom's pub was just . . . well, not coincidence as much as simply convenient. I'd tried to talk to Birk at the end of the meeting to ask if he'd had a message delivered by a messenger too, but he'd left quickly, and I hadn't had time to give him a call.

"Ye should have Tom go with ye," Elias said.

Aggie tsked. "She's a modern woman, Elias. She'll be fine."

"I don't think I'd be invited," Tom said with a wry smile my direction.

"You'd be invited," I said to him. I didn't add, *But not to save me.* Instead I looked at Elias. "I really will be fine, though."

"Weel . . ." Elias took an authoritative sip of his hot chocolate.

Tom sent me a furtive wink.

We finished our drinks and chatted a little longer. Elias and Aggie went to bed early, even earlier than their normal hour. It was clear they thought Tom and I should have plenty of time alone. We'd told them that we enjoyed having them there, but they still bade us goodnight and retired to their room early in the evenings.

Tom had changed his schedule since we'd gotten married. He used to work most nights, but now he worked only a few, leaving the evenings to Rodger and some part-time employees.

The pub had been running fine, but I knew if things started to change or too many of the regulars missed Tom, he'd go back to working nights. I'd known his schedule when we married, but I was pleasantly surprised by the change. If he returned to the old ways, I'd hide my disappointment.

For now, though, I'd enjoy our evenings watching television

or reading in my new garret library. Tonight, after a few minutes of looking at the foam on the dark ocean, we decided we were tired enough for bed too.

As we were making our way to our room, though, Elias came out of his.

"We've been watching the telly," he said, a concerned look on his face. "Have you?"

"No," I said. "What's wrong?"

"Come in."

We followed him into the bedroom, where Aggie was bundled up under the covers. She even wore a nightcap.

"Look," she said as she nodded toward the small television set on the old dresser.

A newscaster was speaking.

"It seems the burglar was caught on CCTV. Please take a look at this video. If you have any information regarding who this person might be, please call the police immediately."

My mouth fell open as we watched the grainy video that had been captured by a camera across the street from the house that had been robbed. The burglar was dressed similarly to the person Tom and I had seen hiding in the shadows by his car.

"Tom, do you think that's who we saw?" I asked.

"I have no idea, but it sure looks like them. I think," Tom said.

"I'm not sure either."

"Wait," Aggie said as she used the remote to turn off the television. "We wanted ye tae see this because we were talking about Shelagh earlier, and the person on the telly looks to be dressed as Shelagh dressed back then. What are ye two talking about?"

We hadn't shared our encounter in the parking lot with our houseguests. It hadn't even occurred to me. And even if it had,

I still wouldn't have brought it up to them. They were worried enough about me touring an eccentric woman's library in broad daylight. They'd be mightily concerned about someone potentially lurking in a dark car park.

However, we told them now. And then I called Inspector Winters.

SIX

Against his will, and probably his better judgment, Inspector Winters and I had become friends.

I had his cell number, but I tried the police station first. He was there, and pleased I thought to let him know what Tom and I had seen. It was a quick call.

I tossed and turned the whole night, grateful when it was finally time to go to work and even more grateful that Rosie was already there when I arrived so I could tell her everything.

"Not much tae the call with Inspector Winters, then?" she asked when I took a breath from sharing the story.

"Not really. He thanked me and told me goodnight."

"He didnae want an official statement or anything?"

Rosie and I were the only two in the shop, both of us there early again. We decided to use the time to dust bookshelves.

"No, but we only saw what we saw briefly," I said.

Rosie halted her feather duster. "Lass, ye didnae tell him aboot yer meeting with Shelagh?"

I frowned. "No. I thought it might muddle things, maybe make the police look at her again when she's surely just as innocent as she was the first time around. I mean, they might look at her anyway but it's an old story and maybe the past should just stay in the past. I didn't want to make it worse." I cringed.

"Aye," Rosie said doubtfully.

"I don't think it was her we saw, Rosie. She's old and small. This person moved like someone younger, and they were bigger, masculine. I think."

Rosie shrugged. "Old people can surprise ye sometimes, and she could have added layers."

"I know, but . . . it just doesn't seem like it was her." I sighed and changed the subject. "Oliver McCabe was the man who was killed back then—he and Shelagh had some sort of relationship. I still don't understand the details, but I believe it was something like he wasn't good enough for her parents. I don't know why, though. Do you remember anything else?"

"'Tis probably that *no one* was good enough for Shelagh, but I dinnae ken. I'd even forgotten his name." Rosie stopped dusting.

I nodded. "There's not much online."

"It's a shame that we all talk about Shelagh still but the dead man seems tae have been forgotten. I would like tae know more aboot him."

"Me too."

After Tom and I had told Elias and Aggie goodnight for the second time and then retired to our bedroom, we'd discussed if it might have been Shelagh we'd seen. Tom wasn't as sure as I had been, but he ultimately agreed that he didn't think the figure was a woman. We also discussed whether I should tell Inspector Winters about the meeting at Deacon Brodie's Tavern but agreed that there didn't seem to be any need to point a spotlight on Shelagh again. At least, *yet*. Just because it was top of our minds because of the events of the day didn't mean we needed to make it important to the police.

But neither of us had been one hundred percent sure of much of anything. After my tour of Shelagh's library, I thought I might call Inspector Winters back and tell him about the hunt for the book, if there was anything to tell.

The bell above the front door jingled. Rosie and I turned, feather dusters aloft.

"Brigid?" I said.

She stood in the doorway and sent me a scowl I knew I didn't deserve.

"What in the world happened?" she said.

I shook my head. "When?"

I walked toward her, setting the duster on Rosie's desk. Hector, sensing the animosity that Brigid wasn't trying to hide, trotted to my feet and sat protectively—all seven inches or so of him—in front of me.

"Yesterday. Did you meet with Shelagh O'Conner?"

It was my turn to scowl, or at least frown a little. "What do you know about it?"

"I'm the one who told her about you."

"You are? Well. Thank you?" I said.

"And the evening of the meeting, Edinburgh has a new Mr. Hyde roaming around town, stealing and who knows what else?"

So much for the past staying in the past. "Um . . . I didn't have anything to do with that."

"Ladies, would ye consider sitting in the back for yer discussion," Rosie intervened. "A customer could come in at any moment, and I dinnae want tae scare them away right off the bat."

Brigid and I did as Rosie suggested and sat across from each other. Rosie offered to cross over to the other side and gather refreshments. I didn't take the time to acknowledge that she wouldn't offer treats if she weren't warming to Brigid.

Brigid had attempted to remain immune from Hector's charms, but I witnessed her scowl melt a little as the dog propped himself on my lap. She normalized quickly enough.

"You told Shelagh about me?" I asked. The scowl had returned, though only at about sixty percent.

"I did. I wrote a story about her a few weeks ago—"

"I read it. It was very good."

"Thank you."

"But you didn't mention anything about her long-ago trouble. Did you know about her disguises?"

"I did."

"You didn't put that part in the article."

"No, I didn't mention it because it seemed wrong at the time. The article was about the good that Shelagh has done over the years, how she's used some of her wealth to benefit Edinburgh." Brigid paused and blinked at Hector before she looked at me again. "I don't know that it mattered. Now, apparently, I might have stirred up the old story anyway."

"Because of . . . what happened last night?"

"It looks like we might have a new monster, a new Mr. Hyde." Brigid crossed her arms in front of herself. "Do you really think we would have one if I hadn't written the story?"

"Well, who knows? But unless you're the person playing the part, none of that is your fault. Shelagh's story from those days isn't easy to find."

"But people still remember it."

I thought about Rosie. Yes, she remembered some parts of it, but not all. "It's not your fault," I repeated.

Brigid shook her head once. "No, not my fault, but this is

just a prime example of why a journalist should always tell the whole story. I should have mentioned her past problems, Delaney. I shouldn't have held back. Now I look like I wasn't doing my job thoroughly."

Ah, it was about her. Was she losing her ruthless ways? I didn't think so.

"Brigid, it was a great article. Now you just might have more to write about, but good job."

"Thank you," she said with some forced humility.

"How did my name come up?"

"As we were talking, she asked me if I'd had any dealings with local bookshops and if there was one I could recommend."

"You recommended The Cracked Spine? Thank you."

"No, in fact, that's not exactly how it went. I said I knew people at this bookshop, and though the owner often seemed to be up to something suspicious, there was an employee from Kansas who seemed to always want to do the right thing. Honestly, I didn't mean to compliment you, but it came out that way."

"Well. Thank you again."

"She called me two days ago, telling me she'd have another story for me but first she was going to conduct a meeting—that was to be scheduled for yesterday. That happen?"

"It did. I was invited and I went." I waited for her to ask me about the specifics of the meeting, but she didn't.

She nodded. "Good. But if it wasn't because of my article, something happened there to turn one of the attendees into the new Mr. Hyde."

"I don't know . . . seems a stretch." My eyebrows came together.

"Someone who was dressed as Shelagh dressed back in the

late 1960s story broke into three homes last night and stole valuable items—silver, artwork, money."

"Three? I saw the video on television last night. I was under the impression that it was one home, and I saw no mention of Shelagh."

"The investigation is ongoing."

"The face wasn't clear. Do you know if the police *think* it was Shelagh?"

"I don't think so. Some of the television journalists do remember the story and are using it. They are calling her the old monster and saying we now have a new monster."

"Oh. I missed that." Aggie had turned off the television quickly the night before, and I hadn't paid any attention to the morning news. "That's pretty harsh, maybe an overstatement."

"It's not me saying it, and someone *was* killed back then. Who was at the meeting?"

"I promised I wouldn't tell." Not true, but maybe Shelagh hadn't wanted us to share. I'd ask her later.

"I was afraid of that. Care to break that promise?"

"Not at the moment, but I might. Let me think about it."

"Really?"

"Yes, really. I don't know Shelagh. I don't know what's going on, but if it's something that's a threat to the citizens of Edinburgh, I can't keep her secrets." I didn't add that I'd first tell Inspector Winters everything and then maybe call Brigid.

She looked at me a long moment. She didn't completely believe me. "Good. Thank you."

"What do you think of Shelagh? Do you think she got away with murder all those years ago?"

"I don't, but there was a time when she seemed guilty. As I've researched, I've come to the conclusion that she was just in the wrong place at the wrong time, but I don't know. I didn't want to rehash false accusations, which was another reason I didn't mention that part of her past."

"What can you tell me about Oliver?"

"All I know is that Shelagh fell hard for him back then, but he was older than her—in his late twenties—and knew her family would never welcome him. I believe he's the one who broke things off, said they should go their separate ways."

"How do you know that much?"

Brigid smiled. "I have my ways."

"Was his killer ever caught?"

"No. Never."

"That's not good. Were there other suspects?"

Brigid cocked her head and squinted at me. "Any chance you'd ask Inspector Winters for some of those old police records?"

"No." In fact, I might ask him, but I wasn't going to tell *her* that.

"Do you know what her new story for me is?"

"I have an idea, yes, but I can't tell you that part either."

"Makes sense. She asked me to stop by this evening and we'd talk. Sound about right?"

"Yes."

"I can be patient."

"You can?"

She shrugged. "I can try. Listen, Delaney, you need to be careful. I don't know if all of this is tied together and I don't know what it will turn into, but I really didn't mean to get you involved in something dangerous. Please be aware."

"I will be. I don't think there's anything to worry about, though." I kind of did, but I couldn't put my finger on it exactly, and it would take something pretty big for me to show any fear to Brigid.

"Okay, then." She paused before she stood. "Stay in touch."

"I will."

She started to turn but paused again, "How's married life? And I'm not asking to find out if there's something bad. I *have* grown up, and I wish you and Tom only the best." She cleared her throat. "Really."

I smiled. "Married life is great, Brigid, and we wish *you* only the best."

Rosie made a funny noise as she came around with a tray full of treats.

Brigid grabbed a couple of cookies off the tray and thanked Rosie.

"We'll talk later," Brigid said to me before she left.

She sent a quick smile to Hector.

Rosie set the tray on the table. "Most of the cookies are stale anyway."

I smiled and took one too. "Thank you, Rosie."

"Ye're welcome, lass."

The bell jingled again as Brigid left and customers entered. We were busy for hours.

SEVEN

I took a bus to Shelagh's house. Elias offered to be available for the day, but I knew that much of his attention would be on his cottages, where the people who'd been working on the electrical system were "daupit."

He'd translated the Scots word for me. *Stupid.* I felt a little sorry for the workers but hoped they'd up their game—not because I wanted Elias and Aggie to leave my house but for the sake of Elias's blood pressure.

After I disembarked, I stood on the distant curb and looked up at Shelagh's mansion. No, I think it would be called an *estate*.

An expanse of manicured green and a now only lightly snow-covered lawn—a garden, as it's known in Scotland—sloped upward toward three buildings. Perfectly round flower beds dotted the ground here and there as if a random design had been at play, but I doubted that anything in this garden had been done randomly.

The building on the left was a blue, barnlike structure, the one to the right a giant glass-paned greenhouse—or would something that size be a conservatory? A garage was attached to it—four single doors wide. It was the structure in the middle that was the true stunner, though.

The three-level house had white siding and blue-shuttered windows. Though it wasn't modern, it had sharp angles reminding me of a stark version of homes built in the 1980s. It looked as if all the windows were uncovered. I glanced along the sloping driveway. From the bus stop down the road, I hadn't been able to see the property because it was hidden behind strategically planted tall trees; it didn't seem likely that anyone could peer inside the bare windows from the other side of the treeline.

The home was beautiful, I thought as I continued up the driveway. I liked stretching my legs and was both grateful for and surprised by the fact that it wasn't currently snowing or raining. I'd forgotten to grab an umbrella, which meant it would surely do something weathery when I made my way back to the bus stop.

I didn't spot any vehicles until I came around a curve at the top of the drive.

"Oh, hello, Delaney. I'm sorry I didn't see you sooner. I would have come to gather you."

Shelagh O'Conner sat in the driver's seat of a golf cart that had been threaded with feather boas around the top roof panel. "That's a steep walk"

"Hello," I said, glad I wasn't breathless. "I enjoyed it."

"If I had security cameras, I would have caught your arrival. Apologies. I'm not a fan of all the things we do to watch everyone all the time."

"No problem." Of course, I wondered if she might not be a fan of the cameras because a picture had once exposed her strange behavior. But surely I was reading too much into the moment.

"I've been tending to one of my horses. She was a wee bit off last night. I wanted to make sure she's okay."

"Is she?"

"Right as rain."

"Glad to hear it."

"Since you're the last one to visit, we have some time. Would you like to meet my animals?"

"I like animals and books almost equally. I would love to meet yours."

"Climb aboard."

Even the golf carts in Scotland had steering wheels on the wrong side. I hopped into the passenger seat next to Shelagh, and she told me to hang on.

She pressed on the gas pedal, and we quickly veered over and around more shrub-lined asphalt pathways until we came upon a giant pasture and another blue-and-white barn set even farther back from the front structures.

"I'm fond of the color blue, if you couldn't tell," Shelagh said.

She had a lead foot, and I was holding on to the front pole for dear life.

"You like many different shades of blue," I said.

She laughed. "I like all blues. Do you know what my family did, how I became so ridiculously wealthy?"

"I do know." I'd found out about the roots of her fortune online. "Manufacturing."

"Yes, but specifically manufacturing something called Magic Blue."

I looked at her but still held on as we approached the barn. "It's quite a product."

"Aye, lass."

Magic Blue was a product I still saw on store shelves, one

my family back home in Kansas probably still used. You poured it down your drain every month or so to prevent clogs and buildup. Afterward, blue foam came up through the drain. After a few minutes, you turned on the water for approximately thirty seconds, and then you could be practically guaranteed to have clear pipes for at least a month. My parents used it religiously, and I suddenly had an urge to buy some to use at the house by the sea. The blues would complement each other.

"You must be rich beyond comprehension," I said.

Shelagh laughed. "My bank account does not suffer. My father was a chemist. He invented the product, patented it. It's not just snake oil—it really works."

"Oh, I know. He must have been brilliant."

"He was." Shelagh smiled sadly. "Not the kindest of men, though. He wasn't abusive, but he wasn't affectionate either. My life as an only child was lonely and quiet."

"Your mother?"

"Distant, addicted to some drug or another that they gave back then so women would remain in their place—docile and without opinions."

"I'm so sorry," I said.

"A long time ago now, and I found ways to amuse myself. Not all of them got me in trouble with the law." Her smile transformed into something wry.

I nodded as she steered the golf cart into the barn, wood chips snapping under our wheels as we came to a stop.

Three horses were inside, each in its own stall, along with one tender, a man with a quick smile.

He patted a horse on the nose and then hurried to give Shelagh a hand out of the golf cart. I watched her as an image of the person Tom and I had seen in the car park popped into my mind. Yes, that person had definitely moved like someone younger, someone who wouldn't need help getting out of a vehicle. Someone male.

"Ta, Winston," Shelagh said. "This is my stable man, Winston. Winston, this is Delaney Nichols. She's from America."

"A pleasure tae meet ye," he said as he extended a hand my direction.

He wore an old brown-billed cap. Its fit over his thick gray hair made me think he'd had the cap for a long time. Along with his big nose and thick, wrinkled skin, the friendly light in his blue eyes made me smile.

"Nice to meet you too," I said.

He nodded politely and then turned and walked to a narrow storage closet in between two stalls. He crouched and busied himself with taking things out of his pocket and putting them into the closet. I couldn't help but notice the key ring he used to lock the closet; it was a big round one with a macramé tail. There had to be at least fifty keys on it.

"She's still doing all right?" Shelagh nodded toward the horse Winston had been tending to.

"She's grand, ma'am," he said.

"Good." Shelagh walked toward the stalls, and she and the horse greeted each other over the half wall, cheek to cheek. "This is Gin. Well, she has a much longer name, but we just call her Gin," Shelagh said to me. "The other two are Willa and Bouquet."

"May I pet them?" I asked.

"Of course."

I hadn't been around horses in a long time, and their brown-eyed wisdom was like food for my soul. They were beautiful and friendly. My heart swelled, and I cooed at the animal. Winston stood and smiled at me again.

"Do you ride much?" I asked Shelagh.

"I ride, though not as much as I used to. Do you?"

"I grew up on a farm, and we had a couple horses at one time or another, but I haven't ridden for years."

"You are invited to ride any of these lovelies at any time you would like."

"That's very kind," I said. "I would enjoy doing that someday."

I looked at her as she kept her attention on Gin. She adored these animals. Anyone who loved creatures as much she did couldn't be a bad person. That was one of the rules, wasn't it?

"She does seem fine," I said.

"Aye," Winston added.

"Aye, she's fine. Thank you for taking care of her, Winston," Shelagh said.

He nodded at her.

But there was something to her voice that gave me pause. Yes, she was grateful the horse was in good health, but was there a hint of coldness in her tone? Or was I imagining it? She changed the subject too quickly for me to decide.

"All right, then. How about the tour of the library?" she said to me. "Come back anytime to see my girls."

"I appreciate that. And I am very ready to see the library."

As we reboarded the golf cart, she sent Winston a frown. He didn't notice as his attention was fully on the horses.

"Everything okay?" I asked quietly after she backed the cart out of the barn.

"Aye," she said abruptly. She frowned again. "I think Winston was drinking through the night. If something had happened to Gin . . ."

I didn't see any sign of a night of heavy drinking. I'd seen him putting things away in the closet, but I didn't notice what the items were—I'd been too interested in Gin. Had Winston been hiding a bottle—perhaps one filled with booze? I didn't think so. I had an urge to go back and look, but I squelched it.

I put my hand on Shelagh's arm. "Gin seems okay."

"Aye. I think so." She shook her head and then forced a small smile. "I'm looking forward to showing you the library."

Shelagh steered the golf cart to the side of the house. She led me through a door, on the other side of which was what I would have called a mudroom, if it weren't so fancy. There were plenty of pairs of wellies lined up, only some of them muddy, but this was nothing like a good old Kansas mudroom with a warped screen door that slammed shut in the ever-present prairie wind.

We moved into a kitchen that was as large as I might have predicted. It was pristine, but I thought I smelled the remnants of recent cooking. Another door led out to the back grounds. It was closed, but I could see the barn through the window that took up the top half. I hadn't noticed the door from the other side.

I wanted to ask how many people lived in the house, but I suspected that it was only Shelagh. I knew she'd never married. It was a beautiful, expansive place, but it was also big enough for a person to get lost in. I felt a tiny bit sorry for her, but she didn't behave as if she wanted sympathy.

Once through the kitchen, we followed a long, white, wood-paneled hallway toward the back of the house. Shelagh stopped outside some closed double doors and looked at me.

She nodded at the large multipaned window at the end of the hallway. "I have a security system, but I don't always remember to arm it. I need to better care for these books, which is part of the reason I think it's time to do something else with them."

"In recent years security has become much more convenient. Have you had someone show you any new options?"

She shrugged. "Some."

"Well, you might want to consider looking at everything that's out there. It's really is much easier than it used to be."

"I'll keep that in mind," she said, as if she wouldn't. "Here it is. Here is the library, Delaney." She turned the knobs and pushed the doors so they swung open with just the right amount of speed and flair. She probably always opened the doors with such drama.

I followed her inside.

The library extended up the entire height of the house.

Rich wooden shelves and floors covered with vibrant throw rugs filled the large space. There were more books in here than in the bookshop.

Couches and chairs were set up in a U formation, each seat given its own lighting as well as a table where mugs of tea or coffee probably magically appeared. Each of the two upper levels had its own walkway with a wrought-iron railing, and each wall was adorned with a rolling ladder.

It was a place of both opulence and comfort. You had everything you would ever need inside this library. You wouldn't even need to eat; the books would be enough.

"Wow." My eyes went wide.

"Aye. Wow. It's my favorite place in the whole world. I don't even enjoy traveling, because it takes me away from here."

"I understand." A tiny part of me silently acknowledged, however, that I liked my new garret library even better, but that was for less material reasons. Maybe there was a perfect library for everyone; you just had to be lucky enough to find it. Or find the perfect someone to make it for you.

"You may take a slow look around when we finish our business. Sit."

We sat on opposite ends of the couch. I tried to rein in my focus and direct it at my host, but it took me a few seconds. She seemed to understand and waited.

Just as I nodded that I was ready, a gentleman in a tuxedo and a cap walked in with a tray. I didn't recognize Louis at first, but once he greeted me, I did.

"Oh, hello!" I hadn't meant to sound so surprised, as my mind tried to figure out exactly what his roles for Shelagh included. He seemed to understand.

"I do a little bit of everything," he answered my unasked question. He lifted the hat, exposed his bald head, and lowered it again. "I didn't fix the refreshments, but I'm still solid enough on my feet that I can deliver them."

"It's good to see you, Louis," I said.

He poured us each a mug of tea and then left again. A tray overflowed with small cookies in more flavors than maybe even Rosie and Aggie could bake. Since Shelagh didn't fill a plate immediately, I didn't either. I eyed them, though.

"What do you know about Robert Louis Stevenson, Delaney?" Shelagh asked after she took a sip of tea.

"Other than the books he wrote, I don't think I know anything. I've never researched him. What do you find most interesting about him?"

"Oh, everything. Did you know he wrote *Jekyll and Hyde* in three days, after a dream?"

"I didn't."

"He did. And he battled ill health all his life, through writing all his stories. Bronchial tube troubles—things that we could handle fairly easily these days, but not then. He searched his whole life for a place he could live and not suffer as much. Ultimately he moved to Samoa and then died there."

"Interesting." I took a sip too.

"Yes. He was a celebrity during his lifetime, much like Charles Dickens was. It was a different time, of course—back then popular writers were some of the biggest celebrities."

"Like Stephen King these days?"

"Aye, but there were fewer popular writers back then, of course, and printing presses were less reliable. As I believe I mentioned to you, *Jekyll and Hyde* was set to publish one year, but many of the first-edition copies didn't get delivered until the next. Nowadays, as you know, digital copies have changed everything . . . but I digress. Mr. Stevenson was popular and considered prolific, but nothing happened as quickly back then as it does these days. He didn't write as many books as you might think, but of those *The Strange Case of Dr. Jekyll and Mr. Hyde* is undoubtedly his best known. Perhaps it and *Treasure Island* have equal places in history." She cleared her throat. "But in my heart there is only *Jekyll and Hyde*."

"Why?"

"From the first moment I read it, it spoke to me—the imagery, the secretive life, the idea of man's true self being tamed only by the constraints of civilization. I just love it. I've lost track of how many times I've read it over the years, but each and every time it still hits me in all the right spots." She smiled. "I savor each word."

"I think it must be wonderful to have something like that. I've reread a few books over the years, but I don't have one that I go back to again and again. In fact, some of the books I loved as a girl I don't like now. The old-fashioned writing isn't enjoyable for me any longer."

Shelagh turned and nodded to the bookshelves immediately behind us. "Understand that when I read it the first time, for whatever reason, I hadn't ever heard of it. I had somehow bypassed all the spoilers, if you will. It was a new story to me, and that might have contributed to why I fell in love with it. Please just go have a look at that shelf."

I set down my tea and made the short trip to the shelf. There were probably three hundred copies of *Jekyll & Hyde* on it.

"So many different editions," I said.

"Yes, and most of them aren't valuable at all. They are just copies I purchased here and there. I once stopped by The Cracked Spine, but there were no copies there at the time."

"I heard you'd stopped by, but I don't think you've been back."

"Ah, I suppose people do notice those sorts of things sometimes, but that doesn't mean I haven't sent in others to search. In fact . . ." Shelagh stood and came over to my side. Gently she took hold of my arm. "This way."

We walked toward the back of the room and to some other shelves. Shelagh paused dramatically and sent me a conspiratorial smile. "You're going to love this." She pushed on a book, and just like in old movies the bookshelf swung open. "In here is where I keep my favorites. They aren't the most valuable of my books, except for one, but they are definitely the ones that mean the most to me. Louis has been inside your bookshop many times. He has spoken about the lovely older woman you have working there."

"Rosie?"

"I don't know her name, but Louis adores her."

"Everyone does."

"I'm not surprised." She gestured to the shelves. "Some of the books from your bookshop are in here, but some are also

out in the general population of my library. This place is a secret, Delaney. I'm showing it to everyone involved in the hunt,
but I haven't told a soul outside my immediate circle about it
in years."

"I'll keep the secret."

We walked into the small space behind the moving bookshelf. Inside were more shelves, but only the top one was filled.
An old typewriter sat up on a pedestal in a corner. A row of
books ran along the shelf. My eyes scanned copies of modern
mysteries as well as older versions of the classics.

"Is that a first-edition Austen?" I nodded toward a copy of
Persuasion.

"A second edition, sadly, and with no autograph inside, but
I love the feel of the cover. It's worn perfectly."

I smiled at my fellow book nerd. "It's lovely."

"Aye." Shelagh sighed.

"The typewriter?" I said. "Is that yours?"

"It is!" she exclaimed as she smiled at the old machine.
"It's an Underwood. Only slightly valuable, but it means a lot
to me. It was my first typewriter back when I was young. I've
had it for so long, I expect it has witnessed all my secrets. At
one time I imagined I could be a writer. I pounded out a few
short stories on this." She pushed a key. "I decided I was more
of a reader, though. I'm fond of the old machines, and they're
headed the way of the dinosaurs, so I kept this one."

"And this room is where the book that we will be hunting
for was kept? One of your favorites."

"No. My *most* favorite. An old and valuable copy of *Jekyll
and Hyde*."

I frowned.

"You think I'm being naïve, perhaps careless with my most
prized possession."

"I just hope it's being hidden in a safe place."

"Of course it is."

"Good."

"Anyway, I wanted you to see where the book had been kept. It's my secret room, Delaney. I don't advertise it. It might be silly, but sometimes they speak to me, my books. If they speak to you too, perhaps this will give you an advantage. Perhaps there's still something of its spirit here that might tell you where to find it."

I looked at her. Yes, books spoke to me, but I doubted it was in the same ways they did with her. My bookish voices, those tricks of my intuition, had a knack for speaking up more when I least expected them than when I wanted them to. I turned up my intuitive ears for a moment to see if they were trying to communicate now. They weren't.

"Ah," Shelagh said as she smiled at me knowingly. "I see they do speak to you."

"I suppose."

"Come along. There's more to this, I promise. I'm sending you on a treasure hunt, but not a wild-goose chase."

I followed her out of the room. She closed the shelves by pushing gently on them, and we moved back to the couch.

Shelagh reached into her pocket and pulled out a folded piece of paper. "I gave everyone else the same note." She handed me the paper.

I unfolded it and read aloud:

"'Pierce my hart and blood will flow. Not red nor black, but aye, read all o'.'" I looked at Shelagh. "Clue number one?"

"Aye."

"A riddle of sorts."

"Maybe." Shelagh shrugged.

"I'm not from Edinburgh, Shelagh. I'm still kind of a tourist. I'm not sure I'll be able to figure out one clue, let alone a trail of them."

"I disagree. Based upon what I have learned about you, you are very smart."

"Brigid told you that?"

Shelagh looked surprised. "She did. She told you about talking to me?"

I nodded. "I appreciate her vote of confidence, but I still don't know my way around all that well."

"Something tells me you might know people who could help."

I opened my mouth to protest, but she was correct; I knew several people who would not only be good at such a game but would enjoy it too. I closed my mouth and nodded.

"There. See! I knew what I was doing." Shelagh reached into another pocket and pulled out a different piece of paper, holding it in her hand as she continued. "Delaney, whoever finds my book shall receive my entire library upon my death. However, each of you will also receive a sum of money just for trying. I've written that sum here." She extended the paper to me. "If this amount is disagreeable to you, let me know now and we will go our separate ways."

I looked at the dollar amount she'd written down and gulped. Any museum or library or school would be beyond blessed to receive such a sum. If I won, I'd follow Edwin's lead. He gave money away all the time; this would thrill him no end. "Shelagh, this is very generous."

"I have the money, and I like my money to do some good. You may do whatever you want with it."

I would never keep it. "Very generous."

"So you'll do it, then? You'll search?"

"I will do my best." I would, but I was more thrilled by a

future donation than motivated by the contest. Shelagh's library was beyond impressive, and hopefully all the books inside it would go where they'd be best taken care of and viewed, but in truth the hunt might also be plain fun, particularly if I could get my friends and family involved.

"That's all a person can ask for. Now . . . I have something else I want to tell you." Shelagh's voice became more serious than I'd yet heard it.

The double doors to the library burst open, startling us both.

"Gracious," Shelagh said as we struggled to understand what was happening.

"Shelagh O'Conner," a police officer said as four of them marched toward us with Louis following behind, his expression one of panicked fear.

"Aye, of course." Shelagh said.

"We need you to come with us," the police officer said.

I stood. "Is she under arrest?"

The police officer sent me a level but angry glare. "Not yet, but it's imperative that we speak with Ms. O'Conner immediately."

"You can't do that here?" I said, plopping my hands on my hips.

"We. Would. Prefer. Not. To."

I nodded at him as a voice sounded in my head. The bookish voices had just been waiting for the right moment.

The single biggest problem in communication is the illusion that it has taken place.

I thought it might be George Bernard Shaw, but I wasn't sure. It was a rare moment that I couldn't place exactly where the bookish voice had come from, but it had happened. No matter what though, my intuition was trying to tell me *something*.

"Do you have an attorney?" I asked her.

"Louis, please call Frank."

"I will," Louis said.

A moment later Louis and I were alone inside the library, looking at the open doors where Shelagh and the police had departed.

I hadn't heard any sirens approach the house, and I didn't hear them peel away in retreat.

"I had so many questions, and she was about to tell me something very serious, Louis. It felt important. Do you know what it was?"

"I have no idea, lass."

"You should call the attorney."

"Aye. Of course. You'll show yourself out?"

"Yes." And that's exactly what I did.

EIGHT

I could have retraced my steps and gone back the way Shelagh had brought me in—down the hallway, through the kitchen, and then out the mudroom. But there was also a front door, and my curiosity quickly concluded that it would be fine for me to go that route instead.

In the hall, I listened for where Louis might have gone. Was there a landline he was using somewhere? I didn't hear any voices, but I kept my ears pricked to all noises as I hurried along, passing the entry into the kitchen and continuing toward the front of the house.

The hall turned right and then to the left before I came upon more living spaces. The library seemed far off, very hidden from view, from curious eyes. The design had probably been on purpose, but Shelagh and I hadn't had a chance to discuss it, or much of anything for that matter.

On my left was a giant living room. It was so large that there were three different gathering areas; a television hung on the wall above a fireplace in the middle of the room, in front of a couch and a few comfortable chairs. The room didn't feel overly formal, but there was no sign that it was well used either. No old mugs, no misfolded newspapers.

On my right was a room with a grand piano as well as another hall that led to a distant staircase. I didn't dare explore that far off the beaten path.

Other than a small loo, there were no other nearby rooms. I didn't know if there were other hallways going other places, but looking would entail much more than the small detours I'd already taken. I hurried to the door.

Windows bordered it, and through them I spied dark clouds coming in this direction; rain clouds, not snow, I thought. An old wooden coat cabinet held several umbrellas, but it didn't feel right taking one.

The knob turned easily, and I let myself out. After another glance up to the clouds, I hurried toward the drive in hopes of making it to the bus stop before a storm hit.

Of course, I wondered why the police had wanted to talk to Shelagh, but I suspected it had something to do with the burglaries from the night before. If the burglar and the person Tom and I had come across in the car park were the same, there was now no doubt in my mind that it hadn't been Shelagh we'd seen. None of the elements fit—the size of the person, the agility. And there really was something distinctly male to the figure, something Shelagh couldn't even fake.

I wasn't worried for her—I didn't believe she would be arrested, but maybe that was just denial on my part. I would call Inspector Winters later and see if I could ask as well as tell him the things I hadn't mentioned before.

As I approached the long driveway, lightning struck somewhere close by, and then thunder rumbled a few seconds later. I sped up to a jog, wishing it had been snow and not rain heading toward me.

The noise of a car's engine coming from the direction of the house caught my attention. I looked behind. I didn't know my expensive car models well, but I was pretty sure it was a Bentley.

I kept to the side but didn't stop jogging. The Bentley slowed, and the window rolled down. Findlay Sweet was behind the wheel.

"Louis sent me to find you," he said. "I can give you a lift."

I fake-smiled at him. "I enjoy walking."

"Well, certainly, but the rain's coming. You'll be drenched."

"The bus stop is just past the end of the drive."

"Which is a long way off, and then you'll have to wait for a bus." The car was moving at my jogging speed.

"I'm okay."

"Tom told you about our past, didn't he?" Findlay said a moment later.

"I'm okay, Findlay. Thank you for offering me a ride, though."

"I'm over all that resentment. It was a long time ago, and I only stopped by his pub yesterday because I was in the area and thought I might see if we could bury the hatchet. I was the one driving and delivering the messenger. You were his last de- livery, and I waited in the pub to watch and make sure he went inside, and then I just enjoyed being there. It's a lovely pub, and your coming in gave me a better opportunity to have a brief conversation with Tom. Truly, you'll be safe with me."

Isn't that what all the serial killers said?

Lightning struck again, so bright I closed my eyes and held my arm above my head a moment. The thunder followed only a second later.

"It's becoming unsafe out there, Delaney. Hop in. It will be fine."

"Well, a lift to the bus stop wouldn't be terrible." Against about fifty percent of my better judgment, I hopped into the front passenger seat of the Bentley. The other fifty percent was glad to be out of the rain that started coming down in sheets the second I closed the car door. Findlay had to hurry to get his window shut.

He sent me a quick, somewhat impatient smile. It occurred to me that he probably hadn't wanted this duty and had only come out in the rain because Louis told him to.

"Thank you," I said.

"No problem."

"Do you know anything about why the police wanted to talk to Shelagh?" I asked a few long, silent beats later.

"I'm sure it has something to do with the robberies."

"You mean because of her behavior decades ago?"

"Aye. It seems we might have a new Mr. Hyde, a new monster."

I cringed. That moniker was shocking. "That might be over-stating."

Findlay shrugged. "The name? Oh, aye. It's what all the newspeople are saying, though. They said it back then too."

"Weird timing, huh?"

Findlay thought a moment. "You mean it's strange because you just met Shelagh yesterday?"

"No, it's strange because Shelagh set up the treasure hunt at the same time someone dressed at least similarly to how she was dressed robbed some homes. The timing feels . . ."

"Forced?"

"No, just strange."

He didn't comment further, but I couldn't tell if it was because he agreed with me or if he just didn't want to argue.

We'd come to the end of the driveway. Catercorner was the bus stop, an aluminum awning protecting a gathering of riders who'd huddled together.

"I really don't mind taking you home or back to work or to the pub. It's cold out there, and you'd have to get in close to all those people to stay warm and dry."

He had a point, but still . . . "I'm okay. Thank you very much, though."

Findlay squinted at me. "Call Tom. Tell him you're with me. I'll talk to him too. If something happens to you, there'll be no way for me to hide."

I didn't like this man. I didn't trust him, but his idea also made me smile with a little embarrassment. Tom knew where I'd gone. Louis had told me to show myself out. Supposedly he'd told Findlay to come get me.

"I wouldn't mind a ride to the bookshop. Thank you, Findlay," I finally said. However, I pulled out my phone. "I'll text Tom and let him know I'm on my way back."

"Aye, that should work."

Findlay skillfully steered the car through the heavy rain and busy streets.

"Do you still fish in the summer?" I asked.

"Aye. Less and less as the years go by, and Shelagh pays me well to be her driver."

"How long have you worked for her?"

"About seven years. It's been good."

"Did you . . . ever remarry?"

He turned to look at me. "No, never did. I enjoy the company of a lovely lass every now and then, but I'm not meant to be tied down. There was a time I would have said the same about your husband."

"We're fine." I wished I'd just ignored the bait.

"Well, time will tell."

I nodded.

A text came through on my phone. It was Tom.

Let me know the SECOND you get back.

Will do, I texted back.

Yikes, he was genuinely worried.

Anxiety clenched my jaw. Was there really a reason to be concerned here? For someone who lived by her instincts, either I wasn't listening well or they weren't speaking loud and clearly enough.

I knew my way around this part of Edinburgh well enough that when Findlay turned left when I was certain that he should have taken a right, my anxiety ramped up even more.

"Are you bringing me back to the bookshop?"

"Aye. This is a shortcut. You'll see."

I put my hand on the door handle. Findlay angled a side-eye but kept driving.

"Are you familiar with the closes?" he asked.

"Of course."

"You really don't drive though any of them, but there is a wider one this direction, one that Shelagh always has me take to get her to downtown or to Grassmarket."

"Okay." It didn't make sense, but I wasn't ready to jump out of a moving vehicle yet.

"You know, Tom never did apologize to me. I had come to accept that he wasn't sorry for what he did."

"I don't think he was. I think he cared about your wife."

Findlay laughed. "Aye, I think so too."

I didn't like the insinuation, if that's what I was hearing. It had all happened a long time ago, and I wasn't interested in hearing his side of this story.

"I'm good here, Findlay. Stop and I'll hop out."

"We're almost there."

I didn't think we were. "It's okay. Please stop."

"One more turn." Findlay took another right.

And suddenly we were back to the world I knew. The statue of Greyfriars Bobby, the infamous dog who'd guarded his person's grave after he'd died was right there—how had I not known about this "shortcut"?

We were also next to Grassmarket. It was still raining, but we were almost to the pub, which meant we were also almost to the bookshop.

"There we are." Findlay nodded toward Tom's pub as it came into sight.

The car stopped at an intersection.

"I'll get out here. Thanks for the ride." I was out of the car before I could register any response from him.

Relief washed through me as I hurried toward the pub. The rain hadn't stopped, but it was no longer blinding.

My reaction was probably ridiculous, but I couldn't help being glad I was out of that car and safe from whatever frightening things my imagination had conjured. I wished I hadn't gotten into the Bentley, but I had.

I stepped into the pub, grateful for the small crowd so that Tom didn't spot me immediately. I normalized my face, took a couple deep breaths, and finally wove a path to the bar.

Relief lit his eyes when he saw me. "Ah, lass, there you are." He put down bottles he was using to pour a mixed drink and came around the bar. "Happy you're here."

"Were you truly worried about Findlay doing something or

just generally concerned?" I took a towel that Rodger handed me over the bar.

Tom saw his own anxiety mixing with the remnants of my own and sighed. "I'm sorry, Delaney, but I was truly worried. I've seen a side of Findlay that isn't pleasant. My issues with him are from a long time ago, though, and maybe I shouldn't judge anyone by what happened then. I didn't mean to frighten you."

"It's okay." I smiled. "I shouldn't have gotten into the car."

"All's well that ends well."

"Hush, hush, everyone. There's been a murder!" A customer's voice rose above the noise of the crowd, his words silencing us and directing our attention to the television set.

A newscaster was on-screen, a picture to his left.

"Police have just released a statement regarding last night's robberies by this man." A CCTV shot of the same person in the shabby coat and big hat we'd seen on the television the night before expanded to fill the screen. "It seems that the burglar is now under suspicion of murder as well. The victim is an Edinburgh man recently known to tend bar at our world-famous Deacon Brodie's Tavern. Ritchie John was last seen alive at the pub yesterday afternoon, though it's unclear if he was there as an employee or a patron. CCTV caught the burglar making his way into Mr. John's flat. A couple hours ago, police went to the flat to investigate and found Mr. John's body."

"Oh, Tom, I met him." I steadied myself by grabbing on to the bar.

"Aye?" Tom stepped closer to me.

"I need to call Inspector Winters," I said.

He held on to my arm as my knees buckled a little. "Take a minute, then we'll call from the back."

NINE

"A book?" Inspector Winters said. "She's sending people on a treasure hunt to find one of her books?"

"Yes," I said.

"And this has been set in motion just as a new threat has come to Edinburgh?"

"I know, it seems odd timing, but I don't know if it's related or if it's all just coincidence. I can't imagine Shelagh's a murderer. Is that why she was taken in for questioning?" I'd asked the same thing more than once now, but he still hadn't answered.

This time he just shook his head, but I didn't think it was in response to me.

We were inside The Cracked Spine with Rosie, Tom, and Hector. The rain had given way to a cloudless, starry darkness so cold it seemed like a bad idea to go out there, even with the twinkling sky.

"I'm sorry I didn't tell you all this before," I'd said at the beginning of the conversation. This time around I even mentioned the part about Louis seeming to know the victim but Ritchie behaving as though he didn't know Louis.

Inspector Winters's phone dinged. He read a text message silently to himself and then put the phone back into his pocket. "In answer to the question you've asked a number of times now, it looks like Shelagh wasn't arrested for anything. The officers who came to talk to her simply wanted to discuss what might have been behind her behavior all those years ago and if she could think of anyone who might want to repeat her actions. They do not think she killed anyone." Inspector Winters scratched his head.

"What?" I asked.

"I need more clarification as to why they don't think that, but I'll ask in person. According to the text I just got, she's been released and was of very little help."

"I'm glad she wasn't arrested," I said.

"Will you still hunt for her book?"

"I think so." I shrugged.

Inspector Winters sat on the corner of the front desk and rubbed his chin. "I'll meet with the officers on the case this evening and tell them what you've told me."

"Okay."

"How is this treasure hunt supposed to begin?"

"Oh, I was given a clue." I reached into my pocket for the piece of paper with the clue that Shelagh had given me. I'd already shown it to Tom and Rosie.

Inspector Winters read it and shook his head once more. "I have no idea."

"May I see it again?" Rosie asked.

Inspector Winters handed her the paper.

"H-A-R-T, not H-E-A-R-T?" Rosie said.

"Yes," I said.

"I should have realized it before, then. Och, 'tis verra easy," she said.

We all, even Hector, blinked at her.

"Aye. The White Hart Inn. The spelling is the key. H-A-R-T, and 'a white kiss' is from a poem that Robert Burns wrote when he visited his lady at that verra place long ago."

En masse we moved from the back of the bookshop to the front and looked out the window. Multiple businesses had storefronts on the bottom level of the buildings all the way up and down the long part of Grassmarket. The pub at The White Hart Inn was one of those establishments; so was Tom's pub. Tom and I had joked a few times that if I'd first stopped inside a pub closer to the bookshop than his, I might have met a different pub owner and I'd be married to someone else. It was just a joke, but every time we laughed about it, the hairs on my arms rose, as if the Fates were reminding me of how good they'd been. I didn't want to do anything to offend the Fates.

Besides, I *had* visited The White Hart Inn, but only once, though I hadn't met the pub owner. My bookish voices had been noisy in there.

"Really?" I said as we all looked toward the lit windows of the now busy establishment.

"I think you're onto something, Rosie," Tom said. "It seems obvious now."

"I wonder how many others have already figured it out," I said.

"Shall we go see?" Tom asked.

"I think we should," I said. "Want to come with us?" I looked at the police inspector and Rosie.

They both declined but wanted an update later. I promised I would let them know what we found.

As Tom and I grabbed our coats, I decided I was going to

have to share something with him on the way. I should have shared it a long time ago, but now it might become important, depending upon how noisy my head found the pub this time. Hopefully the crowd of real people inside would drown out the imaginary ones that lived in my mind, but it made perfect sense that they would have lots to say inside The White Hart Inn.

Wooden beams hung along the pub's ceiling. Robert Burns's words had been painted on them. I'd read everything Burns had written, starting back when I lived in the States. I loved his work. The words on the beams had come together with the voices in my mind and made my first visit to the pub loud and almost unbearable.

As we hurried toward it and the cold bit at my nose, I said, "Tom, you know how sometimes I seem a little spacey?"

"Aye." I could hear the smile in his voice. "It's an endearing trait."

"I'm not sure my mother would agree, but I'm glad to hear you think so. Anyway, something is going on inside my head when I appear to be zoning out sometimes."

"Aye?" Tom stopped walking, so I did too.

It was too cold to stand still for long, but we both sensed it was the right thing to do. We faced each other, our breath fogging around us.

"Words from books come to me. The characters speak to me. It's the way my intuition works—using the words I've read, with voices that seem appropriate, to tell me something I should be paying attention to."

"Aye?" Tom said again.

"Yes. Aye."

"Interesting."

"Again, probably not how my mother would describe it."

"Different voices?"

"Yes, some male, some female. Of course, I've never heard most of the real voices, but my mind gives them all unique qualities."

He smiled. "I think it's wonderful." He reached up and ran the back of his index finger along my jaw. "Lovely."

"Well, thank you, but now you know, and there's a chance it will happen in there tonight." I nodded toward the pub.

Tom's eyebrows came together, but he continued to smile. "Was that something you were afraid to tell me?"

"Not afraid, really. Okay, maybe a tiny bit. It's a little odd."

Tom laughed. "Delaney, you could tell me you're the new monster and I couldn't love you any less than more than everything."

I closed my eyes tight and then opened them a moment later. "Nope, not a hallucination. You're still there."

Tom laughed again. "I will be forever. Come on, it's cold. Let's get to the pub."

I'd noticed the carved white stag above the front door many times as I'd walked by. I glanced up at it tonight as we entered. The well-stocked bar was at the back, on the left, and tables and chairs filled the rest of the homey, smallish establishment. A black-and-white rendition of the Grassmarket of old, along with the castle on the hill, had been painted on the green wall to the right, above a long, floral-cushioned bench.

A good-size crowd filled the place, which might have been why no bookish voices spoke to me immediately. In fact, I focused on keeping them at bay and sensed it would be fine.

However, we were greeted by someone we knew.

"There you are! I've switched to coffee so I could manage

my way home. Why did it take you so long?" Birk sat at a table just to the left of the front door. "Why is it taking everyone so long?"

Tom and I shared a look.

"You figured it out?" I said.

"Hours ago. Sit."

We looked around the pub but then joined Birk at his table. Behind him a television had been mounted up in the corner, similar to how Tom had mounted the TV in his pub. An old American show was playing—*Gunsmoke* maybe, but I couldn't be sure.

"How long have you been here?" I asked.

"Since about two this afternoon."

"Why didn't you just call me?"

"Because I thought everyone should figure out this first clue on their own, see if they all were game. I just didn't think it would take so long."

"I didn't figure it out. Rosie did."

"And here it is, right by the bookshop. Goodness." Birk tsked.

"Has anyone else shown up?"

"No."

"Why did you wait?"

Birk shrugged. "I thought it would be more fun to do this as a group—if everyone else is agreeable, that is."

"Really?"

"Aye. Why not? I think it's the best way, really. We need to make sure the books get the proper care. I'm here to do my part in making sure that happens."

"I agree," I said, though I hadn't given the idea of a group effort any real thought. "Sorry it took me so long." I glanced up at the television. "Have you been paying attention to the news?"

"I heard about the murder, aye."

"Did you know the man killed was our bartender yesterday at Deacon Brodie's Tavern?"

Birk's eyes got wide. "I heard that he might have worked there, but I didn't put it all together. Gracious . . ."

I nodded and then told him about Shelagh's being questioned by the police.

"I had no idea," he said. "But she was released?"

"Yes."

"Who do they think is doing all this?"

"I don't know."

Birk paused and then took a sip of his coffee. "This *might* all be somehow tied together, but I don't know . . ."

I shrugged. "Maybe. We can probably talk to Shelagh tomorrow. I'd hate to bother her this evening. But if the monster has anything to do with her, maybe we should hold off looking for this book."

"Why?" Birk asked.

"Maybe we're being set up for something."

"I suppose that's possible." Birk hesitated. "But I'm not willing to stop searching."

"I don't really want to stop either," I said.

A server appeared with another coffee for Birk and two more for Tom and me. I hadn't seen Birk order them, but my hands were glad for the warmth.

"So is this the place we're supposed to be?" I asked. "Is this the answer to the clue? What next?"

"Aye." Birk nodded toward the bar. "The barkeep has an envelope with the next clue for each of us. This is mine." He reached into his coat pocket and pulled out the envelope. "Run and get yours, just in case they're different. You'll have to show your identification."

I bobbed and weaved a little to make it to the bar. The bartender was an old guy with flyaway white hair and round wire-rimmed glasses.

"Help ye?" he asked.

"My name is Delaney Nichols. I believe you have an envelope for me."

"Och, just a minute."

He finished pouring two pints, deposited them onto a tray, and then, with a hitch in his step, moved to the end of the bar. He reached down to a shelf and pulled out some envelopes. I spied a total of three, which confirmed for me that the other two participants hadn't been in yet. The bartender put two of the envelopes back on the shelf and walked toward me with mine in his hand.

"Identification, please," he said.

I showed him my ID.

"Verra good. Here you go." He handed me the envelope. "What's this all about?"

"I believe it's some sort of treasure hunt. Who brought these in for you?"

"Well, I'm not sure I'm supposed tae tell ye." He scratched his head. "But it was an older gentleman. Bald as a billiard ball. Dinnae tell anyone I spilled the beans."

Must have been Louis. "I won't. Thank you."

"Ye're welcome. Good luck to you."

I went back to the table, opening the envelope along the way.

Second Clue:
You always have to pay, perhaps with your very soul.

I read it aloud after I sat down again.

"Well, that's creepy." I looked up at Tom and Birk.

"'You always have to pay, perhaps with your very soul.' Mine said the same," Birk told us.

"Make anything of it?" Tom asked.

"Not offhand," Birk said.

"I have no idea." I handed Tom the note.

He read it again and then looked up at me. "It sounds ominous—or just purposefully mysterious."

"Yeah." I fell into thought.

"What, lass?" Birk asked.

"Do you think there is any way at all that Shelagh truly is a burglar, a killer?"

Tom put his hand over mine. "Lass, you can just walk away from this at any moment."

"I could . . . but I *truly* don't want to." Tom nodded as I turned to Birk. "What do you think? She's no spring chicken. Could one of her people be doing her bidding? You knew her before, right?"

"I knew her some, a long time ago but I don't know her people well, but she would never instruct them to do any of what's going on. I'm sure," Birk said.

I looked at Tom again. "I don't want to stop searching. It's not just that I want Shelagh's library—though don't get me wrong, it would be wonderful—but what if she's in danger too? I'll talk to Inspector Winters."

"You're concerned about Findlay?" Tom said.

"Who?" Birk asked.

Tom and I told Birk about Findlay Sweet and Tom's past with him. Birk didn't like hearing what had happened all those years ago, but he stuck by his guns that Shelagh would never ask anyone to do anything illegal or even somewhat harmful. If Findlay was behaving badly, he wasn't doing it because Shelagh had told him to.

"We'll work together, lass," Birk said. "I don't need the library either, or the money, of course, but I'm curious too. We'll do it together, the two of us. If the others want to be included, we'll welcome them also."

"I like that," I said.

"So do I," Tom added.

The door opened, and in unison the three of us glanced toward it. Tricia came through. She stood in the doorway a moment and looked around. Her eyes didn't land on us until after she'd scanned the rest of the pub.

I waved. She didn't wave back. She didn't smile either but walked toward us.

"Hello," she said. "I see you've all figured it out."

"Your envelope is behind the bar. Grab it and come join us," I said.

"You'll need identification," Birk said.

When Tricia returned to the table and I introduced her to Tom, she sat and read her message aloud. It was identical to the others.

"We've been discussing the robberies and the murder from last night," I said, trying to gauge if she also thought the events might be somehow tied together and if she was as hesitant to join in as she'd seemed the day before.

Tricia nodded. "It's terrible, and I didn't like what was going on, so I called Shelagh a wee bit ago. The police questioned her but let her go. She's pretty sure they don't think she was in any way involved in robberies or a murder. She said she wasn't. She told me the solution to the first clue, or I might not have ever figured it out. I'm not good at these sorts of things, but I'm going to keep trying. My school could use the funds that selling her library would give them."

We looked at her. I hadn't wanted to bother Shelagh, but that hadn't mattered to Tricia. She seemed different from the day before—either bolder or more comfortable, I wasn't sure. Maybe it was as simple as the idea of a new library being motivation enough for her to jump in with both feet now, but it was an interesting change.

"Delaney and I are going to work together," Birk said. "Want to do this with us? If we find the book, we're willing to figure out something fair."

In fact, I'd ask Birk if we should just let Tricia have the library if she did something good with it, but kept that to myself for now. I didn't tell Tricia about the fact that Louis seemed to know the murder victim either. For some reason I was glad Birk also chose not to.

"Oh. Well, I like working alone," she said. "That sounds rude, I'm sure, but I do prefer to work alone, even if I don't succeed. I'm not a team player at all. Go ahead and do what you want to do, though."

"Aye, all right," Birk said, no offense to his tone.

"Do you mind if I order something to eat? I'm starving, and . . . I could move to another table, but I need to eat something," Tricia said.

"Certainly," Birk said. "Good idea. Let's eat and see if our fourth arrives. If he does, we'll make it a grand party."

We ordered food, and as we ate, we discussed *Dr. Jekyll and Mr. Hyde* and the secrets men (and women) keep. People could be so many different things, in secret or not. It turned into a more philosophical conversation than I think any of us intended, but it sure seemed that though we all held the second clue inside our envelopes, we should consider the story more, think about those secrets and about possible clues within it.

We didn't stay too late, and our fourth never did show up, but I decided I'd find Jacques the next day and tell him he could join me and Birk.

There was safety in numbers, after all. Wasn't there?

TEN

"I suppose the good news is that there hasnae been another murder," Rosie said as she came through the bookshop's front door the next morning. She held Hector over one arm and a book in her other hand.

"Yes, that *is* the good news," I said.

But there was plenty of bad news.

There had been another string of robberies overnight, but the perpatrator, now *officially* dubbed "The New Monster" or "The New Mr. Hyde" by almost everyone in the media, had been caught on only one camera. Shelagh's past exploits were also mentioned, though not with much detail, and I heard one newsperson call her "The Old Monster."

The police suspected that the perp had broken in and stolen items from three different places, but he'd managed to duck and hide from nearby CCTV cameras at two of the locations. The one picture that was captured was even grainier than the first group of images.

However, it *did* seem that no other murders had been committed, which was undeniably good news.

"The city is going to become terrified." Rosie set Hector on the floor.

As he trotted toward me, the weight of the stress lifted a little. Everyone should have a Hector in their life. I picked him up and let him kiss my cheek.

"The newspeople aren't helping much."

"Aye." Rosie walked toward one of the bookshelves. "Do we have any copies of Robert Louis Stevenson's books? We'll need to gather them. I think people will be thinking about him and his books—they might be all the rage today." She waved the book she carried. "I found this one at home. I've had it for years and am not willing tae give it up. But I read it again last night."

Still holding Hector, I walked toward her and looked at the book. It was an old copy of *Jekyll & Hyde*, but not rare or overly valuable. The cover picture was illustrated with a well-dressed, dapper man and a monster's shadow looming behind him.

"What did you think?"

Rosie shrugged. "I thought the same thing I thought when I read it the first time. The language is stunning and beautiful, even with the older style. I enjoyed it, but my impressions haven't changed over the years despite all the other influences—the movies, the television. It's good but not my favorite."

I nodded. "Shelagh told me that when she read it the first time, she hadn't heard of it beforehand, so she read it without knowing anything about it. It fascinated her, and she fell in love with it."

"Aye. I cannae imagine not knowing something about the story before reading it. It's a part of our culture."

"Me either, and I wonder if we missed out on the best

experience because it has been such a well-known story for so long. Imagine the 'twist' being a true surprise."

"Aye, and with no computers, all the secrets werenae spilled as quickly as they can be now."

"It spoke to her back then, and she hasn't been able to let go of it."

Rosie frowned. "Do ye suppose she has a laboratory in the gigantic house? Maybe she's come up with a potion."

"The laboratory is certainly a possibility. It's a huge place, but I don't see her as the potion type." I shrugged, thinking about her father and his potions—but those were created a long time ago. "Who knows, though?"

"Do we have any other Stevensons?"

"We do. I've already arranged them on a single shelf." With Hector in the crook of my arm, I walked in that direction.

"How many *Jekyll and Hyde*s?"

"None, unfortunately."

"Aye? I was sure we had at least one."

"Not that I could find, but I'll keep looking if you want."

"Och, lass, I'm not sure of anything anymore. How long have ye been here?"

"A few hours. I woke up early."

"Ye didnae send an update last night. What happened?"

I told her the events of the evening, including the newest clue in the hunt for Shelagh's book. "*You always have to pay, perhaps with your very soul.*" Surprisingly—Rosie's very superstitious— she was more intrigued than bothered. I thought she'd encourage me to pull out of the hunt, but she didn't. She did, however, think that it was a good idea for Birk and I to hunt together.

"Tricia's an odd one, aye?" Rosie said.

"I'm not sure. Maybe she's just not overly friendly, which

is okay. We ate, shared lots of small talk, discussed the book some, and then left. She had no desire to work with either us or Jacques, Shelagh's nephew."

"Jacques didn't show?"

I shook my head. "Our first time was cut short. I'm going to visit Shelagh again to check on them both. He's from France, so he might not know Edinburgh enough to get the clue, but Shelagh told Tricia. She would have surely told Jacques too, you'd think."

Rosie fell into thought. "I think ye should take Birk tae visit Shelagh this morning. Talk tae her in person."

"Birk's busy until late this afternoon. We were planning on brainstorming later."

"Take Edwin. He'd enjoy visiting with Shelagh."

I thought a moment. "Good idea. I'll call him right away."

But then the front door opened and customers poured in before I could gather my phone. I couldn't remember a morning as busy as that one. Bookshops all over Edinburgh were probably experiencing the same; those with copies of *Jekyll & Hyde* were ringing up some extra sales. Rosie had been correct in predicting that many people would be looking for *any* Robert Louis Stevenson book. And once we ran out of those, many people just wanted something good to read. We had plenty of that in stock.

Hamlet arrived at ten, just as the rush slowed. His eyes were wide and bothered, but we couldn't ask him what was the matter until the bookshop emptied. I managed a quick call to Edwin, who said he would be at the shop to pick me up soon, but my immediate concern was for Hamlet. Something was wrong.

"What is it, lad?" Rosie asked when it was just the three of us and Hector. The dog had hurried to Hamlet's feet and panted up at him expectantly.

"I think I met the murder victim," he said as he pulled his laptop from his backpack and opened it on the table. "I knew the name was familiar, but I didn't remember the details until this morning. He spoke in one of my classes last year—an introduction to veterinary medicine, something for those of us who just wanted a little more information. He knows horses—*knew* horses."

"Oh, Hamlet, I'm so sorry," I said. "How did he know about horses?"

"He worked with them, but he didn't tell us any more than that. Just that he'd been around them all his life. He spoke about their personalities, their strengths and frailities, lovingly."

"Sorry, lad," Rosie said.

"Hamlet, I met him briefly two days ago, at Deacon Brodie's pub. He was a bartender."

"You did?"

I nodded. I hadn't seen Hamlet for a few days, but that wasn't unusual. He was a student, so his schedule was flexible.

"I don't remember him talking about tending bar."

"I'm sorry, Ham," I said. I wanted to say something complimentary about Ritchie John, but other than his kind smile I didn't know him at all.

"It's okay." He looked at us, tried to blink away the unsettling tears that had brightened his eyes. He picked up Hector. "I'm okay. It was strange to remember him, though. He was funny." Hamlet scratched behind Hector's ears. "His daughter was in the class too. I saw a young woman who appeared to be upset today. We passed each other. That's when Mr. John's talks came back to me. I'm pretty sure it was her. I'm going to double-check." He nodded at the laptop.

We sat around the table just as the front bell jingled again.

"I've got it," Rosie said. "Ye two see what ye can discover. And tell Hamlet the new clue, Delaney."

I told Hamlet the clue as he arranged Hector on his lap.

"*You always have to pay, perhaps with your very soul.*"

"That sounds ominous." Hamlet's eyebrows came together.

"Which makes me think it might not be, not really. Clues just sound better if they're scary, right?"

Hamlet smiled. "You have a point." He turned to his computer. "Here, yes, here she is. Darcy John. This is the woman I saw today. I remember him teasing her a little in the class."

Hamlet had pulled up pictures of university students from one of the student organization's Facebook pages. The people in the pictures were all tagged.

Darcy John was stunning, with a bright smile, long dark hair, and happy brown eyes.

"She's lovely. And really tall," I said.

"Aye, she's very tall," Hamlet said.

"Does everyone who gets tagged know they're on this page?"

"Aye. It's all part of the university's social activities. We're told going in that our names will be public if we attend certain events, and we're welcome to untag ourselves."

"How did you find this so quickly?"

Hamlet frowned. "I might have thought she was attractive and looked her up before, back when her father spoke in class. I didn't stalk her, but I did find this, then forgot all about her until today. Well, mostly. I might have looked around for her for a few days back then, but when I didn't see her anywhere . . . She never appeared in that class again, so I assumed she was just visiting it that day."

I smiled. "I see."

"Aye."

Hamlet was twenty-one and could talk to anybody. I'd observed him in conversation with highly educated people about everything from space travel to crayon colors. He was extraordinarily smart and handsome in the artistic way that Shakespeare had probably been. But he didn't date much—that I'd seen anyway.

Edwin said that Hamlet's past as a child living on the streets of Edinburgh had turned him into a loner. I thought that was sad, but Edwin thought Hamlet would grow out of it, probably after university.

"If I run into her again, I won't just walk by without inquiring if she needs anything. I'll give her my condolences, something more than an awkward smile at least."

He was also an old soul who just might not ever be able to connect with anyone good enough.

I put my hand on his arm. "That would be nice."

"I'm sure she's devastated. They were sweet together in the class. He teased her about being the teacher's favorite and such. I wish I'd . . ."

Hamlet might have had a crush.

"I'm sorry, Ham," I said again.

Hector put his front paws up on Hamlet's chest and demanded that Hamlet let him kiss away whatever pain he was going through.

Hamlet and I laughed.

Edwin called shortly afterward, telling me he and his Citroën were right outside the shop. I gave Hamlet a quick hug and confirmed with Rosie that it was okay for me to go.

"Tell Edwin the clue too," she said quietly as two customers searched the shelves.

"I will." I went through the door, the bell jingling again.

It was neither snowing nor raining. There wasn't a cloud in the sky. It was cold, though, and I pulled my collar up tight around my neck as I hurried the short distance to the car.

I hopped into the passenger side and filled Edwin in on the latest, including the newest clue.

"All right." Edwin said as he steered the car toward Shelagh's street. "What is worth the price of your soul?"

"Deal with the devil?"

"That's possible." But he didn't sound convinced.

We speculated, but none of our guesses seemed to have any meat to them.

We also updated each other on our personal lives. I was happy to hear that he and Vanessa were still going strong—Edwin had everything a person could ever want, and I was glad he had someone to share it with now. I told him about my garret library, and he said he wanted to come see it soon. He had a grand library in his grand house, but I would proudly show him mine, and I knew he'd want to spend some time inside it.

"The house is up that long driveway." I pointed at a break in the trees.

Edwin turned onto the drive. "Should we have called first?"

"Probably, but I think this will be okay."

"The element of surprise?"

"Maybe a little."

"I can work with that."

"Rosie mentioned you might know about the quirks in Shelagh's personality."

Edwin parked the car at the top of the drive. "Aye."

I looked at him. "Other than her love for *Jekyll and Hyde*, is there something else?"

Edwin shook his head. "I don't know her so very well, lass. Well, I don't know her at all now, but many years ago she was part of the Fleshmarket Batch."

"The auction group? I don't know why that surprises me so much, but it does."

"Aye."

I thought a moment. "That's how she knew Birk?" If that was indeed how they knew each other, Birk wouldn't broadcast it, particularly around others. Fleshmarket Batch was a long-kept secret.

"Probably. They were friends. We . . . we had to ask her to leave the group."

"Why?"

"She was . . . bossy."

"Bossy? In that she wanted to take charge or something else?"

"Aye. She didn't like that we weren't better organized. She didn't like that the auctions could be spontaneous. She thought everything should be planned and scheduled. We tried to explain to her that we didn't work like that. She kept fighting our methods, so we had to ask her to leave. It was awkward and terribly uncomfortable."

"And she and Birk remained friends anyway?"

"It seems so. It's been years since I've seen her, years since Birk and I have had any conversation that included her. You'll have to ask him."

"Interesting." I looked at the house and grounds. No one was around. "Let's go knock."

As we got out of the car, we heard neighing from behind the house. The noise made me smile.

"Horses?" Edwin asked.

"Three beautiful ones."

It was less than a half hour ago that Hamlet had told me about Ritchie John sharing his knowledge of horses with Hamlet's class. It had crossed my mind that perhaps that's why Louis had seemed to recognize Ritchie, something to do with horses. I wasn't sure how I could look into that possible connection, but I'd try.

"I would enjoy seeing them," Edwin said.

"We'll ask."

Edwin knocked, but there was no answer. I peered in through the window next to the door, and then I knocked too. I couldn't see anyone.

I wasn't ready to give up. "Let's go around back. Maybe Winston, the guy who works with the horses, can track her down."

Edwin followed me around. We came upon the golf cart in the same parking spot Shelagh had used during my visit. I thought about knocking on the door to the mudroom or even just opening it and going inside, but Shelagh and I didn't know each other nearly well enough.

As we came upon the back grounds, we noticed one of the horses trotting around a corral. Winston was riding Gin. I looked at the back of the house as we walked toward the corral. From this angle I saw the library windows and the door that led into the kitchen. Just as we stopped outside the corral, that door burst open.

The noise of it smacking into the house made such a cracking slam that even the horse stopped to see what was happening.

Jacques Underwood, Shelagh's nephew, was stumbling toward us. At first I wondered if he was drunk, but then he took his hand from his forehead, where blood seeped and shone bright red against his dark hair.

"Jacques!" I ran to him with Edwin at my heels.

He went down just as we reached him.

"Jacques!" I said again as Edwin and I slowed his fall to the ground. Winston ran over too, crouching with us.

"*Aide-la!*" Jacques said once his eyes found mine.

"What?" I said.

"He said 'Help her,'" Edwin translated.

"Shelagh?"

I looked at the house as we crouched next to Jacques.

"Help my aunt," Jacques said in English. "He took her!"

"What?" I hurried to stand up and ran inside the back door, Edwin following close behind.

"Where to?" he said.

"This way." I led us to the library.

The double doors were wide open. We hurried inside, only to be greeted by the aftermath of what looked like a struggle. The seating area had been disturbed, the chairs and couch all in slightly different spots than they should be. Two lamps had been knocked off the tables, and the glass from a broken light-bulb was scattered across the floor.

There was no sign of Shelagh.

Without really knowing what I was doing, I pushed my way around Edwin and hurried toward the front of the house. The main door was now open wide, and bloody fingerprints shone stark against the white trim around it. We rushed outside.

"We were just here," I said.

"Aye."

There was no sign of Shelagh anywhere. There was no sign of anyone. We hadn't seen any other vehicles around the house when we'd arrived, and there was no sign of any now.

It seemed we'd missed seeing Shelagh being taken from her house, by mere seconds.

ELEVEN

The police who arrived to investigate the scene weren't officers I knew. I also called Inspector Winters, who hurried over too. He asked the investigating officers if they needed help and then told them he was going to talk to Edwin and me.

Winston, Edwin, and I had already given our statements by then, so the officers gave their okay. Winston hadn't even known that Jacques was in the house. He hadn't seen Shelagh for over an hour and had spent his morning with the horses. Visibly shaken by the whole incident, he turned his attention back to the animals after giving his statement. They were okay but agitated, probably keying in on everyone's panic.

"Jacques is going to be fine," Inspector Winters said as he joined Edwin and me. "The hospital called, and he's being attended to, but he doesn't have a concussion."

"Can you tell us what he said happened?" I asked.

"The best I understand is that Jacques was visiting Shelagh. He calls her his aunt. They were in the library when someone ran inside. According to Jacques, the person was dressed like the Monster"—Inspector Winters frowned; he didn't like the moniker either—"who has been terrorizing the city. He and

Jacques fought, but he hit Jacques, knocking him off his feet, though not unconscious, and then took Shelagh."

"Was she hurt when Jacques saw her go?" I thought about the blood on the doorframe.

"It's unclear. He said he heard her yelling but doesn't know what else happened to her. An alert has been sent out through all possible avenues."

I nodded. "Edwin and I missed them coming out of the front door by only a couple minutes."

"That's what the other inspector said. And you saw nothing at all? Did you hear anything?" Inspector Winters looked between Edwin and me.

"We saw Winston on the horse, but nothing seemed wrong or out of place," I said.

"Winston was riding in the corral when we came around," Edwin added.

"There were no other vehicles anywhere. How did they get away?" I asked.

Inspector Winters shook his head. "I wondered the same thing. Apparently there are places where cars can park in spots hidden in the trees out front. The abductors could have been parked there. Shelagh used to use them for parties. There are no vehicles in any of them now, and it's difficult to tell if any have been parked there recently."

"Did they check the garage and the greenhouse?" I said, but I knew they had.

"Aye. No sign of her anywhere. Three cars inside the garage."

"Who else is on the property?" I asked.

"Just you two and Winston."

"Shelagh has an . . . assistant, Louis Chantrell, and a driver, Findlay Sweet. They aren't here?"

"I don't think so."

"Her driver, Findlay, is . . ."

"What, lass?" Inspector Winters asked.

"It's nothing pertinent to the case, but he and Tom had a few troubles some years back."

"What do you mean?"

I told Inspector Winters and Edwin about Tom's past with Findlay. They listened closely.

"And you got in the car with him?" Edwin said.

"It was fine, and it might be that I just don't like him—this might not be fair. But he does seem . . . creepy."

"Noted," Inspector Winters said sincerely.

"If the . . . Monster took her, this must all be connected to her past," I said.

"Don't jump to conclusions, Delancy. Not enough proof yet. Copycats take advantage of timing." Inspector Winters's eyes were moving around the property.

Out of the corner of my own eye, I spied a person circling around the house in a hurry. She was blonde and pretty, and she looked right at me.

"Delaney, what the hell?" Brigid said as she plopped her hands on her hips.

The investigating officers started walking toward her, an urgency to their steps.

"Uh-oh," I said quietly as I hurried behind the officers.

"I'm a friend of Shelagh's and a journalist," Brigid said with way too much sass. "I heard about the commotion on the police scanner. The public has a right to know what's going on."

I jumped in and said to the inspectors, "I know her. Can I just take her up front? I'll talk to her?"

The inspectors glared impatiently at Brigid as she stood her ground.

"Aye. Take her out of here," one of them said.

"Let's go," I said to Brigid.

She turned, and I followed her bouncing curls back to the front of the house.

There were now more vehicles out front. Three police cars, a fire truck, and an ambulance that was no longer needed. I spied what must have been Brigid's car at the rear of the pack—an old yellow Fiat.

"I swear, you are like a magnet for trouble." Brigid faced me, replunking her fists on her hips.

"It does feel like that sometimes," I admitted.

Brigid took a deep breath and let it out shakily. Was she angry or upset or both?

"You okay?" I asked.

"No, what happened to Shelagh?"

I put my hand on her arm. There was a tremor there too. She was shaking all over. "It's okay, Brigid. . . ."

"I shouldn't have written that story, Delaney. I told everyone about that amazing library. I set her up to be . . . whatever has happened to her, maybe whatever is happening in Edinburgh."

"No, it's not your fault there are awful people in the world. And I'm working on the premise that she's okay. The police will find her."

"I hope so."

I nodded. I hoped so too. This was not a good situation, no matter what. Brigid was very upset, though, and I would put on a brave face if that'd help calm her down. It truly wasn't her fault.

I'd never known her to take the blame in the past. She'd written several stories that had stirred up lots of trouble, but she'd stuck firmly by the fact that the public always had a right to know the truth about everything.

"You like Shelagh." I said.

Brigid glared at me, but then her face eased into a worried frown. "I do. She is lovely, and forthcoming in ways most people aren't. I really like her."

"Your article told a good, interesting story. You didn't hurt her." I leveled my gaze.

A few beats later, Brigid seemed to relax. "Tell me what happened, please. You said you would call me, give me an update. I haven't heard a word."

I'd forgotten, but I didn't tell her that. Instead I told her everything I knew. I even told her what Tom and I had come upon in the car park. Her eyes lit with the news, and I was surprised she didn't pull out a notebook to record the event.

"Tell me the second clue again," she said when I finished.

I shared the ominous words.

"Hang on." She drew her phone out of her pocket and started searching. "That's what I thought." She held the phone so I could see it too. "You went to a pub to meet her. The first clue was in a pub. Maybe it's all about pubs. What about The Tolbooth Tavern? You have to pay at tollbooths, right? And this place used to be a prison, so maybe paying with your soul was the only way to get out of there, at least for some."

I took her phone and scrolled through the site on her screen. "Impossible to know, but this might make sense." I looked back at the house and wondered if there was something else I could do that would help find Shelagh. I couldn't think of anything. "I need to get to this pub."

"I'll take you." She retrieved her phone and turned.

I grabbed her arm, gently. "Brigid, hang on. No. Listen to me. I'm not going to just go with you. I have to talk to Edwin and Inspector Winters, and I have to call my friend Birk. I made a deal. You can go without me if you want, but technically you weren't invited to this hunt. I know you want the story, but you can't just swoop in and take over."

For a long moment, her eyes told me that she thought that's exactly what she could do, what she had the right to do. But then she nodded. "I'll wait in my car but I'm going too."

"Good enough." I let go of her arm. She sent me a squinted glare, yet said no more.

I hurried around the house again. The investigating officers said Edwin and I were cleared to leave, but we needed to remain available via our mobiles if other questions arose.

I told both Edwin and Inspector Winters about the possible answer to the clue. Edwin agreed to go with me, but Inspector Winters had other commitments. He wanted another update later, though.

On the way around to the front again, I called Birk, who seemed pleased by a possible solution to the second clue and said he'd meet us at The Tolbooth Tavern. For a moment I thought Brigid had left, but it turned out that her car was hidden by the fire truck. I waved. She rolled her eyes and waved back.

"I can't believe she waited," Edwin said as we got into his car.

"I'm sort of surprised too."

I *was* surprised, pleasantly, but I also wondered what she'd ask of me now. No matter that she'd done the right thing, it was rare that Brigid did *any*thing without an ulterior motive.

The Tolbooth Tavern was located off Canongate, not far from Grassmarket. Edwin drove with speedy, precise skill, and so did Brigid; I thought it must be difficult to do such a thing in an old Fiat.

I'd never visited this tavern, but even before Brigid mentioned its onetime incarnation as a prison, I knew a little of the history surrounding it. It was located on the bottom floor

of an old building, on one side of an arched tunnel, a close—
Old Tolbooth Wynd—that had once served as an actual toll-
booth. Atop the tunnel was a clock tower that had a fairy-tale
quality, evoking images of both royal battles and Rumpel-
stiltskin. The tunnel led the way back to other buildings that
had served many official functions over the last few hundred
years, including courthouse and prison. Time had worn the
stones some, but the buildings were still impressive, retaining
their Old World beauty. In the 1600s Oliver Cromwell had im-
prisoned several Scottish enemies in the upper floor rooms of
the clock tower. The prisoners made their escape by tearing
up blankets and tying the pieces together, using them to lower
themselves out the windows.

As Edwin and Brigid parked, Birk appeared from the tunnel, his hands in his pockets and a scarf pulled up around his
chin. He made his way toward the front door.

"Lass, Edwin," he said. He nodded at Brigid. "Lass."

"Birk, this is Brigid. Brigid, Birk," I said. "Come on, let's get
inside."

They followed me into the warm pub. Though smallish like
the other pubs, this one was decorated with more reds. Red
upholstery as well as red-painted walls and some rich cherry-
wood for the bar. From the outside the tavern looked to be another small pocket space, but it extended far back, with a few
steps up to another seating area.

"What can I get fer ye?" a server said as she stood next to
the bar. There were only two other customers in the place.

I wanted to talk to Birk before asking if there was a clue anywhere nearby. He needed to know what had transpired.

"A pot of coffee?" I asked my friends.

Everyone nodded, so I turned to the waitress and repeated
the order.

"Ayc? Whatever ye say. Have a seat, and I'll bring it tae ye in a moment."

We sat, keeping our coats on to ward off the inside chill.

"Birk, we think the third clue might be here," I said.

"I figured as much." He looked at Brigid but didn't ask why she was there. "What're your thoughts?"

I shrugged. "The hunt might be all about pubs, and the clue somehow makes sense for this place. Paying a toll and such. Maybe."

"Aye. Should we just ask the barkeep?"

"First I wanted to fill you in on something else that has happened."

"I'm listening."

Both Brigid and Birk listened closely to everything Edwin and I said as we told them the story of Shelagh's abduction, each of us filling in any details the other left out.

"This makes no sense. Took her from her house?" Birk was visibly bothered as we finished sharing events.

"Yes, in broad daylight."

"That seems so unreal."

"Nevertheless," Edwin said as he put his hand on Birk's arm, "that's the way it is. The police are searching for her."

"This is truly terrible." Birk frowned, and it seemed he was going to stand up. But a moment later he relaxed back into the chair, probably realizing that searching for Shelagh by himself didn't make sense. "All right, everything must be tied together. The sooner we find that book, the better. Why does it feel like if we don't find the book, we won't find Shelagh?"

I nodded. "I know, but that's just because we're in the middle of all of it. It's impossible to know if this is connected."

"And the police will find her," Brigid added. "We'll find her if we have to."

Birk squinted at her. I could see uncertainty in his eyes—
Who was this woman and why was she involved now?—but he
appreciated her determination.

He also hadn't protested that Edwin had joined us. I couldn't
help feeling the same way he did, that Shelagh wouldn't be
found until the book was discovered.

"I'll ask the bartender," I said. I looked at Birk. "Want to
come with me?"

"No, go ahead. If I need my identification again, I'll join
you."

I scooted the chair back and made my way to the bar.

"'Elp ye?" the man behind the bar said. He reminded me a
lot of Ritchie John, but maybe all older-men bartenders took
on the same wiry, bright-eyed look.

"My name is Delaney Nichols," I began.

"Aye? Benton's mine. 'Elp ye?" he repeated.

"I wondered . . . My friends and I have been sent on a treasure hunt of sorts, and we've concluded that we might be able
to find a clue here at the pub. Do you by chance have anything?"

Benton hesitated and then put down the glass he'd been
holding. "I can't say that I do. But let me look."

He turned and made his way back to the other end of the
bar, which wasn't far. He glanced at some narrow shelves, pulling a box out from one of them. He rifled through it, stirring
up what I thought was probably forgotten winter wear that
had been left behind. My heart fell when I realized he really
didn't know anything about a possible clue. Whatever it was,
I didn't think it would have been tossed into a lost-and-found
box.

He put the box back and rubbed his chin as he returned to
me. "Lass, I dinnae ken anything about a clue. I'm sorry."

"Thanks for looking. What about a manager or something? Would anyone else know?"

"No. I'm yer man," Benton said. "I own and run the place, pour most of the drinks."

I smiled. "It's a wonderful pub. Thank you for looking."

"Aye. Want tae give me a contact number in case something comes in?"

"Sure."

He handed over a pen and a paper napkin. I wrote my name and the bookshop's phone number and gave him back the note. He stuffed it into his pocket without looking at it, and any hope I had that he really meant to let me know about a potential clue dissipated.

I returned to the table just as the waitress was delivering the coffeepot and mugs. I couldn't help but smile at the mugs. They were something I would expect in America, not in Edinburgh. Each was painted with an old advertisement reading GOOD TO THE LAST DROP.

The waitress caught my smile.

"It's all we had. Apologies if ye were looking for mugs with our name. That's what most people who visit want. It seems we're either plum out of them or they're dirty—they do get stolen."

"It's okay," we all said.

"They're kind of wonderful," I added, enjoying the reminder of home.

"Well?" Birk said when the waitress was gone.

"Nothing," I said. "He took my name, though, in case something comes in."

"Maybe it's not like the previous clues—maybe it's not as convenient as a note tucked into an envelope," Edwin said.

"Aye. Let's look around the pub," Brigid said. "I'll take the ladies' room. Birk, you take the men's, and, Delaney, you and Edwin look around in here." She stood and headed toward the back. Birk followed behind her.

"Goodness," Edwin said as he watched Brigid hurry away. "She's a little bossy."

"A wee bit," he agreed. "Let's get to work."

Edwin and I separated as we looked around the pub. It wasn't a big space, and we tried not to be too intrusive. Nonetheless, we examined pictures on the walls, peered under tables and chairs, paid way too much attention to one dusty corner before we realized we were overthinking.

"Look at his sweatshirt." Edwin nodded toward Benton.

"It's an Edinburgh Castle sweatshirt," I said.

"Do you think the clue could be something like that?"

"I don't know. Let's keep it in mind. He didn't seem to be particularly anxious for me to notice it. He seemed genuine in not knowing what I was talking about."

"Aye."

Our common thread of desperation made us willing to turn almost anything into a clue, but we ultimately had to admit that nothing seemed like it was trying to speak to us. For an instant I even closed my eyes and tried to summon my bookish voices. But of course they weren't talking. When my eyes were closed, though, I did happen to notice that the coffee smelled exceptionally good . . . to the last drop, I ruminated as I opened my eyes, went back in my chair, sat down, and took a sip.

Brigid and Birk rejoined us at the table.

"Anything?" I asked.

"Nothing," they both said as they sat.

"Nothing around here either," Edwin said.

"Maybe something will come to one of us," I said. "We've looked around. Maybe our subconscious will bring something up to the surface later."

"Maybe," Brigid said doubtfully.

"Birk, are you still good friends with Shelagh?" I said, but then I put my hand up to halt him from speaking. "Before you go into detail, you need to know that Brigid is a reporter. If you want something to be off the record, you need to mention that."

"Aye? Where do you work?" Birk asked Brigid.

Brigid mentioned her alternative newspaper, the *Renegade*.

"Lass, are you the reporter who wrote the article about Shelagh's library?" Birk asked.

"I am. Why?"

"It was a wonderful article," Birk said. "I hadn't spoken to Shelagh in years when I read it. I thought she must have been very pleased. When I received her message to come talk to her about her library, it all seemed like some sort of synchronicity."

"I hope I haven't contributed to . . ." Brigid said.

"Brigid . . ." I began.

"What? You think your article had something to do with her disappearance or the New Monster? No. Whatever's going on here, it is somehow of Shelagh's doing. If she's hurt, it's not something she wanted to happen, but she's extraordinarily good at manipulating situations. She set something in motion that has gotten her into trouble, I'm afraid. If that's unkind, I don't mean to be, but it's a big part of why we couldn't stay together," Birk said.

"Stay together?" I said. "Were you more than friends?" I looked at Edwin, who sent me a small shrug. I understood— he'd felt it hadn't been his place to tell me that part.

"Aye." Birk took a sip of his coffee. "We were, but Shelagh . . . well, she just thinks she has an overactive imagination. To the rest of the world, her imagination seems like lies and manipulation. It was all too much work." Birk shook his head. "It was also the most difficult decision I've ever had to make, even more difficult than asking her to leave . . . a group we were a part of. I loved her, maybe still do a wee bit, but I just couldn't live with her as my partner in life."

"What group?" Brigid asked.

"I promise I'll tell you another day," Edwin said to her.

She frowned at him,

"I'm sorry, Birk," I said quickly, before Brigid could get us off track. "But she's going to be found, and she's going to be fine."

"I hope so."

"I'm going to the hospital to check on Jacques. He might know more than he told the police," Brigid said, sounding now as if she was ready to move on.

I looked at Edwin and then back at Brigid. "Can I come with you?"

"Aye, but I'm going now." She stood and turned, making her way toward the door.

"Edwin?" I said.

"Aye. Birk and I will enjoy another coffee and ring you if we figure out the next clue."

It seemed futile, like we'd come to a dead end.

"Maybe a different pub?" I said.

"There are a few of those around," Birk said.

"We will figure this out."

I told the men hurried good-byes and then sprinted outside to Brigid's car. The engine was already running, but she had waited for me again.

"How do you know which hospital?" I asked, noticing that her car smelled of gasoline fumes.

"I'll find it."

Brigid might have been a good driver, but she was also a fast one. As she drove, making unsafe calls from her mobile on the way, again I found myself holding on for dear life.

TWELVE

Logically, the hospital ended up being the one closest to Shelagh's house. Brigid figured it out after talking to someone at her office. She parked the car in a spot that was clearly not a parking place, but I didn't bother to mention that.

We jetted up toward the building just as Jacques Underwood and Tricia Lawson were exiting through the emergency-room doors.

"Hello," I said, surprised but relieved to see him upright and walking.

"Hello," Tricia said as if it were her we'd come to see.

"Hello," Jacques said uncertainly.

"I'm Brigid McBride, a reporter with the *Renegade Scot*," Brigid began. "Can I ask you a few questions about what happened to you and Shelagh O'Conner in her home today?"

She cut right to the chase.

"Hang on," I said as I raised a hand. "Jacques, are you okay?"

"I'm fine. Thank you." He seemed to suddenly realize who I was. "Delaney, you were there. You helped. *Merci.*"

"I was worried."

Jacques shook his head and gave me a weak smile. "I'm fine. They didn't even want me to stay overnight."

"Can you tell me what happened?" Brigid asked.

"No, I don't want to talk to a reporter, but off the record I don't remember much anyway. *Pardon*."

He made a move to step around us, but Brigid sidestepped and got in his way.

"What's the *last* thing you remember?" she said.

I was torn between wanting to drag her away and wanting him to answer.

He wasn't going to answer. He sent her a glare that would have melted a lesser reporter. But Brigid wasn't a lesser reporter. She stood firm, and for a reason I might never understand, her method worked.

"I remember sitting on the couch, talking to my aunt," Jacques said a moment later. He sighed as he spoke and then looked at Brigid as if he'd like her to help him remember more.

She nodded. "Okay, go back to that conversation you were having on the couch. What were you talking about?"

Jacques's eyebrows came together, and his gaze moved to the sidewalk where we stood. It was cold, and I wanted us to go inside somewhere, but other than the hospital there didn't seem to be a reasonable choice. At least it wasn't raining.

"It must have had something to do with the hunt for her book, but I don't remember the specifics," Jacques finally said.

"Did you figure out the first clue?" I asked.

"No, but I can't even remember if I told her that or not. I know we hadn't spoken long before. . . . It's all so fuzzy."

"My friend and I were at the front door around the same time all of this must have been happening. Did you hear us at the door?" I asked.

"Not that I remember. . . . It was chaos, though, that much I'm sure of."

"You knew that the person who attacked you was dressed in a shabby coat and hat? You said that to the police," Brigid said.

"Well, I think so. The more time that passes, the less sure I am," Jacques said desperately.

I put my hand on his arm. "It's okay."

"Do you think they'll find her?" His voice sounded choked.

"Yes, I do." I wasn't sure at all, but I hoped.

"What are you doing here?" Brigid asked Tricia.

"Brigid, this is Tricia Lawson. Tricia is a librarian. She's part of the hunt for the book," I said.

"Where are you a librarian?" Brigid asked.

"Firrhill," Tricia said.

"Did you call her?" Brigid asked Jacques as she nodded toward Tricia.

"No . . ."

"I heard about what happened at Shelagh's house," Tricia said. "I thought Jacques might need some help."

"How did you hear?" Brigid asked.

"I stopped by the house just as the police were leaving, and they told me." Tricia didn't seem bothered by Brigid's questions.

I would ask Inspector Winters if he'd still been there when she stopped by.

"Jacques, truly, are you okay?" I said.

"I'm fine. Just a small hit on the head."

"Okay," I said, thinking that any hit on the head wasn't good but relieved he'd been released from the hospital.

Tricia cleared her throat. "The news on the telly in the waiting area mentioned that the police were on the hunt for the

New Monster *and* the Old Monster," Tricia said. "I just knew that Shelagh's past behavior would somehow lead to trouble."

Jacques shook his head.

"What?" Brigid asked him.

"Auntie has never been the most honest person."

Brigid and I shared a look. Birk had said something similar.

"She lies a lot?" Brigid said.

"She exaggerates the truth, makes things up because she thinks it's fun." Jacques shrugged again. "That's the best I can explain it."

"Can you give me a recent example?" Brigid asked.

"The Hyde Monster nonsense is her biggest lie of all. Back when she dressed up—how ridiculous was all that? I agree with Tricia, I'm worried that she's done something to bring all this back," Jacques said.

"What could she have done?" Brigid asked.

"I don't know," Jacques said. "I have no idea, but . . . I just wouldn't be surprised."

"Can you give me another example of her lies?" Brigid pushed.

"No, not at the moment. I'm tired," he answered quickly.

"Jacques," I said as gently as I could, "can you remember when you first arrived at the house? Was Louis Chantrell or Findlay Sweet there?"

"I didn't see anyone."

"Winston?"

"Who's that?"

"The man in charge of the horses."

"No, I didn't see him either."

Jacques needed to rest.

"Can I get him back to his room now?" Tricia asked.

"Sure," Brigid said. She gave Jacques her card and told him

to call her if he remembered anything else. To her credit she *did* say to call the police too, though she didn't mention to call them first.

I decided not to tell them about our visit to The Tolbooth Tavern. It just didn't seem to matter at the moment. Brigid must have felt the same, because she didn't mention it either.

Besides, it looked like we'd hit a dead end anyway.

We told them good-bye, and without much more conversation—because Brigid used the time to call into her office and ask questions I couldn't hear the answers to—she dropped me off at the bookshop. I was certain she was up to something too, but she didn't want me along.

I was just fine with that.

THIRTEEN

Considering everything, it was a surprise that my dreams weren't filled with visions of monsters and murderers.

Instead I dreamed about coffee—the aroma of it, the taste. In the dream I drank the best coffee I'd ever had. Normally I drink coffee without anything extra, but in the dream I added loads of cream and sugar and then other good things that don't normally go into coffee—chocolate, cheese crackers, hot dogs—and everything tasted delicious. Somewhere deep down I thought, *Oh, maybe I should try that.* After I'd enjoyed the nocturnal journey for a while, the dream's real message became clear. I opened my eyes, sat up in bed, and gasped.

"What?" Groggily, Tom sat up too.

"Oh, Tom, The Last Drop pub."

"Aye, what about it?"

I looked at the time. All the pubs had probably just closed.

"I need to make a call."

In the dark I looked up the number for The Tolbooth Tavern and hit Dial.

" 'S'late, what can I do for ye?" a voice answered.

"Benton?"

"Aye?"

"Hello, I know it's late, but . . . I'm Delaney, and I was in earlier."

"Aye. The treasure hunter."

"That's me. I have a question. The mugs we had today with our coffee—they had an old advertisement painted on them, something about 'good to the last drop.' They aren't the mugs you normally use, right?"

"No, they arenae. Someone brought them in last week, offered me a thousand quid if I used only those mugs for a few weeks. I thought it was a clever advertising idea."

"And you took the deal?"

"Aye, do I look daft tae ye? 'Twas easy money."

"Can you tell me who brought them in?"

"A man called me on the phone and then had the mugs messengered over. My waitress told me that a lad dropped them by, didnae say much of anything."

"Can you tell me more about the messenger?"

"I can ask my waitress tomorrow. Call me back in the afternoon. I've got tae go now, though. Time tae go home. Goodnight."

He clicked off before I could say anything else.

"What?" Tom said after I didn't explain.

"I don't know how the person who left the clues did it, but this one, I'm almost one hundred percent sure, was meant to lead us next to The Last Drop tavern."

"Another pub? Another one in Grassmarket?"

The Last Drop pub *was* in Grassmarket, in between Tom's pub and The White Hart Inn.

"I think so. I think all the clues are inside Edinburgh pubs."

"Might be a long hunt."

"I hope I'm on the right track. . . ." I shook my head and

told him about the mugs. As I explained what had happened, it seemed like a pretty weak story, but it was all I had.

"Someone paid him to use them?" Tom asked.

"Yes."

"How in the world would they know you'd order coffee?"

"Maybe it was just a chance they took, but not only did we order coffee, we ordered a carafe of it, along with the four mugs. Maybe Shelagh thought we'd stop by during the day, and it's cold. . . . I don't know. If we hadn't ordered warm drinks, we'd have nothing, which might actually be exactly what we have anyway. I'll stop by The Last Drop pub tomorrow and see if there's another clue there."

"You'll call Birk?"

"Of course. I'll send him an email tonight and have him meet me there."

"Good plan."

I kissed my husband. "Go back to sleep. I'm wired. I'm going up to my wonderful library to email Birk and do some reading. If I'm not here in the morning, send a search party to the attic."

"Are you sure you don't want me to come too?"

"No, rest. But thanks for asking."

"Very well. Goodnight, love."

I kissed him again, and I was pretty sure he was back to sleep by the time his head hit the pillow. I was going to have to re-member to leave the bedroom when I had middle-of-the-night epiphanies.

I wrapped myself in a thick robe and made my way to the pull-down door. It whooshed open and I climbed up.

I switched on a table lamp, lighting the space with a warm, bright glow. Though the light didn't extend to illuminate all the books on the shelves, I knew exactly which shelf I wanted to go to and the approximate spot where a certain book was located.

The Complete Short Stories by Robert Louis Stevenson. It wasn't a valuable book, but one with a few of Stevenson's stories, including *The Strange Case of Dr. Jekyll and Mr. Hyde*.

I opened the book to the monster story. It was short, probably only about seventy or so of today's pages, but it was still astounding that the author had written it in a mere three days. I started reading.

It wasn't long before I became swept up in not only in the story but the writing too. Yes, the language was somewhat old-fashioned, as were the characters' behavior and speech. But Stevenson's words were crafted beautifully, his imagery vivid. I could see the monster. I could feel the fear, the devastation some of the characters felt when they began to understand that their friend Dr. Jekyll was in fact also Mr. Hyde.

The narrator of the story is an attorney, Utterson. An intelligent and levelheaded man, he's compelled to find the answers to what is happening in his city and what he himself has witnessed. Who is this villain, a man who he eventually discovers is living in his friend Dr. Jekyll's home? Dr. Jekyll is a good man, a good doctor, so the idea that he is also the monster doesn't occur to Utterson until another friend of theirs, so shocked by what he has discovered about Dr. Jekyll, sinks into depression and death.

The ending is a statement by Dr. Jekyll himself—written before he disappears forever. Having wanted to explore the dark side of human nature, he concocted a potion that turned him into the violent Mr. Hyde. But that first potion had been made with something the good doctor couldn't find again. As a result, as time went on, the dark side of the man kept winning, and Jekyll couldn't get back to being himself so easily.

Dr. Jekyll had to kill Mr. Hyde—but there was no other way to do this than kill himself, because there weren't two different men, only one, made of both good and bad elements, like all humans.

I closed the book. There was no happy ending, but it touched something inside me. Fear? Sure, but it was more than that. It made me wonder about my own dark side, about that of the people I thought I knew.

Dark and light had been used more times than I could remember in books and movies to portray good and evil. There was nothing unique about those descriptions. So what was it about this book that had captured Shelagh's heart? Was it simply the fact that she'd read it without knowing anything about the story beforehand and learned the twist in real time, or was it something more disturbing? Something about her own darkness?

But that's not the way it works. Most people who enjoy reading books about serial killers aren't serial killers themselves. Maybe *Jekyll & Hyde* was pure escapism for Shelagh, and maybe her behavior long ago really was something she'd done because she'd been a rich, curious, and bored young woman.

My sense of it was that there was more, but I was far from figuring it out.

I dug into more internet research on my phone, starting with the author himself. Not only had Stevenson written the story in three days and not only had there been a rumor that he'd based his character on Deacon Brodie, there were other interesting things too.

He *had* dreamed the book, his wife waking him in the middle of it as he was screaming at the monster. I smiled. I'd just been awakened by my own dream, though visions of coffee weren't quite as exciting as Stevenson's fantasies.

When I read the next part, though, I exclaimed aloud. Though Deacon Brodie was often thought of as the inspiration for the story, there was another source of inspiration mentioned too. Stevenson had been friends with an Edinburgh-based French teacher who was convicted and executed for the murder of his wife, Mary. The teacher had appeared to live a normal life in the city, meanwhile poisoning his wife as well as maybe other people throughout France and Britain. He'd serve them his favorite dish of toasted cheese, but with lethal doses of opium added to it.

Stevenson had been present throughout the teacher's trial, shocked and terrified by what his friend had done, much as Dr. Jekyll's friends had been.

The part that caught me off guard the most, though, was the teacher's name. It was Eugene Chantrelle. Was it a complete coincidence that a man who worked for Shelagh had the same surname? Who was Louis Chantrell, and was he somehow related to the nineteenth-century killer whom Stevenson had known? How much difference did an *e* make?

Louis was my next search, but I found nothing online at all. As far as I could tell, Louis was in no way involved with social media. But that didn't necessarily mean anything. Neither was Edwin, after all.

I could find a few things about Edwin on the internet, though. He was well known. Though Louis might not be, I was surprised that I couldn't find even one thing about him anywhere. I pulled up a couple of Chantrells who lived in France, but no one I could guess was local to Edinburgh.

I thought back to those first few moments in Deacon Brodie's pub, when Louis seemed to recognize the murder victim, Ritchie John. I wished I'd asked him what had seemed so familiar, but at the time I hadn't thought it would be something important.

Where had he been yesterday afternoon when Shelagh had been taken from her home? What about Findlay Sweet? And did Ritchie's tie to horses also tie him to Shelagh?

A chill shivered through my limbs. Where had she been taken? Was she still alive? If so, she was probably terrified. I sensed she was still living, but that might have only been wishful thinking on my part. I hoped she was. I considered that we all might too easily have been somehow blaming her for whatever had happened to her. That was a mistake. Because even if she held some responsibility for her own disappearance, it should not change the fact that priority one was finding her and assuring her safety.

My eyes were tired, yet adrenaline still coursed through me. I had so much I wanted to do, so much I wanted to think about and figure out, but it was far too late—or maybe early—to do anything.

I emailed Birk, telling him I'd meet him at The Last Drop tavern at 10:00 A.M., and then I shut my eyes. As I fell asleep, I was sure I heard the faraway howl of a wolf, but there weren't wolves in Scotland. Maybe it had been a dog.

Or maybe it had been something else altogether.

FOURTEEN

"Do you think it's all about Grassmarket?" Birk asked as we looked toward the front of the pub. Snow was flying again—sideways this time, because of a strong wind.

The name The Last Drop had nothing to do with old coffee-advertising campaigns. The sign outside was one of the things most commonly photographed by tourists in Edinburgh; along with the name of the establishment, there was an illustrated noose. Grassmarket had at one time been the location of many hangings, mostly for those determined to be witches, and this "last drop" referred to that particular last drop, down from the gallows.

"Maybe. Let's go in," I said over the wind.

I'd also been in this pub a time or two, though I'd never stayed long. It was a large place, with the door in between two large front windows. The inside had rich woods and old lanterns hanging from the ceiling, giving the space a darkish light. As part of the decor, there were plenty of pictures of nooses and gallows on the walls, the sorts of terrifying true historical things that Edinburgh tourists also enjoyed.

As we came through the door, a woman nodded at us from behind the bar. There were no other customers inside.

"It's a wee bit early. Our cooks aren't here yet, but if you want a pint, I'll accommodate you. I can put some coffee on too if you're just wanting to be out of the weather, for which, by the way, I wouldn't blame you one wee bit."

I looked at Birk and then back at the woman as we walked toward her. "Actually, we just have some questions, if that's okay."

She shrugged and stood straight, wiping her hands on a towel. "Depends on the questions, I s'pose."

She was middle-aged, with beautiful green eyes and dishwater-brown hair pulled back in a smooth ponytail. A pencil was stuck behind one ear, and the apron she'd tied around her middle was currently spotless.

"My name is Delaney, and this is Birk."

"Good to meet you," she said. "I'm Sarah."

I scooted up to a stool. "We are on something like a scavenger hunt, but it's more of a treasure hunt with clues. The last clue we got led us here, we think, and we're wondering if there's something here for us."

Her eyebrows came together. "A wee bit old for such things, aren't ye?"

Birk sighed. "You have no idea. Nevertheless, here we are, and we feel compelled to see it through to the end."

She smiled at Birk. I liked his charming side too.

"Well, I wish I could help, but I don't think I know of anything that might serve as a clue. Would it be a note or something?"

"Maybe," I said. "The last clue came in the form of an old advertisement on a mug. 'Good to the last drop.'"

"Och, aye, I've heard that one a time or two." She fell into thought as she plunked her hands on her hips.

"Someone might have asked you to use something different than you normally do. Carry a different product? The last clue showed up on mugs that were delivered. The pub owner was paid to use them for a couple weeks."

Sarah laughed once. "Good job if you can get it."

"Aye." Birk smiled.

She shook her head a few moments later. "I'm so sorry, but I can't think of one thing. I apologize."

"It's all right. We weren't even really sure we got the last clue right to bring us here. Mugs might be a long shot."

Sarah's eyes went to a spot above our heads. "Excuse me a moment. I've been wanting to hear the latest on this." She grabbed a remote control and turned up the volume on the television that was mounted above us.

Birk and I turned and watched the story too.

"Still no sign of missing eccentric Edinburgh resident Shelagh O'Conner," said the newscaster. "She was taken from her home, leaving a bloody trail in her wake."

"Well, not a trail," I muttered. "Bloody fingerprints on the doorframe."

"What's that?" Sarah asked.

"Nothing. Sorry."

The newscaster continued. "The police are working from the assumption that Ms. O'Conner was taken by the New Monster, a man who continues to evade the police even after committing another string of burglaries last night. Please look at these pictures." More grainy black-and-white pictures showed on the screen. I squinted and tried to see if I could spot anything familiar. I couldn't even estimate the real-life size of the person under the shabby winter wear.

Another newscaster took a turn as the pictures snapped back to half screen. "There is no indication that the New Monster has anything to do with the Old Monster, even though it was Shelagh O'Conner herself, fascinated by the *Jekyll and Hyde* story, who dressed and played the part all those years ago. A man was murdered back then, but Ms. O'Conner was never arrested for the crime and later expressed regret for ever having pretended to be someone she wasn't. There's no indication that she is in any way responsible for the burglaries and murder that have occurred this time around, but our investigators have uncovered some new information.

"It seems that the man who was murdered two nights ago might in fact have had a tenuous tie to Shelagh O'Conner."

"Uh-oh," I muttered quietly.

"Aye," Birk said over my shoulder, and just as quietly.

The newscaster continued. "At one time Ritchie John worked caring for horses, and though we don't think he worked for Shelagh O'Conner, we are investigating a lead that might still connect Mr. John and Ms. O'Conner because of their shared love of equines. We will report details as they unfold."

"That's how Louis knew him!" I said.

"Shh," Sarah said.

A grainy picture of the New Monster filled the screen, and once again the newscaster continued. "If you see anyone resembling this man or if you have any information regarding him or Shelagh O'Conner, please contact the police immediately. We'll be right back."

Sarah turned down the sound. "Terrifying, but at least there hasn't been another murder."

"It is," I agreed as Birk and I turned to face her again. She looked at us expectantly, but I didn't have anything else to ask. "If I leave you my name and number, will you ring me in case something comes in that might be considered a clue?"

"Certainly."

For the second time in as many days, I was handed a paper napkin and a pen. I scribbled my name and number.

"Delaney," she said as she read it. "Happy to."

"Thank you."

"You two want some coffee before you step back out into the storm?"

"No thanks. We don't have far to go," I said.

"Very well. Good luck to you both."

Leaving the pub was just like walking into the exaggerated wind in an old black-and-white movie. The force took the door and pulled it open so hard that Birk and I had to put both our backs into it to get it to shut. Once we did, we silently made our way toward the bookshop, being pushed along comically by the the wind.

"Delaney!" a voice called from behind, seeming to fight the wind to reach us.

We turned to see Sarah running in our direction. She was holding a stack of papers, or maybe cardboard. We tried to meet her partway, but the wind knocked us back a couple steps instead.

Sarah's neat ponytail was now blowing in her face. "I realized that something odd might have happened. These came in two days ago. I thought it strange, because they're advertisements for another pub. The gentleman who brought this stack in said that the papers were to advertise a band, and since we didn't have live music, would we mind giving them out. I argued a moment, but I've heard the group and they are good. I begrudgingly agreed, but I've kept them behind the counter."

I took the flyers, their ends flapping. They advertised a pub named Whistle Binkies—but it was the band's name that garnered my and Birk's full attention: Hyde and Seek.

"This is definitely a clue," I said to Birk over the wind. I glanced up at Sarah. "Can you describe the man to me?"

"I'm not sure I can. He had no distinguishing features, rather average-looking, I think, but my pub was crowded, and I probably didn't pay him much attention."

"Do you think you could recognize a picture of him?"

"I doubt it. Sorry. I'm going back inside. Keep the flyers. They're my only guess as to your clue, and I don't need to give them out anyhow." Sarah turned and made her way back to The Last Drop. She had to wrestle the door too.

Without speaking Birk and I turned again and rode the wind as we headed to the relative calm and quiet of the bookshop.

FIFTEEN

"We're going to a pub called"—I looked at the flyers again—"Whistle Binkies."

"I know that one," Hamlet said. "Good music."

"Have you ever heard of the group called Hyde and Seek?"

"I don't think so."

Other than the noise of the wind blowing outside, the bookshop was quiet. Grassmarket was quiet. It was as if Birk and I had been the last ones to find our way inside and out of the elements. It had taken a few moments to warm my fingers enough that I could show the thick flyers to the others.

Rosie, Hamlet, and Hector had been inside the shop but not working. They'd taken chairs to the front and had been watching out the window. Someone had put a red sweater on Hector, and I realized that the cutest dog in the world could actually be even cuter.

The scent of chocolate cloaked the other normal shop smells of old ink, paper, and bookbindings. Rosie had filled her desk with a carafe of hot cocoa and treats from the bakery next door, so we all could enjoy watching the storm out the window, certain that customers would either join us or wait elsewhere until it passed before resuming shopping. Soon we all had our own filled mugs.

"We think that's where we'll find the subsequent clue, though I'm not sure we can call them clues as much as instructions on which pub to visit next. Considering the number of pubs in Edinburgh, this could go on forever," I said.

"There must be a pattern, a reason for the pubs chosen," Hamlet said.

Standing by the front window, Birk turned and nodded. "I agree, but we haven't been able to figure that out, other than maybe a tenuous tie or two to *Jekyll and Hyde*."

"The storm, lass. Ye cannae go yet." Rosie said.

I nodded. "I know, but I really do think that the sooner the book is found, the sooner Shelagh will be found and that then we'll also know who the New Monster is. I don't know how this is all tied together, but it must be. We just heard on the news that the victim, Ritchie John, might have known Shelagh because of their shared love for horses. Learning that felt like another piece has been put into place, even if we've just got one small corner of the puzzle. The book might only be another corner, but . . . well, the sooner the better."

"Aye," Hamlet said doubtfully.

"What?"

"He seemed like a nice man."

"Hamlet, I need to tell Inspector Winters about Darcy John. The police have probably already talked to her, but I feel like I should let them know what you've told me about Ritchie speaking in class. I don't know why, but just in case it would help."

"Already done." Hamlet smiled. "When I first heard the news, I rang Inspector Winters myself. He was surprised it wasn't you ringing. He asked if you were okay. I told him you were fine."

"Good job," I said.

Birk faced us again. "At least there are no places more public than pubs. It's not like we're exploring the underworld city."

"Aye," Rosie said.

"However . . ." Hamlet looked at his phone. "Whistle Binkies doesn't open until later. Not until six this evening."

"That's good news. Ye'll stay in and the storm will pass." Rosie crossed her arms in front of herself, and Hector, sitting on her lap, sneezed in solidarity, once again pushing the boundaries of cuteness.

"Yeah, I agree. Maybe get some work done," I said, smiling at Hector.

"I'm going to go home, lass," Birk said. "Ring me and I'll pick you up later. Let me know."

"All right."

"Don't go, Birk." Rosie glanced outside again. "Not yet."

"I'll be all right. I've been in worse, and no one else out there is driving. I'll be fine."

I watched Birk as he left the bookshop. He'd parked his car near where Tom parked his, up toward Tom's pub. He walked into the wind but seemed to make it there just fine.

"More hot chocolate, lass?" Rosie held the carafe in my direction.

"Thank you." I took the mug with one hand and punched Inspector Winters's number on my phone with the other.

He answered quickly, and I filled him on what had happened since I'd last seen him. He didn't have a problem with Birk and me going to the pub that evening, which surprised me a little. He hadn't been bothered by our other pub visits, but there was something else to his tone, something I couldn't immediately identify. He mentioned that he appreciated Hamlet's calling him earlier.

"What's up?" I finally asked.

"We've made an arrest, lass. We think we have the man who killed Ritchie John and who's been robbing homes. The New Monster." He cleared his throat.

"Really! That's great. Who is it? Does he know anything about Shelagh?"

"I can't tell you yet, Delaney, you know that. I will share with you, though, that we haven't found Shelagh and we are still very concerned about her well-being."

"Oh, I hope she's found soon."

"We do too. I'm sure the media will be informed as soon as the police are certain they have the right man in custody. You'll know soon enough."

"Okay," I said again. "This is good news."

"Be safe, Delaney. Let me know what you find at the next pub."

"Will do."

We disconnected the call, and I slipped the phone into my back pocket. It occurred to me that Inspector Winters might actually be happy I had something to do to keep me out of his way.

"What is it?" Hamlet asked.

"They've arrested someone, but Inspector Winters wasn't at liberty to tell me who."

"For what? The robberies? Shelagh? The Monster?" Rosie asked.

I shook my head. "The robberies, maybe Ritchie John, maybe Shelagh, but I think they're still trying to figure it all out."

"Och, no matter, an arrest is wonderful news."

"Yes, it is," I said absently. I looked up and noticed Rosie and Hamlet looking back at me. "It's not that I'm disappointed they've arrested someone, but it's just occurred to me that maybe there's more than one person doing these terrible things."

"I'm sure the police are considering that," Hamlet said.

"They'll get the answers, lass," Rosie said.

"I know. I know." I paused.

Maybe I was listening for bookish voices, maybe I just needed to take a moment, but nothing spoke to me, nothing tried to right itself inside my intuition. I sighed. "I need to get some work done in the warehouse. I'll be over there for a while."

"Let us know if ye need anything," Rosie said as I made my way to the stairs.

First though, I picked up Hector and greeted him properly. I wished I could take him over to the dark side with me, but it wasn't the best place for him, and he would miss Rosie and Hamlet too much.

I put him down again and then walked up and through the doorway. I flipped the switch that illuminated one single bare bulb on the high ceiling. The bulb had needed changing a few months ago. Tom had brought over an appropriately tall ladder and done the task. He'd asked if we wanted him to install a real fixture over the bulb, while he was there and all, but Edwin had said it wasn't necessary, that he wasn't sure we could handle something so sophisticated after decades of austerity.

I walked down the stairs, feeling the typical chill, and hurried to the big red door. I inserted the blue skeleton key and turned it three times to the left. The bolt slid open, and I pushed. Once inside, I flipped up another switch and closed and locked the latch behind me.

The chill was then gone. Somehow Edwin had made sure this old space in the back of the building was perfectly temperature-controlled. It was never too cold nor too hot—not that it was too hot in Scotland very often anyway.

I was home. Well, *one* of my homes. Edwin had created the warehouse—with painstaking remodels—as a place where he could keep his treasures, items he'd collected over the years. Objects filled the tall shelves, some books but other things too—old-fashioned mousetraps, stuff from Egyptian tombs, coins, artwork, et cetera. He'd always meant to organize the space, but it had been more fun to put things in it than to organize them, so the tall room had turned into more of a retreat for him than a proper archive. When he decided it was time to get serious about organization, he searched for a new employee to help. I was the lucky new employee.

I'd made a dent in my job, but it would take me years to get on top of everything—maybe forever, I sometimes joked with Edwin. He didn't argue and in fact seemed to like the idea of my never leaving. It was always good when employers and employees were on the same page regarding employee retention.

I looked at my desk. It was covered in jewelry cases and boxes. My latest task in here had been to evaluate the surprisingly large number of jewelry boxes that had been stored on the warehouse's packed shelves. The project was only at its beginnings, and I still wasn't quite sure how to figure out what all needed to be figured out. The day I'd received the message from Shelagh, I had become diverted, and I wasn't ready to get back on any other track yet again. I scooted the boxes to one side of the desk and fired up my laptop.

As things were loading, I glanced at the time and then made a call to The Tolbooth Tavern.

"Tolbooth, how can I help ye?" the voice said.

"Benton?"

"Aye."

"It's Delaney. I'm calling to see if your waitress remembered the messenger who brought the box of mugs."

"Och, aye. She did. She said it wasnae even a man a'tall but a lass."

"Did she describe her?"

"All she had was 'nothing special.' She said the woman wore sunglasses and a cap over what was probably brown hair."

"Short, tall?"

"Neither."

"A real messenger with a company or just a woman?"

"She said she didnae see any sort of official anything on the woman's shirt. I asked."

It seemed the world was suddenly full of average-looking people who didn't make impressions, except for the Monster.

"Thank you. Would you call me if you learn anything else?"

"Aye. Got tae go now, though."

The call disconnected before I could tell him thank you or good-bye.

"A woman?" I said aloud. "Shelagh?"

I wondered if Benton had a camera running anywhere. I called the number again, but there was no answer. He probably had caller ID and was tired of me. I'd try again later.

For now I had other research to do.

I hadn't found anything about Louis Chantrell the night before, but I tried again anyway. Still there was nothing. It was weirdly quiet.

Findlay Sweet was a different matter, though. I found so much about him that I wondered if he knew how much of his personal information was available at the touch of a few keys. It seemed he'd made a small habit of getting into trouble. I didn't find anything back as far as the days when Tom told his wife on him, but there was plenty of other bad behavior.

Eight years earlier Findlay had been arrested for petty theft. He'd later been released on bond. In fact, he'd stolen from quite a few shops—jewelry, clothes, food. They weren't things that would necessarily make the news, but he'd been involved in something that had—a car accident. As a result of that high-profile wreck, his crimes had made their way to any search that included his name.

The car accident had taken place just outside Edinburgh. Findlay's car had been hit by a truck, but it seemed Findlay might have neglected to stop at a stop sign. The truck driver had been hospitalized for a long time, but he was surprisingly still alive, though no longer working for the trucking company. Though Findlay's vehicle was the smaller one, it seemed he hadn't been injured at all—one article mentioned that only a front fender had been damaged, but the truck had tipped over onto the driver's side.

Findlay had been sued, and he in turn had sued both the trucker and the company. The court cases had been newsworthy for a week or so according to a few articles I found, but all lawsuits were thrown out because nothing could be proved either way.

There'd been no witnesses.

One reporter had delved deeply into Findlay's background, going so far as to mention his ex-wife. There was even a picture of her, though just like all important pictures lately, it was grainy.

I enlarged it.

Hang on. Jessica Sweet looked familiar. How did I know her? With short brown hair and a grim expression pulling on her mouth, there was something deeply familiar about her. Did I know her, or was I trying to make something of nothing?

I couldn't place her. She looked nothing like Shelagh O'Conner, but I *had* seen her somewhere, I was sure.

That had been happening to me a lot lately.

When you live and work someplace for a while, all people start to look familiar. We had enough loyal customers that I recognized most of them most of the time, but I wasn't looking at a customer now.

How did I know Jessica Sweet? Maybe I didn't. Maybe I'd superimposed a familiar face over hers. Wishful thinking?

A few months earlier, I'd become acquainted with a woman who looked like me, as well as the martyred Mary, Queen of Scots. Our time together had been interesting as well as rife with tragedy. We'd remained acquaintances but had never been able to quite become friends.

What I'd noticed after we'd been out together in a few public places was that some people paid attention to what other people looked like, some simply didn't. The contemporary Mary and I could go to a restaurant and a server might not be able to take her eyes off us, but in another restaurant with another server we weren't given a second glance.

I was somewhere in between. Sometimes I paid attention, sometimes I didn't. But I was pretty sure I'd seen this woman somewhere recently.

It would come to me eventually.

I sighed and moved on to something else. I spent some time searching for connections among all the people I'd met recently, but didn't find much. Finally I opened my few-days-neglected email and went through it.

My phone suddenly buzzed.

"Birk?" I answered.

"Shall I come by the bookshop to pick you up?"

I looked up at the windows along the top of the warehouse. It was dark outside. I pulled the phone away from my head and checked the time. It was just after six. The afternoon had flown away.

"How's the storm?"

"It let up a couple hours ago," he said. "You okay?"

"Fine, just got lost in some work. Yes, I'll meet you outside the bookshop."

I grabbed my phone to call Tom as I made my way back to the other side, but he was calling me at the same time. It seemed my luck in having him home in the evenings had run out tonight, which was just as well since I was headed to another pub anyway. Rodger was working, but with two big groups of customers—one a wedding party, the other a girls' night group—still inside the smallest pub in Scotland, it was going to have to be all hands on deck. I told him I'd found something to keep me busy. When I shared the name of the pub we were visiting, he laughed, saying even he hadn't been to that one yet. I told him I'd try to memorize the details. He was just pleased I was going with Birk and not by myself.

Before we hung up, I managed to let him know that the police had arrested someone. He said he hadn't heard about that. I wished I'd thought to pay attention to the news again to see if the police had released the information yet. The day had truly gotten away from me.

I came through the door to the light side, where Rosie, Hamlet, and Hector were still working. Though they'd noticed the improvement in the weather, they'd lost track of time too.

"One of those days," Rosie said as she stood and stretched.

Hector had been on the floor next to her. Still in his red sweater, he stood and stretched too, one leg at a time. Yep, even cuter.

I noticed Birk's car outside, so I said good-bye quickly. Birk was just stepping out as I left the shop.

"I can get my door, Birk. Thanks, though," I said as I jogged toward the car, glad for the milder weather.

Birk hesitated but then slipped back into the driver's seat and closed his door. Just as I made it around to the passenger side, I heard a sound from the end of the row of buildings that housed the bookshop.

It was a distinct growl, maybe like a dog's but with a higher pitch. I stopped and looked but saw nothing. No one was walking in that vicinity. A few people were walking across Grassmarket Square, some going into the pubs I'd recently visited. I glanced up the street to Tom's pub, where a line of customers snaked out the door.

Birk got out of the car again. "What's going on?"

"I thought I heard something."

"What?"

I looked back at the end of the street, where I was sure the noise had come from. Okay, maybe not sure. There was no one there, and I knew that my imagination was on fire.

"Nothing," I finally said before I hopped into the car.

SIXTEEN

I would never tell my husband, but Whistle Binkies was maybe one of the coolest pubs I'd ever seen.

To be fair, it was impossible to go wrong with any Edinburgh pub, but since my heart belonged to the smallest pub in Scotland, it took a lot to turn my head. Whistle Binkies had enough to do it.

We were no longer in Grassmarket but not far away from either the Royal Mile or my blue house by the sea. I felt like we'd come upon a place that should have required a secret knock. The inside of the space was long, with the stage area at one end and the bar and leather banquettes jutting and alcoved off the main area. Old brown tiles, some of them chipped and broken, covered the floor, and in some places old casks had been repurposed as chairs for tall tables.

A band was warming up when we entered through a door next door to a pizza place. The pub was already crowded, most of the chairs filled, the hum of voices and some raucous laughter adding more layers of noise to the band's jaunty rhythms.

Birk and I made a quick beeline to the bar. It was the first ~b we'd visited where we had to raise our voices. I introduced

myself and Birk to the bartender, a young woman calling herself Sprout. I ordered two pints and then asked Sprout if she
had any clues for us.

She didn't consider my question for more than a second or
two before she laughed. "I have no idea what you're talking
about. Let me know if you need anything else." And then she
turned and gave her attention to another customer.

Birk and I grabbed our pints.

"Let's go talk to the band," I suggested.

"Right behind you. The ale is agreeable."

The four-man band reminded me of the Beatles, at least
in the way they looked. Their sixties-throwback clothing and
shaggy haircuts were cute and nostalgic.

Birk and I weren't your typical groupies, I decided as we
passed by a table of young women who all seemed to be glanc-
ing at the band members as casually on purpose as possible. I
smiled at the women, but they didn't smile back as we walked
by the table, blocking their views momentarily.

We stopped just to the side of the stage. Birk was the first to
raise his pint in salute when the lead singer noticed us.

The singer's eyebrows rose. I smiled and waved. To his credit
he said something to the drummer and then walked toward us.

"Help you?" he said, his accent British rather than Scottish.
He reminded me more of John Lennon than Paul McCartney
in looks, but there was something playfully Paul about him.

Again I introduced Birk and myself and gave him my now
well-practiced spiel about our hunt. He told us his name was
Todd.

"That sounds fun." Todd smiled.

"Well, maybe a little. Our last clue led us here and, we think,
specifically to your band. The people who set up the hunt
are particularly fond of the book *Jekyll and Hyde*. Is the

anything you might want to share with us that would send us to wherever we need to go next? Has anyone given any of you a note to pass along? Or a message? Something?"

His eyebrows came together in genuine thought as he shook his head slowly. "I can't think of one thing. I'll ask the others."

He wasn't far away, but we couldn't hear him as he spoke to the other band members. They all shook their heads in response.

"Sorry, nothing," he said as he rejoined us.

"What's the story behind your band's name?" I asked.

Todd shrugged. "Hyde's my last name."

"What about your songs? What are some titles?"

"They're all original. Tonight's set will be the same set we've been playing for a while."

Todd told us the titles of the songs, but it was clear they weren't well-known songs, not publicized and not printed on the back of a CD case or a record sleeve. Hyde and Seek hadn't made any such recordings. They were simply a bar band, and that's the way they liked it. They all had day jobs doing things that didn't seem in any way tied to our hunt. None of them worked with books nor inside laboratories where potions to create monsters might be mixed.

We overstayed our welcome, but Todd remained polite and as helpful as he could be. The audience started to get antsy for the band to start playing for real. As we turned to walk toward the back of the pub, Todd stopped us and said, "Tonight's our only night this month."

"What's that?" I said as Birk and I turned around again.

"We're a popular band in this pub, many pubs, but like I mentioned, we all have day jobs. We don't do as many gigs as the pubs would like us to do. They always advertise with flyers d such. It's usually a pretty big night for them."

"Aye," Birk said. "You think that whatever clue might be here, it's here only tonight?"

Todd shrugged. "If you're on the right track, I guess."

I nodded. "Makes sense. Thank you."

"You're welcome. Good luck." Todd moved back to his microphone.

With our pints we stepped away and found a corner where we could stand. We listened to the band and looked around for something that might be a clue. Maybe someone was coming in tonight to talk to us. Did we just have to wait?

Hyde and Seek were great and sounded more country than Beatles. Birk and I had fun. Their fan base was loyal. The pub became very crowded, but the audience was more interested in hearing the music than talking over it.

We might have stayed later, but after a couple hours we lost steam and decided we weren't going to find anything else. In fact, we weren't sure if we'd found anything to begin with. We were punting, just going where we thought the clues *might* be sending us. Nothing had been confirmed.

I wondered at what point on the hunt Jacques and Tricia were. No one had mentioned to me that others had come searching, so I assumed they hadn't made it as far along as Birk and I had, or that they were on a different scent—maybe the correct one.

I followed Birk as we weaved our way through the crowd toward the stairs. I bumped into him when he stopped suddenly. He was looking at something on the wall. It was an old poster, a painted depiction of the galaxy. I'd noticed it when we came in, thinking there was something very "ancient astronomers" about it.

"Lovely," Birk said.

"It is," I agreed.

I'd been with Birk a few times when he'd become intrigued by a work of art. It could be anything from a fine masterpiece to a stamp. He'd once carried around an ad from a local plumber for a couple weeks just because he liked the colors used. It wasn't surprising that he needed a moment to take in the beautiful poster.

He finally nodded and led the way up the stairs and out to the cold—but still not stormy—night.

"Now what?" he said once we were inside his car again.

"I don't know. I wish I did. I wonder if the police have mentioned who they arrested."

"I don't know. We'll listen to the news as I run you home."

"Tom's pub if you don't mind, please."

Birk turned on the radio, and we first heard the latest weather forecast. Nothing new or surprising there. The newscaster answered our burning question a moment later.

"Though the local police had arrested someone they suspected was the New Monster, the city won't in fact be allowed a breath of relief, because the suspect has been released. We are working to gather further details, but officials aren't disclosing the name of the man they brought in for questioning. We'll keep you up to date. In other news—maybe tied together, maybe not, local philanthropist Shelagh O'Conner still hasn't been found." The man on the radio cleared his throat. "Let's keep aware, folks, and let's find Shelagh."

With agitation Birk turned off the radio. "Damn, none of that is good news."

"No, it's not."

Birk left the radio off, and we took the rest of the trip in silence, both of us probably wondering what to expect or prepare for next. It was impossible to know.

The only place available to pull over was on the far side of

Grassmarket Square. Birk let me out and waited as I looked down toward the bookshop. It was closed, and nothing seemed out of place. I waved at Birk and then hurried across the square to the pub. There was no line of customers anymore, but it was still crowded inside.

Birk waited until I waved at him again before he took off.

As he drove away, though, I spotted something that froze me in my tracks.

The Monster was there, watching me.

SEVENTEEN

My eyes were on the far corner of Grassmarket-Canongate. I was sure I'd seen a person in a shabby coat and hat peeking around the building on that corner, watching me. But that certainty wavered a little as I continued to stare and didn't see anything else for a few long beats. Nevertheless, I grabbed on to the arm of someone walking into the pub.

"Pardon?" the man said.

"Get Tom, right away," I said.

"What?"

"Please. Get Tom. Now."

"Aye," he said. He hurried inside as I barely blinked, keeping my eyes on that now-dark spot, afraid I'd miss more . . . something.

An eternal half a minute or so later, Tom stepped out of the pub.

"Delaney?"

"Tom, come with me," I said.

"Aye."

We took off, across the square and toward the corner.

"I think I saw the Monster," I said.

"Let's call the police."

"I'm not sure, though."

"All right. Let me lead." Tom moved ahead of me.

"Right around that building."

We stopped and peered carefully around the corner. The brick-paved road led up to and under a bridge in the direction Birk and I had just come from—toward Whistle Binkies. A close was located in between the buildings about thirty feet way. I'd been in the close before; it was steep and frequently used on haunted tours. As we looked up the meagerly lit road, it seemed we briefly saw the flap of a coat at the close's entrance.

Tom and I looked at each other.

"You saw that?" I said.

"I did."

"Let's follow," I said. "I'll call Inspector Winters as we go."

Even if he'd wanted to argue, there wasn't time to think. We were together, and we would be as careful as we could be.

"All right." Tom led the way, and I pulled out my phone as we approached the close.

"Delaney?" Inspector Winters picked up just as Tom took out his phone and clicked on the flashlight app, shining it into the close. We didn't see anyone, but the steep close was intimidating.

"Tom and I are chasing someone we thought might be the . . . Monster."

"What? Stop immediately."

"It's okay, we're keeping a distance." I told him where we were.

"All right. Don't go into that close, do you understand? I'll get someone out there immediately."

"Got it." I ended the call and said to Tom, "We have strict instructions not to go in there."

"Aye." He held the light steady.

On each side, old brick buildings were stacked and angled atop each other, and metal fire escapes glinted off Tom's light.

The slam of a door echoed around us.

Tom tried to move the light toward the direction of the noise, but because of the crazy angles of the buildings some doors were hidden from view, and echoes were weird anyway.

It couldn't have been fifteen more seconds until a police car, sirens blaring, came to a stop behind us.

We identified ourselves and told them what we'd seen. On foot they took off up the close, with much stronger flashlights than the one on Tom's phone.

"Stay back," one of the officers commanded over his shoulder.

We did, but not far. We waited at the curb, where Inspector Winters soon pulled up and parked his car.

"Glad you two are okay," he said.

"We're fine," I said. "I was pretty sure I saw something, but I just didn't know," I said. "And then both Tom and I saw something here."

"I have no doubt we saw the flap of a coat," Tom said. "But that's it."

"The person who was arrested was released?" I asked.

"Aye."

"Was it someone we know?"

"Aye, I believe it was."

When he didn't continue, I tried not to look too eager.

Inspector Winters took a deep breath and rubbed the stubble on his chin. "Aye. We arrested Findlay Sweet, but I'm requesting that you not share that information. We only had circumstantial evidence, so it didn't really hold up, but there might be more for the police to find. We hoped he could help us find Shelagh, but now we believe he had nothing to do with her disappearance."

"When you say 'we,' do you include yourself?" I asked.

"I watched the interview recording. I believe him too. I know more about Findlay Sweet than I ever wanted to, including the fact that he once worked with Tom and that he was the one who delivered the messenger to you, Delaney."

"What about his ex-wife?" I asked. "Jessica Sweet. I saw her picture on the internet, and I feel like I've seen her somewhere, but I couldn't place her."

"He hasn't been married for a long time. I don't think we've talked to her," Inspector Winters said as he reached for the notebook and pen he kept in his shirt pocket.

"If you do, I'd love to know where she works or lives—I really do feel like I've seen her somewhere." I looked at Tom.

"I haven't seen her since the day I talked to her about her husband's behavior all those years ago. I can't remember what job she did or even if she had one back then," he said.

"Well, I can't imagine it matters at all, but just to satisfy my curiosity I'd like to know where I've seen her."

The other officers exited the close.

"Anything?" Inspector Winters asked them.

They shook their heads. "Nothing. We're going to do a walkabout, though, check the surrounding area."

"Very good. Be safe."

Once the officers left, Inspector Winters turned to us again.

"The officers on the case have some new clues to explore, but I'm not at liberty to share them with you. At this point mostly we'd like to find Shelagh O'Conner. Of course we don't want any other burglaries or murders, but we do suspect that the appearance of the New Monster has something to do with

Shelagh's disappearance. We want her safe. Come along. I'll get the two of you back to the pub. Be aware. Don't go out alone."

"You do believe we really saw something?" I asked as we crossed Grassmarket. I was shaking out my arms, still tense and wired.

"Aye. Can't tell you if it was the Monster or not, but . . . just be careful," Inspector Winters said.

"We will be," Tom said.

I wondered if Tom was going to insist on being with me now 24/7. Not that I would mind hanging out with him that much, but we both had things to do.

Inspector Winters told us good-bye and then jogged back to his car. Tom and I watched him turn and wave in our direction.

"Are you all right, lass?" Tom pulled me close.

"I'm fine. Please don't worry."

Tom laughed. "I'll always worry, but I'm glad you had someone come get me, that you didn't go alone."

I pulled back. "You saw the coat flap, right? You're not just saying that to support me?"

"No, I saw it." Tom looked toward the corner, his eyebrows coming together. "I don't know what's going on or why it seems—and it does seem like this—that whoever is doing all this wants you to see them. You, specifically."

I hadn't thought of it exactly that way, but Birk hadn't mentioned any in-person Monster sightings. I hadn't asked the others.

"Hello," a familiar voice said.

We jumped and turned. Tricia stood in the pub's doorway, her arms crossed in front of herself.

"Tricia?" I said.

"I've been waiting. I saw you leave." She nodded at Tom and then looked back at me. "What were you guys doing? Did I see police cars down there?"

"Hello, Tricia. Good to see you again." Not missing a beat, Tom stepped toward her and extended his hand. She was so petite that even though she stood on a step, he was still a little taller than her.

They shook.

"You know, I wanted to tell you that you are extraordinarily handsome," she said with no flirtation at all as she pushed up her glasses.

"Thank you," he said. "Come on in, drinks are on me."

The crowd had thinned even more since Birk dropped me off. The three of us moved to the bar, Tom letting Tricia and me pass first. He and I exchanged some conspiratorial raised eyebrows as I moved by. We weren't going to share the details of what had happened at the other end of Grassmarket— according to our eyebrows at least.

Tricia and I sat on tall stools and both ordered Cokes as Tom moved to the other side of the bar. Rodger was there, as well as a young man I hadn't met yet. I would introduce myself when he wasn't so busy.

I was still rattled, but I thought I was hiding it well. I clasped my hands together to conceal any leftover shaking. There was no indication that Tom might be distracted or bothered. He was good at this.

"What's going on?" I asked Tricia.

"That's why I'm here, to ask you. After that night at the pub, I haven't been able to figure out anything, and I was in the area, knew you guys owned the pub. I know I said I wanted to work alone, but I'm wondering if you've gotten any farther on the hunt."

I thought the person Tom and I had seen in the coat probably hadn't been Tricia, probably not even female, but I was still wary. The timing might be uncanny—or it might not be.

I shrugged noncommittally. "It's been difficult." I took a drink of the Coke that Tom put in front of me. "I feel like I'm onto something and then I'm not. I don't think I have any real answers. What about Jacques?"

"What about him?"

"You made sure he got back to his room. Is he okay? Did you two decide to work together?"

"I dropped him off outside is all. We aren't working together," she said almost defensively. "I don't think Jacques cares about the books. I think he just wants one of us to find the treasure so he can get the money from Shelagh and go back home." Tricia paused. "I mean, if Shelagh is ever able to pay out. I guess she'll have to be found first."

"I guess. Would you mind sharing what Shelagh said to you during your tour of the library? My time with her was cut short."

"Oh. Sure." She took a drink too. "She told me how important her library was to her, how important that story of *Jekyll and Hyde* is to her."

"What did she say as to why she loves the story so much?"

"I don't think we talked about that part."

I nodded, thinking it very well could have just been because I always like to know the reasons people love their favorite books that Shelagh and I'd had that discussion.

"I asked her about her staff, about that man named Louis and the driver, Findlay something," Tricia said.

"Yeah?" I said, sitting up a little more. "Why?"

"Don't really know, except they both set off alarm bells with me. She said that she trusts them both completely. I asked about any other people who work for her. I was just curious, you know. It's such a big house, and I wondered how she kept it all going."

"And?"

"She said she has a housekeeping service, her cook is a woman who comes in every other day and makes the most delicious food. They barely see each other." Tricia paused. "She did, however, mention that she was bothered a little about the guy who tends the horses. Winston, I think. She wouldn't go into detail, but when she went missing, I told the police what she'd said."

I remembered Shelagh's being bothered by what she said she thought had been Winston's night of drinking.

"Good. What else did she say about him?" I asked.

"Nothing that I remember."

"Did the police tell you anything else that day?" I asked.

"No."

"Did Shelagh talk about anyone else?"

"No, did she to you?"

"No, but our time was cut short," I repeated.

"Because the police came and got her?"

"Yes, but she was released."

"Oh, I know. Personally, I don't think Shelagh has done anything wrong. I think her past life is being used as an excuse for someone to misbehave in the worst ways possible. I knew that it would happen, though, or something like it. It's just too good of a story for someone not to remake it. You know, copycats?"

Was it possible I could like Tricia? "I do know."

"So you haven't figured out anything else?"

"I'm sorry, I haven't." Well, I only *might* like her.

"Okay. I haven't either." She shrugged.

Companionable silence isn't too difficult in a pub, but it wasn't easy to achieve with Tricia. She seemed uncomfortable and anxious, and not really interested in conversation. I suspected she wasn't one to visit many pubs.

Finally, she looked at Tom. "May I use the loo?"

"Aye. Just down the hall."

When she returned, she finished off her Coke and told us she needed to head home. Tom and I watched her weave her way through the pub and then out the door.

"Maybe that's her way of trying to be friends?" Tom said when she was out of sight.

"Maybe," I said. "Do you suppose she wanted to tell me something but couldn't get around to it?"

"Lass, I have no idea."

I nodded. "All right, let's go over what we saw out there again. Do you mind?"

"Not even a little bit."

EIGHTEEN

"Ye're going back there today?" Aggie asked as she spooned some scrambled eggs onto my plate.

"Yes. Birk is picking me up. We'll go together."

"Do ye think Elias should go?"

Elias, sitting next to me at the table, looked up. "Happy tae drive anytime, ye ken."

"I think I'm okay." I took a bite of the eggs and looked at Aggie. I was going to miss having them around. "Elias has plans."

"Och, he doesnae need tae help the electricians. They can figure oot their jobs themselves," Aggie said as she looked at her husband. He pretended not to notice.

He would happily go with me, but he really did like supervising the people working on his properties. Tom had already left so he could get a jump on some deep cleaning at the pub, but Aggie had made sure he'd eaten first.

I smiled to myself and then looked at Aggie. "Birk and I will be all right."

"Whatever ye think." Aggie sat and finally started eating her breakfast.

"Aggie, do you remember anything else about Shelagh O'Conner? What about the victim back then, Oliver McCabe? I can't find anything at all about him."

Aggie fell into thought as she chewed. "I have been thinking, lass, and I do remember more, but mostly about her. Shelagh was funny, delightful, except when she wasn't, I suppose. She could change in an instant."

"Moody?"

"Aye." Doubt lined the word.

"What?"

"A wee bit more than moody. Extreme sometimes. Large mood swings, even for seventeen."

"Oh?" I put the fork down. "Do you think she had some sort of illness, something like bipolar disorder?"

"I couldnae tell ye, but when she was younger, her moods were most definitely extreme, and her imagination was so . . . big."

Maybe another small piece of this big puzzle had just fallen into place. Was Shelagh afflicted with a mental illness? Did the swings in her mood somehow help her relate to the story she loved so much? It was all pure speculation on my part, but I could see the connection.

I decided early in graduate school that I needed to do something about my moods. It quickly came down to a choice between seeing a psychiatrist or buying a horse.

The bookish voice came from a memoir I'd read. It didn't really do credit to the full thought the author was trying to convey, but the voice in my head only wanted me to have that part of it. *An Unquiet Mind* by Kay Redfield Jamison. Yes, this was all somehow connected—Shelagh's past, what was happening now, even her horses. Even if I wasn't certain of it, my subconscious was. The problem: I still didn't understand the connections.

"Lass?" Elias said.

"Sorry." I came back to the moment and grabbed my fork. "What else, Aggie, anything?"

"Shelagh and her parents, more particularly her father, had issues. He was a strict man. They were a successful family, and they were in the news aftwhiles—often. Of course, back when Shelagh dressed up and pretended tae be a copy of Hyde, her father spoke out and said how disappointed he was in her, after the fact." Aggie tapped her fingers on her mouth. "It was embarrassing for Shelagh, I'm sure, but I don't remember ever talking to her aboot it."

"I'm sorry she had to go through that."

"She did bring it on herself some, though I wish her father had shown her more understanding publicly. Maybe he did in private."

"How did her parents die?"

"I think they were just old and passed in their sleep, both of them. I think I remember reading their obituaries. I'm not sure though. It's been a long time. I also remembered a little something about the man who was kil't, Ollie. He was kil't at the museum. He worked there, and that's where they found his body—on the museum steps, I think."

"What? At Joshua's museum?" I asked.

"Aye, I believe so."

"That's great news! I mean . . . well, that sounded terrible. It's just that I'm sure Joshua knows the story, then." I reached for my phone to call my brilliant young friend who, thankfully, still worked at the National Museum of Scotland. "Wait. Why couldn't I find that in the research that I did? I didn't find out much about him at all."

Aggie shrugged. "Dinnae ken, but the story back then, even with the murder, was more about Shelagh than the dead man.

I think I remember learning that he wasn't the kindest of men, but that was later, and, lass, I'm afraid that Ollie got forgotten. Shelagh was much more interesting."

I started a text but was diverted by a knock on the front door—Birk. I decided to grab him and have us go see Joshua together before we went to Shelagh's house. I stood from the table and grabbed my plate.

"I'll get the dishes, lass," Aggie said.

I kissed them both on their cheeks and then put my plate in the sink. I was definitely going to miss them.

Somehow I managed to talk Birk into a detour to the museum. He'd had a detour of his own in mind, but when I greeted him with the request, he decided to save his surprise for later. He did smile and tell me I'd like where we were going next. After I'd texted Joshua, he replied saying that he was going to be at the museum for only another couple hours or so because of meetings he was required to attend off-site but that he'd love to see us and tell us what he knew about Oliver McCabe.

Joshua had come to the University of Edinburgh to work on one of his many PhDs a few years earlier; a job at the museum had kept him in town, though now other prestigious institutions were calling him, wanting him to leave Edinburgh and go to work for them. I didn't want him to go.

He'd become like a little brother, one who enjoyed museums as much as I did. We toured them the same way: slowly and with singular focus. He and Rosie had grown close too; she'd become the grandmother he'd never really had, and sometimes I wondered if it was her or perhaps her cookies that kept him in town even more than his job.

Birk parked in front of the wide brown building, and we

climbed the stairs to one of the front doors. The museum wasn't open yet, but I knew to knock on a specific door. We'd done this a time or two—there were simply things Joshua thought I needed to see without the rest of the museum crowd around to get in our way; secret viewings were the only recourse.

In fact, he'd been working on something I'd recently found in the bottom of the priceless desk in the warehouse. Joshua was still in the process of authenticating and transcribing the treasure. He'd assured me I'd get an early look, but he wasn't finished yet, and he wouldn't show me anything before his work was perfect.

The museum door opened a moment later. Joshua smiled. "Come in, come in."

We hugged quickly, and he and Birk shook hands. Joshua closed the door behind us and made sure it locked again before he turned and told us to follow him to his office.

"Gracious, do I have a story to tell you," he said as his long legs moved quickly over the wax-shined floor.

He'd once had an office inside an old closet but had recently been upgraded, and he now had a real office down a hallway full of them. His was a large, beautiful room with windows, but I missed the cramped space. He and I both pretended we liked the new office better than the old one; it seemed like the right thing to do.

We didn't see anyone else as we made our way past the skeleton rendition of an old Viking ship. The museum was hosting a Viking display I still needed to see. I wouldn't ask for a tour today, but someday soon.

Joshua closed his office door once we were inside. "Make yourselves comfortable. The coffee hasn't been started yet, but I can grab us some cups in a bit if you're interested."

"No, I'm fine," I said.

"I'm fine too, but thank you, lad."

"When you sent the text, I almost squealed with delight," Joshua said as we all found chairs. "The story I have for you is incredible. I've thought about telling you a few times, but we've been doing other things and it kept slipping my mind. I'm glad it's time to finally share."

"Wow, you have our attention," I said from across the desk. His silver blinds were shut, so I had no view of the close and the building behind him. His desk was, as was typical, cleared off except for the computer monitor, a keyboard, and a yellow notepad, which was turned facedown.

Joshua opened a drawer and pulled out three matching brochures. They were trifolded pieces of paper, yellow and wilted from age.

"I found this when I first started working here. I asked about it but was told it was something we just didn't talk about any longer." Joshua gave Birk and me each one of the brochures. "But I kept a stack of them nonetheless. The story was just too good to ignore."

Holding it with care, I looked at the front of the brochure. The title said, *Come Experience a Real Laboratory Made for a Monster.*

"What in the world?" I said.

"Aye?" Birk said. "Was this a display at the museum? I don't remember it."

"It was supposed to be." Joshua sat up and put his arms on his desk. "Back in the day, Oliver McCabe worked here. Oh, wait." Joshua opened the drawer and reached inside, pulling out a small black-and-white picture, sliding it toward us. "Here he is."

The photo showed a handsome young man—clearly not quite thirty—with dark hair, dark eyes, high cheekbones, and a strong chin. He wasn't smiling, but there was a sense of playfulness in his eyes that made me think it was that—not his handsomeness—that might have attracted Shelagh O'Conner.

Birk and I nodded after we looked at the picture, and Joshua drew it back toward him.

"Anyway," Joshua continued, "Ollie did many things around here, one of them being designing some of the displays. He had lots of wonderful ideas, including one to create attractions about some of Scotland's more famous authors. Here, unlike other museum exhibits devoted to our literary geniuses, Ollie decided to take books and create tableaus taken directly from some of the stories. Of course, he couldn't possibly pass up creating something with the good Dr. Jekyll and the bad Mr. Hyde. It was to be his first author tableau. Then, as he was bringing everything together, he met Shelagh O'Conner, though I'm not exactly sure how or where. They became friendly, I guess. I've been following the story of her disappearance, the New and Old Monsters, et cetera. I spoke to one of the museum directors who was here back then too, Angela, and she told me that Ollie's plans were extraordinary, but then he was killed—on the front steps of the museum, no less."

"I need to understand the timing better." I looked at Birk. "When did you and Shelagh date?"

Joshua's eyes widened as if he were anxious to hear the answer too.

"Shelagh joined a group I was a part of in 1993. She was just over thirty. I was forty," he said. I knew he was talking about Fleshmarket. "She left the group just six or so months later. Our relationship had been established and then cooled just in those few months."

"The Old Monster roamed the streets in 1968," Joshua said.

"Angela thinks Ollie and Shelagh met when she heard about his tableau plans—if he knew she was the Old Monster, she could have been the inspiration for his work. However, I think it's important to note here that chances are that he didn't know, that she didn't tell him. Angela thinks Ollie would have said something if that had been the case. Angela and Ollie were friends."

"Did Shelagh give you any details?" I asked Birk. "Did she tell you if Ollie knew?"

"Lass, she wouldn't speak of that time or of Ollie. I understood."

I nodded and looked back at Joshua.

He continued, "The Old Monster, aka Shelagh, wasn't causing trouble back then, just mystery. There were no burglaries, just odd sightings. Apparently even doing good deeds."

"That's correct," Birk said. "She helped people living on the streets, not harmed them."

"Yes, exactly," Joshua said. "And before Ollie was killed, he and Shelagh became friends, maybe dated secretly from what I've heard. He consulted her regarding the laboratory display—Dr. Jekyll's 'cabinet.' The picture of Shelagh near Ollie's body was developed a couple months after the murder, so that's all the police had at the time. Any other possible evidence was long gone. But Ollie knew how young she was, and Angela thinks he probably came to his senses and put the brakes on anything more romantic developing."

I thought about what Aggie had just told me. "Was Ollie a nice man?"

"I asked Angela that. She said Ollie wasn't a bad man, but he wasn't exactly the friendliest either. He was . . . what was the word Angela used? Obsessive."

"About his work?"

"About everything, or so she said."

"Do you—or does Angela—think Shelagh actually killed Ollie?" I said.

Joshua shrugged. "There's only speculation, but no conclusive evidence. When he was killed, the directors postponed the opening of the display, and then two months later, when the picture was made public, the directors just scrapped the whole idea."

"Other than the circumstantial picture, why would anyone think Shelagh killed him?" Birk asked.

"They argued," Joshua said. "Presumably about Ollie ending the relationship."

"Possibly a good enough motive for murder, but I still don't think she's capable of such a thing," Birk said.

I didn't think Shelagh was a killer either, but I didn't completely understand her.

"I just don't know," Joshua said. He smiled. "But here's the best part." His dramatic pause went on so long that Birk and I shared a look. "We still have the laboratory."

"Aye?" Birk said.

"You do?" I said.

"Want to see it?" Joshua's smile was pure Cheshire Cat.

A few minutes later, we were weaving our way down a staircase and into the basement.

"Ollie was brilliant," Joshua said as he led the two of us. "But also described as odd. From what I can gather, I suspect he was on the autism spectrum. The job in the museum was perfect for him. He could hyperfocus his energy in a creative way that spoke to his brilliant, quirky mind. He was happy, and though not very social, he was most definitely well respected. His social challenges did not stop him from having a few friendships—and, it seems, maybe a romantic relationship with Shelagh, though I don't really know what that meant for them."

"Why did the museum keep the laboratory display?" Birk asked as we turned to take another flight downward.

"The possibility was entertained that we were going to continue with Ollie's idea down the road, but then when Shelagh became a suspect, the directors kept it for possible evidence. The police found nothing they could use, apparently—it wasn't the scene of the murder anyway. But then it just seemed too cool a thing to completely dismantle. Ollie built it in four parts, and each one has all its pieces glued down. You'll see."

We finally came to a spot where there were no more stairs to descend. It was cold and dark and unwelcoming.

"I'm afraid it won't warm up even when we go into the room. We'll make it quick, but I really think you'll enjoy seeing this."

Joshua opened the second door on our right. I wondered what was behind all the other doors too, but I'd ask another day.

We went into an even colder, darker space. Joshua reached around and flipped a switch, illuminating the room with harsh, overhead lights that made us all look gray.

"Oh, my," I said as my eyes took in the rest of the deep chamber.

It was indeed the laboratory of a mad scientist, or at least the representation of one. The display was large, much bigger than I might have imagined, bigger even than I'd imagined Dr. Jekyll's cabinet when I read the story. The lab tables were old-fashioned wooden versions of what I'd seen in the schools I'd attended. Everything else—the beakers, jars, lamps, and such—were also from an earlier time. Shelves had been built into the walls; all of them appeared to be filled with things that were floating in liquid. Yes, the items in the beakers were spooky, but nothing was overtly ominous. There were no detached eyeballs staring at us, no severed heads. That idea seemed woven into the atmosphere of the display. It might have scared a child, but it probably would have simply been fascinating to most any adult who looked at it, particularly if they'd read the story.

There was one part, however, that I did find pretty creepy. Huddled over in a chair with its head tucked downward, dressed in a shabby coat and hat, was a mannequin that was unquestionably meant to be Mr. Hyde.

A chill ran up my spine. "If that thing moves, I'll beat the two of you back upstairs."

"I suspect it will be a lively footrace," Birk added.

"It hasn't moved since I first saw it. I think we're safe." Joshua walked to the middle of the display. "There was an ingredient which Dr. Jekyll thought assisted with his transformation. It was the inability to find that substance again that caused him to ultimately have to rid the world of Mr. Hyde. This"—Joshua pointed to a beaker that seemed to be filled with a green liquid—"was going to represent the liquid. Ollie was planning something interactive, but those details are lost to time."

"Goodness," Birk said.

"I know," Joshua said. "I don't think it tells you anything new, but it's pretty cool."

I couldn't help but imagine Shelagh seeing this—and being both thrilled and intrigued. It would have been a lot to process, but it would have also been right up her alley—or her *close*, as the case must have been.

"Does anyone at the museum have any suspicions as to who killed Ollie?" I asked.

"None whatsoever that Angela knew of. Before the photo

became public, everyone mostly thought he was randomly accosted one dark early morning as he was coming to the museum, a robbery gone wrong. From what I've been told, Ollie wasn't the kind of man to just hand over his wallet. He might not have fought, but he certainly would have been confused, maybe argued, refused, stuck by the fact that stealing was wrong."

"And when the photo became public?" I asked.

"Well, maybe some around here thought about Shelagh, but it all died down after a while." Joshua shrugged. "With what's happening now, everyone is trying to remember the details, but it was a long time ago and most of the people who were around then aren't still here."

"Would you know if Ollie was in any way connected to the current murder victim, Ritchie John? Did Ollie work with horses? Or in any pub?" I asked.

"I don't know, Delaney, but I'll ask around. Maybe someone remembers."

"Thanks, Joshua." I shivered as I leaned over and looked at the mannequin; it was faceless, but dressed so much like the figure Tom and I had seen in the car park and in Grassmarket the night before, and in the pictures on the news. Maybe the garb wasn't too surprising—shabby was shabby—but it felt more uncanny than that.

"Lass, are you all right?" Birk asked me.

I stood straight. "I'm fine. This is fascinating. Thank you for showing us, Joshua."

"My pleasure."

I was glad to better know Oliver McCabe through his work, but now I felt deeply sad about the loss of his life. He was talented, and seemingly kind.

"I'm going to tell Inspector Winters about this. I don't know if he'll want to see it or not, but the police should know, I think," I said.

"No problem. I'll happily show them," Joshua said. "In fact, I really wonder if we shouldn't try to resurrect Ollie's idea—I mean, once everything calms down."

I was glad to leave the cold basement laboratory, and I soaked in the light as we emerged from the stairway. Birk and I thanked Joshua as he let us out the door we'd entered through.

Once he'd gone back in, I paused on the outside stairs and looked back at the building.

"What, lass?" Birk asked.

"That was creepy. Another time, under other circumstances, it might have been deliciously creepy, but today it was just creepy." I looked at Birk.

"Aye."

I took a cleansing breath. "Okay, what's your surprise?"

Birk smiled. "I figured out the next clue."

"Why didn't you say so?"

He laughed. I'd been so anxious to see Joshua that I hadn't given Birk a chance to say much of anything.

"Let's go!" I hurried to the car.

NINETEEN

Though I told Birk about the events of the previous evening—the coat Tom and I had followed and Tricia's surprise visit to the pub—he remained mysterious, not telling me anything else except that we were going to a whole different kind of pub this time.

We came to a stop in front of one in New Town.

"This is definitely different from the Old Town pubs," I said as we looked at the black-painted exterior. It stood out from the lighter-colored stone buildings around it.

"Exactly. Starbar."

"You think the poster we saw of the galaxy last night was a clue?"

He sent me a wry smile. "I know it was. I went back after I dropped you off. I'd been in Whistle Binkies a time or two over the years. The spot where we saw the poster used to have another poster in there, an old cigarette ad. It took me a while to remember that—I just knew something wasn't right."

"Okay."

"Anyway, I went back and talked to Sprout, asking her what had happened to the old poster. She was perplexed, so much so that she came out from behind the bar to investigate with me. She said she had no idea where the galaxy picture came from, that the old poster was something Whistle Binkies was actually known for, and she was sure that the rendition of the galaxy hadn't been there that morning. She wasn't happy. She took it upon herself to peel back a corner. The top poster came off easily. She was angry enough to wad it up and drop it in a bin. I grabbed it, thanked her, and left."

"So you think that poster was put there to tell us to go to this bar?" I tried not to sound overly doubtful.

Birk smiled knowingly. "The poster is in the backseat. Reach around and grab it. Read the writing on the back."

I did as he instructed.

You are almost there. You have almost found the book. Keep going, keep shooting for the stars.

I looked at Birk. "Are you kidding me?"

"No, lass, I am not."

"That's incredible," I said.

"It's about paying attention, I guess." Birk shrugged.

"Well, good work. You think they're open?"

"I think the door will be unlocked and there will be someone in there to give us the next clue."

"Okay. You're way ahead of me, aren't you?"

"Well, I had to make sure someone would be here, and I did wonder if I was on the right track. I rang them and we spoke. I asked about a clue of any sort, and received an encouraging answer. Let's go."

The inside of Starbar confirmed we'd found a whole different kind of place, and I loved it. Furnished with simple chairs and tables—stark and dark was the best way to describe the interior.

"You the one who rang me at the crack of dawn?" a woman said from behind the bar.

She was wearing a housedress, something like what my grandmother would wear only around her home, and her gray hair was pulled back into a tight bun. A large woman with an older but strikingly pretty face, she gave me the fleeting thought that Birk might have finally met his match.

"I am," Birk said. "Birk Blackburn and Delaney Nichols at your service." He extended a hand over the bar.

She shook it, though she didn't smile. "I'm Delta. If you were at my service, you would have let me sleep a wee bit longer. I closed last night."

"Our apologies." Birk smiled. He probably wasn't charming her like he hoped, but he kept trying.

"Well. I suppose it's all right. I've been waiting for you for a week or so. It will be good to get this over with."

"You have?" I asked.

"Aye. I've got this book."

Birk and I both took in our breath, gasping as Delta reached underneath to some shelves. Had we found it?

She lifted it and let it slap down on the bar as if it weren't a treasured item, something that had come off a printing press over a hundred years ago.

Birk and I looked at the book, then at each other, then back at the book. He nodded at me to reach for it.

I picked it up, ever so slowly, so slowly that Delta scoffed.

"It's just a wee book. What's the biscuit?" she said.

I didn't know the phrase, but I assumed she meant *What's the big deal?*

The Strange Case of Dr. Jekyll and Mr. Hyde was written in Times New Roman on the otherwise bland cover. I didn't need to see the date on the inside, but I looked nevertheless.

This was not a valuable book. It was printed in the '90s, the 1990s, and hadn't been well taken care of. It was not the book we were searching for but a later, newer, much less valuable edition. It wasn't the priceless first edition—the print date inside and the green cover told me we weren't looking at the treasure.

"No big deal," I said. I glanced at Birk and then handed him the book.

"It's a clue, though, of course it is." Birk opened the front cover.

"A clue?" Delta asked.

"Can you tell me how you got the book and how you knew it was for us?" I asked her.

"A week or so ago, a woman came in and gave it to me. She said someone would be by asking if I knew about a clue of any sort, and I was to give it to them, give it to the first one who asked. There might be others, and I was to inform them they were simply too late." She squinted. "She didn't tell me that I'd be awakened in the middle of the night. How did you get my number anyway?"

Birk smiled. "I have my ways, but I do sincerely apologize. This was important to my friend and me. Thank you for taking my call this morning and for coming in."

Birk handed me the book again and reached into his pocket, pulling out his wallet. "Do you have a tip jar?"

"No, sir, I don't feel right taking money twice for one task. That would surely be jinxing me in some way. I'll just be glad to have it gone. I don't have a lot of shelf space back here, but I didn't want to risk missing giving it to the person who came in for it."

"Would you mind telling us how much you were paid?" I asked.

"I was told not to tell. I'm a superstitious one, lass. I'll keep my word on that one too."

I nodded.

"Well, there you go, then. Do you need anything else from me, or can I go home and grab a nap?" she asked.

"This is wonderful," Birk said "Thank you kindly. We'll be back sometime soon to enjoy the drinks during the proper hours."

"See you then. I'll show you the tip jar at that time."

It was at once the most obvious and the most mysterious clue of them all, but what it was meant to tell us was a mystery. I still wanted to go to Shelagh's house again. As we drove in that direction, Birk and I tried to figure out what we were supposed to make of this latest clue.

There was no superfluous writing anywhere in or on the book. No ink marks, no erased pencil marks that I could see.

"Maybe there's something stuck in the binding," Birk suggested.

I investigated that avenue from every angle too but couldn't find anything. I couldn't bring myself to tear at any corners, but I probed enough with my fingers to confirm that there probably wasn't anything hidden under the cloth that enveloped the cardboard cover.

"I'm sure it's the clue," I said. "How could it not be?"

Birk pulled in to Shelagh's driveway, and we made our way up slowly to the top.

Clouds filled the sky; they weren't dark, but there was still something ominous about the house, the entire grounds. Even the patches of flowers seemed somehow sad and wistful.

"Goodness, you feel that chill?" Birk asked. "Why are we here, lass?"

"I'm not sure. I felt compelled."

"The house misses her."

He parked, and we exited the car. We didn't even knock on the front door, but I led us around back. Even the golf cart seemed sad, as if it missed Shelagh too.

The back of the house was livelier, but only slightly. I was relieved to see someone, even if it wasn't someone I expected.

"Jacques," Birk and I said in unison.

Jacques was in the corral with one of the horses. He held the end of a tether and guided the horse in circles. He exuded a gentleness I hadn't noticed before. He waved and frowned when he saw us. We'd disturbed something that was giving him peace. It felt intrusive, but I wasn't ready to leave. I was, however, glad I'd left the book in the car as we made our way toward him.

He brought the tether closer and held on to it as he guided the horse to the edge of the corral.

"Jacques. Hello. How are you feeling?" I asked.

"Oh, no worse for the wear. I'm fine." He waved away the question. "How's the hunt going?"

"Nothing new," Birk said easily. "Have you been searching for the book?"

"No." Jacques petted the side of the horse's face. "Not interested. I just want my aunt to come home."

"I'm sure. We're so sorry. Are you staying here?" I asked.

"Not really. Just stopping by. Now that she's not here, I thought someone should watch the place. I'm her only family in town."

"Where are Louis and Findlay? Winston?" I reached up

and petted the horse's nose. My heart swelled a little when she leaned into my hand.

"Louis is around, though not here at the moment. I haven't seen Findlay."

"Is Winston here?" Birk asked.

"No, why do you ask?"

"Just curious," Birk said.

Jacques petted the horse's nose.

"Does Winston have the day off?" Birk asked.

"I told him to take some time away. I decided I would see to the horses for a while. Gives me something to do," Jacques said.

Is this what Shelagh would have wanted? I didn't know the family dynamics, and it wasn't my place to question Jacques, but I was suspicious of everything.

"What do you know about Winston?" Birk asked.

Jacques shook his head. "Nothing, really." He squinted and thought a moment "I recently learned that he and Findlay are brothers."

"What?" I said with way too high a pitch. I cleared my throat.

"Aye. They share a flat near Holyroodhouse."

Did that mean anything? It probably shouldn't be a surprise. Family members helped other family members get jobs all the time. It was just something I hadn't known before, and it felt like it could be important.

I hadn't considered their similar look—older and weathered. I'd liked Winston right off—his smile. I hadn't sensed that he'd spent a night drinking instead of taking care of Gin like Shelagh had wondered. Even over the few short days, I'd spent much more time around Findlay than Winston, though. I didn't know either of them well at all, but learning they were brothers certainly put a different spin on everything.

Once I moved past being somewhat thrown by the news, I said, "What are your impressions of Findlay?"

"Don't know him at all." Jacques's attention was on the horse. He regarded me. "I know he was arrested and then released, but I don't know anything else about that. Can I help you two with something?"

Birk and I shared a look. I'd wanted to talk to Louis, Winston, or even Findlay, maybe take a peek at the library again just to satisfy some curiosity I couldn't quite pinpoint. I wasn't comfortable asking Jacques for a tour.

"Do you think Louis will be here anytime soon?" I asked.

"I don't know," Jacques said. "I can give him a message."

"Sure, just have him call me, if that's okay."

"I will."

"You're really not going to search for the book?" I said.

"I have no desire to own that stupid, stupid book."

I started at his vitriolic words. "Sorry you feel that way."

"Well, I do. Excuse me."

Birk and I watched him guide the horse back to the paddock. Maybe he was simply worried about Shelagh, but it felt as if coming here had been a bad idea. The euphoria from the morning at the museum and finding the recent clue was diminishing as the clouds became darker and frigid air bit at my nose. Our breath was fogging around us, and it was time to leave.

TWENTY

"It's not even a well-taken-care-of book." Hamlet closed the cover.

"I know. There's nothing written in it. I've looked at each page. I've checked to see if any pages are missing. I've done everything but X-ray it," I said, wishing I had easy access to an X-ray machine.

Rosie was helping a customer when I came in with the book, but now she and Hector walked to the back and joined Hamlet and me. I showed her the latest clue—the most obvious of them all and yet the most mysterious.

Rosie grabbed the book quickly and looked at it a moment before she glanced back up at me. "Och, that's ours, lass."

"What?"

"That's our book. Well, I mean that's a book that used tae be in the shop. I remember it well—it's in terrible shape, but I thought it charming. I dinnae remember when it was sold. That's why I was surprised not tae find any *Jekyll and Hyde* copies in here when all this happened. I remember this book." Rosie thumbed through it.

"Are you one hundred percent sure?"

"Aye."

"Do you think it was sold in the last year, since I've been here?"

"I do, though I couldnae be more specific. We had it for years, I think. I cannae remember how we acquired it."

"I wonder what in the world that means." I thought about my spreadsheets, but they were only in the beginning phase. If I'd had them in place over the last year, we'd all have a better grasp on the bookshop's inventory and when exactly this book had been on the shelf.

Rosie shrugged. "Dinnae ken."

Absently I sat down on a chair. Hector trotted to my feet, jumped up, and put his front paws on my leg. I lifted him to my lap. "This can't be a coincidence."

"Or it could be," Hamlet said. "I have no idea what it means."

There was absolutely nothing special about the book.

Hamlet sat down too. "Delaney, I talked to Ritchie John's daughter."

"Oh?" Rosie and I said together.

Hamlet nodded. "I told her I was sorry about her father and asked if she needed anything."

"That was lovely of ye." Rosie put a hand on Hamlet's shoulder.

"It was actually a little weird, Rosie. She doesn't know me at all. Yesterday evening, I happened upon her and approached her at the takeaway across the street from the university library." Hamlet seemed to cringe. "I tried to be delicate, but I think she was put off."

"Why?" I asked.

"Maybe it was strange that I approached her, but there was something more to her reaction, like she was embarrassed to be caught going about living her life. But I don't know for sure. Delaney, you have me looking much more closely at things than I used to. I'm suspicious of everyone."

"Oh. Sorry."

"Not at all. I'm more observant too, and that's good." Hamlet reached into his pocket and pulled out a piece of paper. "However, I'm also doing things I wouldn't have considered before you came to Scotland. I looked up some addresses, though I'm not sure you really want them."

I took the piece of paper. There were three names and addresses listed. Darcy John, Louis Chantrell, and Findlay Sweet.

I looked at him. "This is wonderful. Thank you."

I appreciated the gesture, but I didn't quite know why he'd given me the addresses. I folded the piece of paper, thinking I wouldn't do anything with it. And then, it came to me. Or, it came *over* me—my curiosity. I could feel the paper in my hand and it seemed to buzz with a message: *It wouldn't hurt to check these places out, and maybe you'll learn something helpful. What if you find Shelagh?* I unfolded it.

"Och, lass," Rosie added. "I see the inner struggle, but I know where this is headed. I feel like I'm saying it tae ye all the time, but be careful."

"Aye," Hamlet agreed. "Whatever you do with those, be careful."

"I'm not . . ." I paused a long time.

"It's okay, Delaney, we've got the shop covered," Rosie said.

"Aye. I wouldn't have given you the addresses if I couldn't stick around while you're gone. But, again, be careful," Hamlet added.

I couldn't deny the fact that I was going to somehow look at these places with my own two eyes. Finally, I nodded. "I will be. I know exactly who to call to go with me." I looked at Rosie. "I think I'll take a little more time off."

"Aye? Not a wee bit surprised."

Elias was there quickly, probably happier than he'd ever been that I'd called for a ride.

"Lass, I needed tae get away from my hoose. I ken the electricians are doin' the best they can, but no one works the way they used tae anymore. Everyone needs breaks. People eat lunch, for goodness' sake, for a whole hour. Who needs an hour tae eat a meal?" He shook his head. "The world is changing."

Elias probably wouldn't have done well in a corporate environment with such barbaric things as breaks, lunchtimes, nap rooms, and personal leaves. It was far too late to try to change him.

"Who indeed?" I said.

I wasn't fond of lunches and breaks either, but I didn't really have a job; I had a passion that I got to fulfill every single day. You didn't want to take breaks if you genuinely loved what you did. Well, unless you had some addresses you wanted to explore, some people you wanted to track down, I thought. Okay, so it wasn't that I didn't take breaks—I just had lots of flexibility.

Some university students lived in buildings that were called Roosts. Darcy lived in the Roost at Panmure Court made up of modern black-and-stone apartments that had been built on top of plain stones. Elias didn't remember what had been there before the Roost was built, but he wasn't pleased to see that graffiti now covered the older bottom stones.

"'Tis shamie," he grumbled as he parked the taxi in a convenient spot next to the building.

"A shame, yes," I said.

He peered up and out through the windshield. "Am I coming in with ye?"

"Sure," I said. "I can't imagine I'll run into any trouble in a student Roost, but it will be strange that I'm here. You can be my moral support if Darcy just shuts the door on us."

"I can do that."

We ran into so many roadblocks along the way that I had second and then third thoughts about trying to talk to Darcy John.

First we had to be buzzed into the building. We were greeted immediately by a security officer who asked to see our identifications. When we didn't show him anything that said we were part of the university, he didn't want to let us through the second set of doors.

"Who do you want to see?" he said.

"Darcy John," I said.

"Why?"

Because a woman is missing, and I suspect Shelagh's kidnapping is somehow tied to Darcy's father's murder.

"It's a long story, but I met her father the day he . . . died," I said.

"Let me ring her. Stay here."

The security officer went through the second set of doors. We watched as he made his way to a counter and picked up an old-fashioned telephone handset.

Elias and I shared raised eyebrows.

"I really don't want to bother her," I said, "but that book . . . the Monster, Shelagh. What's going on, and why does it seem the bookshop is involved now? Someone knows something that's going to solve all these things at once, I'm sure."

"I forstaw—understand. I hope she'll talk tae us."

The security officer came back through.

"All right. She'll be down in a few minutes. She'll meet you over in the common area on the other side of the desk inside."

I could tell he was disappointed, that he would have preferred for her to tell us to go away. Frankly, I wondered why she hadn't done just that.

We were buzzed through and found the common area: a sunken space populated with red vinyl chairs and a big square plastic table that showed signs of recent use—rings from glasses and a few stray chips. Ah, the college life.

Several seconds later a young, pretty, and really tall—probably just over six feet—woman came around and toward the pit. Dressed in sweats and a ragged old sweater—something she and Elias would call a jumper—with her brown hair up in a messy ponytail, she was still shockingly beautiful, the type of person you can't help but stare at. I understood Hamlet's crush.

Her heart-shaped face was twisted in sadness and grief, and her brown eyes were glassy. I had the urge to tell her that we were sorry to bother her and that we'd made a mistake. I wanted go back to the bookshop, and leave the mourning young woman alone. But she spoke first, and the course was set.

"You saw my da the day he was killed?" she said as she sat down on a chair next to me.

I finally nodded. "Thanks for coming to talk to us. I'm very sorry about your father, but yes, I did see him at Deacon Brodie's Tavern. He was tending the bar when I was there for a meeting. I'm Delaney, and this is Elias."

"Aye, hello." She waited.

"Did your father work at the pub for a while?" I asked.

Her eyebrows came together. "You're from America?"

"Yes. I've lived here about a year. I work at a bookshop in Grassmarket. The Cracked Spine."

"Why do you want to talk to me?"

"A couple of reasons. First of all, yes, I saw your father that day, but it was as I was walking into the pub with a man named Louis Chantrell. Mr. Chantrell seemed to know your father, but Ritchie said he didn't recognize Louis. The moment struck me as odd, and then so much has happened since then."

"Did you tell the police?"

"I did."

"Good. When you say so much has happened since, do you mean the Monster?"

"Well, yes, but also the meeting I was going to was being conducted by a woman who is now missing. Shelagh O'Conner. I'm just searching for answers, though I'm not sure I know the right questions to ask."

"Aye? I had no idea that woman was there that day. That is strange, but I don't think my father knew her. At least not that I'm aware of." She sat back.

I looked at Elias and then once more at her. "What have the police told you?"

It took her a minute, but she regarded me again. "That there was camera footage of the Monster breaking into Da's flat. They suspect that's who killed him, but they can't be sure. That's literally all they told me. I can't understand who would want to kill my father. None of it makes any sense." Darcy sat forward again. "He was hit with a lamp. He died from blunt-force trauma to his head. The police took the lamp but left the rest as they found it, bloodstain and all. Books had been pulled from a shelf and scattered over the floor. The lamp that killed him was still there, its shade torn. The bloodstain on the throw rug. I couldn't believe the police would leave it like that."

I leaned toward her. "I know you don't know us, Darcy, but I knew who you were because a friend of mine knows you. You go to school with him. Hamlet."

An involuntary smiled pulled briefly at the corner of her mouth. "Aye, a lovely lad. I'm sure I scared him to death yesterday. He came up to me and told me he was sorry, asked if there was anything he could do. I'm so upset and afraid and jumpy lately, I'm sure I responded horribly. Please give him my apologies."

"I will," I said. The last thing on my mind was Hamlet's love life, but I wondered who was in Darcy's life who might be able to help her. Maybe she didn't have anyone she could ask. "I'm sure Hamlet, and those of us who work with him at the bookshop, would be happy to help you clean up."

"No . . . I mean, not right now. I'll take care of it at some point, but I was just so surprised they left it that way. Is that normal?"

"Och, if they've gathered all their evidence, it's probably just the way it's done. They might have offered you the name of a cleaning service or something," Elias said.

She shook her head. "They didn't."

"Darcy, what about the books that were on the floor? Was there anything special about them?" I asked.

"I don't think so. I mean, they were just books that Da had. They weren't valuable, but he liked to read." Her eyes lit momentarily, and she looked at me. "You say you work at a bookshop in Grassmarket? The Cracked Spine?"

"Yes."

"He sometimes shopped there. You have an older woman working there?"

"Rosie."

"I don't know her name, but Da was very fond of her, talked about how lovely she was."

"Lots of people do that. She's the best." I cleared my throat, wondering if Rosie would remember Ritchie if she saw a good picture of him and if him shopping at The Cracked Spine was in anyway important to his murder. I hoped not. "Darcy, do you know if your father had come into the bookshop recently?"

"I have no idea."

"What about the kinds of books he liked to read? Do you know any titles?"

"He liked to read everything. I don't know specific titles, but mostly stuff with lots of testosterone. 'Man books,' he liked to call them." She laughed once but then sobered again. "I don't really know, though."

I didn't want to plant the seed, but considering all that had recently happened, I wondered about the other men of the hour, Jekyll and Hyde. My mind jumped through some ideas. Maybe the book we'd gotten from the Starbar had come from Ritchie John's shelves, but the timing would have been wrong if it was taken the night he was killed. Delta said she'd been holding on to it for about a week.

"Darcy, what about your father's relationship with Louis Chantrell?"

"I don't know who that is."

"Mr. Chantrell seemed to recognize your father, but your father didn't remember him," I repeated. "What did your father do with his days, other than tend bar at Deacon Brodie's?"

"Oh. Well, first of all, that's the thing. As far as I knew, he hadn't tended bar there for quite some time. He used to work there full-time. He did well, earned good tips, but he'd been otherwise employed for at least the last few years. I didn't know he was working at the pub, even part-time."

"What was his job before I saw him at the pub?"

"He cared for horses. He used to work for a man in Glasgow, but that man passed away. We moved here so I could attend university and he could be close by. He found a new stable job about three years ago."

"With who?" *Shelagh,* I thought.

"A man named Birk Blackburn. He's local. I met him a few times, a nice man."

The world around me fell away, tilted a little, and flooded over. Did I know this? No, I was sure I didn't. Why hadn't Birk mentioned it to me? Why hadn't he mentioned it to anyone? Did the police already know?

A funny choked noise came from my throat.

"Are you okay?" Darcy asked me.

"I'm fine. Sorry . . ."

Elias knew Birk, and he kept a much better poker face than I did. He jumped in to give me a moment to compose myself.

"Are you a horsewoman, lass?" he asked.

Darcy smiled at him. It was a genuine smile. "No. I mean, I love them. They are extraordinary creatures, and I truly love them, but I don't enjoy riding them, and I never took to caring for them like my father did."

"Did your father ever work for anyone other than Birk here in Edinburgh?" I was finally able to ask.

"No."

"And he had quit that job?"

"Aye," she answered, but only after a beat too long. It seemed she shut her mouth tightly then, as if she didn't want to say another word about that.

I didn't want to push her. "And you can't think of how he might have known Louis Chantrell?"

"No, I'm sorry. Again, I don't know who that is. How was Da that day? Did he seem okay? Did he seem happy?" she asked.

"Yes, most definitely. He was very sweet and friendly," I said, mostly to make her feel better. "A truly delightful man."

"That's really good to know."

I wished I could take away her sadness, but I couldn't. "I'm serious, Darcy, we would be more than happy to help you clean up. I'm in the bookshop, so is Hamlet. Come see us if . . . well, no matter what."

She looked at me a long time and finally nodded. "Thank you. I will."

She walked us to the security doors and gave us a friendly but distracted good-bye. The security officer was glad to see us go.

"Off to Birk's?" Elias asked as we got in the taxi.

"Yes, please, and step on it." The other two addresses would have to wait.

"I can do that."

TWENTY-ONE

Birk lived in an estate with a large front garden. His interior decorating color of choice was gold. Large gold front doors led into a golden entryway, which in turn flowed to a golden drawing room and kitchen beyond. I realized I'd never seen the kitchen, but it was a safe bet to guess the fixtures there were gold too.

"Delaney, Elias, what a wonderful surprise. Do come in." Birk, dressed in jeans and a simple sweater, held the door open wide.

The first time I'd been to his house, he'd worn a gold robe. At the time I thought he was just trying to be quirky, but I'd come to know that Birk was naturally quirky in everything he did.

"Ingy," Birk called toward the back of the house, "we have guests, please bring refreshments."

From where we stood, I thought I heard the rumble of Ingy's protests. Though she'd worked for Birk for years, she never liked to be asked to do anything, and she would grumble every time a request was made. I was quite fond of her; so was Birk.

"She's been with me forever," he'd once said. "Any crankiness is probably well deserved. I'm not the easiest to be around."

"Fine," she called, a few moments after the grumbles.

Birk led the way into the drawing room and signaled for us to sit on a golden couch.

"Birk, we were just talking to Darcy John," I said. I was watching him closely for recognition or a reaction. There was none. "Her father was the man murdered by the New Monster."

"Aye. Do you know her?"

"Hamlet does, kind of," I said.

There was absolutely zero recognition in his eyes. Instead, what I saw was that he was eager to hear the rest of what I had to say. When Darcy told me that her father had worked for Birk, I'd been shocked at first and then a little angry, but the anger had mostly dissipated as we'd made it to his house. I was sure there was a good explanation as to why Birk hadn't acknowledged that the murder victim had worked for him. However, if after talking to him I suspected he was hiding something important, I was prepared to go back to being angry.

"I'm so sorry. Is she . . . all right?" he asked sincerely.

"Not great, but the real reason I'm here is to ask you about her father, Ritchie John."

"Sure, what about him?" His eyebrows came together.

"Darcy said that her father used to work for you."

"What?"

"With your horses?"

"Aye?"

"Yes."

Birk fell into thought, but he looked up a moment later. "Lass, do you know anything about my stables?"

"I didn't even know you had a horse."

"I have twenty."

"Really?"

"Aye. They're . . . well, they're rescue horses of a sort."

"Oh."

"I have the money," Birk said, with neither humility nor braggadocio. "I love animals, so I try to help them. I have a stable. I can take you if you wish. I'd actually like to talk to my stable manager about Mr. John. Forgive me for not knowing he worked for me. It's not that I don't care, but my stablemen come and go. It can be a transient sort of work. I don't take as much time as I probably should to get to know them all. I know my manager, and I trust him implicitly."

Ingy walked in with the requested tray filled with refreshments.

"Sorry, love, we've got to go. Treats another time."

Ingy's withering look toward Birk was one for the ages, but he didn't seem to notice.

"Apologies," Elias said to her.

She shook her head and turned to leave the room.

"Hang on," I said. I jumped up and hurried to her. "I can't resist those cookies. Do you care if I take a couple?"

Ingy made a noise that might be considered affirmatory.

"Thank you." I smiled at her.

She returned a small, very annoyed smile.

Elias didn't usually let other people drive him anywhere. I noticed his moment of hesitation as Birk directed us to "hop in" his car, but to his credit Elias didn't protest. He slid into the backseat, frowned, and nodded at me to get in the front.

We drove south from Edinburgh for about thirty minutes. The hilly countryside was surprisingly green. All the snow was melted away now, but it was raining lightly.

Birk pulled his car onto a road marked with a large sign reading BLACKBURN ACRES.

"I can't believe I didn't even know," I said.

"I'm not a rider, lass, so you wouldn't have. I don't do much here except pay for it."

"This place is extraordinary." I gazed out at the spread in front of us. Without a house on the property, Birk's stables still reminded me of something that might be used in a television show about a Texas ranch, though nestled in green hills. They would have been adorable if smaller; as is, they were breathtaking and impressive.

"Thank you. I keep this place simply so some animals might have somewhere to live and be taken care of. None of these are Thoroughbreds. In fact, many of them are on their last legs. But they make good steeds for young children or perhaps children who might be otherwise unable to ride."

"That's lovely, Birk," I said.

"Och, not at all, lass. You realize how rich I am? If I didn't do some good with my money, it would be a terrible shame. Of course I hope it's a good thing for others, but it's a good thing for me too—better, in fact, for me than for anyone else."

"Aye, Birk, 'tis a good thing," Elias said from the backseat.

Birk looked at Elias in the rearview mirror. "If Ritchie John worked for me, I have no recollection of knowing the man, which makes me less altruistic than you're giving me credit for."

"No, it's not your job tae ken everybody's name. If everyone's treated all right, that's what matters," Elias said.

"Oh, I do hope everyone is treated all right. It's my number-one demand."

Birk pulled his car into a spot that was marked specifically for him. I could tell he was somewhat embarrassed by the primo golden sign, but he didn't say anything. He and Edwin were both very good at not hiding from their wealth, and at the same time not flaunting it. They were genuine.

"Come along. I'm going to try to find my man, but you're welcome to look around on your own. If anyone asks who you are, just tell them you're with me."

Birk hurried out of the car and away, leaving Elias and me standing beside it in the cold wind and wondering where to go.

"I say the corrals," Elias decided as he brought his collar up around his chin.

I did the same. "Good idea."

The corrals were bordered by the numerous stables and a row of wide bleachers. Once we found our way inside, the wind seemed to become more bearable and it was drizzling only just enough to frizz my hair. We wouldn't get drenched if we weren't out for too long.

We couldn't see Birk, but we were happy to find some horses and a few riders. The horses weren't in bad shape, but true to Birk's word they weren't Thoroughbreds either. The riders couldn't have cared less. Young children smiled and actually squealed as they were guided around corrals. The children all wore thick coats and hats under their helmets as they held on tight to the saddle horns.

"Goodness," I said, taken in by the heartwarming sight.

"Ye ride?"

"I'm not a rider, no, but I've ridden. I grew up around a lot of horses. I love all animals, but I didn't take to horses like some of my friends did."

"Horse people are horse people." Elias said as he and I leaned on a bar of the corral fence.

"That's what my dad says."

"He would know."

"Yes." Homesickness pinged in my gut. I missed my parents

and brother all the time, but the moments when I really felt it, when it shook me some, were now few and far between. I loved my new home, but I wished the rest of my family weren't such a big ocean from me. I cleared my throat and blinked away the surprise tears that filled my eyes. I recovered quickly enough.

We could have watched the riders for a long time, but a moment later we spied Birk and another man walking toward us.

"Delaney and Elias, this is my stable manger, Mort Littleton. Mort, this is Delaney and Elias, two good friends."

"Aye, a pleasure," Mort said as we all shook hands.

Even with only those few words, I could tell I was going to have a hard time understanding this older man's accent. I suspected he'd also pepper his sentences with some Scots. I was glad Elias was there to help translate.

"Mort did in fact confirm that the murder victim, Ritchie John, worked here," Birk said. "He worked here a few years."

"Aye, he most certainly did," Mort said. "The man up and quit his job three weeks ago. I tried tae stop him."

I got most of the words.

"Did he give a reason for quitting?" I asked.

"No, but he was upset, so much so I worrit about him."

"Mort, tell them exactly what you told me," Birk said.

"Aye, he said he was to quit. He behaved afraid, fearsome in a way I havenae seen in a long, long time. He wouldnae tell me." Mort frowned, looked at Birk and then seemed to conclude he would keep talking. "A couple weeks earlier we had an event. The box that we keep the money in for snacks was stolen."

"I didn't know about this," Birk said.

Mort shook his head. "The box was never returned but the money reappeared the next day. I just thought the person who stole it felt guilty. It wasn't much, but enough that we should have been more careful. A couple hundred pounds."

"Do you think Ritchie was the thief?" Birk asked.

"No, not a t'all. The day it went missing he and I were together all day, from the moment we walked inside, throughout the event, and then when it was discovered the box was missing. I ken he had nothing tae do with it, but I couldnae help but wonder if he ken something about it that bothered him so he quit. I couldnae think of anything else—all was well. I . . . I went to his flat the next day tae check on him, I was that worrit. He wasnae there, but the door to his flat was open a wee bit. I heard two voices, angry, aye. I couldnae get the exact words, but I felt wrong aboot listening. I hurried out of there a moment later. After he was kil't, I called the police, I did, but I dinnae think they wanted tae hear what I had tae say. None of them came oot tae talk tae me in person."

"Male or female voices?" I asked.

"Lad and a lass."

"Young, old?"

Mort shook his head slowly. "I couldnae tell."

"You told the police that exactly?" I asked.

"I did. On the phone I told them he used to work here too. They didnae come see me," he repeated.

"Mort, have you ever heard of or did Ritchie ever mention anyone named Findlay Sweet or Louis Chantrell?"

"No, but he and I didnae have such conversations, lass. He was quiet, kept tae his job. I'm the boss and not meant tae be personal friendly with everyone. It's just that he worked here so long that I felt a fondness for him. He was a hard worker, and I really liked working beside him."

"If I call a police inspector I know, would you mind telling him everything you just told me?" I pulled out my phone.

"No, I'd be gled to."

I talked to Inspector Winters first and then passed the phone to Mort. I listened to his side of the conversation as intently as I could.

Mort told Inspector Winters that Ritchie *had* been quiet and a good worker. I got the impression that Inspector Winters didn't know that Ritchie had recently worked at the stables, and he didn't know if the inspectors on the case did or not. Mort said that no one had been out to talk to him.

Mort said that Ritchie had been great with the horses; the animals loved him, the riders did too. Everyone else at the stables thought he was a good man. He would be missed.

When it appeared Mort was finished, Birk took the phone.

"Inspector Winters, Birk Blackburn here. I had no idea the man worked for me. I apologize that we didn't speak to you sooner about any of this. . . . Uh-huh. . . . Aye. Well, I ask Mort to hire men and women somewhat down on their luck if it's at all possible. I believe Ritchie was one of those men, but neither Mort nor I was privy to reasons for it and he was hired a long time ago now. Again, apologies, and we'll let you know if we remember anything else. . . . Aye, and please send anyone out to ask us questions at any time. We'll all speak with you. . . . You're welcome. Good-bye."

"Och, lass, thank ye," Mort said as Birk ended the call. "I believe he listened tae me."

"I'm sure he did," I said.

Birk nodded and then looked at me. "I'm glad you discovered that he worked here, and I really hope we can help."

I nodded. "Did either of you ever meet Ritchie's daughter, Darcy?"

"Oh, aye, I did!" Mort said as Birk shook his head. "She

came tae the stables a couple of times." A frown suddenly pulled at his mouth.

We all waited for him to continue. Finally, Birk said, "What's on your mind, Mort?"

"Last time she was here, when I came around the corner, and when I saw her, I didnae recognize her at first. I'd seen her afore. She'd visited her da a couple times when he and I were working together. She's lovely as a rose, aye. But this last time when I saw her, it took a minute."

"So?" Birk said.

Mort looked up at him, "It was the day of the event when the money was stolen. Ritchie was with me when we came upon her, and he seemed surprised it was her too, but we were so busy, we both just moved on. I just remembered."

"I don't understand," Birk said.

"She was dressed in an old shabby coat and hat."

"Like the New Monster?" Birk asked the question that surely came to all our minds.

"Maybe. Goodness, I'm not sure. I hadnae given it a thought until right this minute, but she looked . . . less like herself, almost unrecognizeable."

I pulled out my phone. "We'd better call Inspector Winters back."

TWENTY-TWO

"Do ye think it's that? Do ye think Darcy killed her own da, that she's the Monster? That she has Shelagh?" Elias asked after we dropped off Birk and were again in Elias's taxi.

The ride to Birk's hadn't been nearly as talkative. Birk was bothered that he hadn't remembered Ritchie John, and he'd been thoughtful and silent for almost the entire thirty-minute drive.

"But why?" I said to Elias.

"That's the question, isn't it? She certainly didnae behave as if she was a killer, but who knows?"

"Mort did say that the coat and hat weren't exactly like the ones he'd seen on television, but it's all strange. Even he didn't want us to jump to the conclusion that it was Darcy."

"But of course we did."

"Of course." I paused. "It would be a gruesome turn of events. What am I saying? It's *already* a gruesome turn of events. And who was in Ritchie's flat—the time Mort stopped by? I wish my mind would quit conjuring Findlay Sweet's face."

"Aye, and his ex-wife is such a delightful lass."

I sat up straight. "What?"

"His ex is lovely."

I shook my head. "How do you know his ex-wife?"

"Lass, ye ken her too. Well, in a manner."

"I do? I mean, I found her picture online and thought she looked familiar, but I couldn't place her."

"She's a server at Vanessa's, Edwin's lady love's establishment."

"Wha—Oh! Of course she is. We know her as Jolie, not Jessica. Maybe a nickname. She is the sweetest of all the servers."

"Aye."

"How did you figure this out?"

Elias nodded knowingly. "Aggie has been spending some hours researching on her laptop. After ye told us aboot Findlay, she wanted tae know everything she could know aboot him. She found his ex-wife and showed me the picture. She couldnae place her right off either, said she just looked familiar. Ye, Aggie, and I had all been oot to dinner a week or so ago. Jolie was our server."

"Yes, she was." I was embarrassed I hadn't been able to identify her quickly. But to be fair, the picture I'd found on the internet was a ten-years-younger version with curly, windblown hair. Jolie didn't necessarily look much older now, but she always had her hair pulled back in an efficient ponytail. And Tom didn't recognize her; because of his previous schedule, he hadn't gone out to as many dinners as the rest of us had.

"It's late, but we missed lunch," I said. "You hungry?"

"Aye."

We didn't know if Jolie would be at work, but at least we'd be able to enjoy some good food and maybe say hello to Vanessa.

Vanessa had come to Edinburgh from Ireland, bringing the food of her homeland with her. Her restaurant, located in Old Town, wasn't far from Grassmarket. Elias pulled the cab onto the long driveway that would take us to a parking lot behind the building.

During the summer Vanessa would set up some tables and chairs just outside the restaurant's back door. A sturdy blue awning kept diners safe from any light rain. Anything heavy and the rear patio would have to be closed. I'd only eaten outside one of the many times I'd been to the restaurant.

We spied Vanessa's car as Elias parked and we headed for the back door.

"Two?" a young woman asked as we went inside. It was crowded, but there were a few seats left, and we didn't know the greeter.

"Hi, is Vanessa in?" I asked.

She smiled. "Can I tell her who's asking?"

"Delaney, Elias!" Vanessa dodged her way around a couple tables. "They're friends of Edwin's." Vanessa put her hand on the greeter's arm. "It's fine. I'll take care of them. Susan is the newest member of our team."

Vanessa's long gray ponytail always fell perfectly down her back. Her bright eyes only seemed to get brighter the busier she became. I'd—we'd all—become very fond of her.

Once introductions were made, Vanessa led us to a table in a quiet corner. We were there to get lunch, but I felt a little guilty about our ulterior motive.

"Stew?" Vanessa said.

"How did you know?" I asked.

"It's your favorite, and it's cold outside. Elias?"

"The same, please."

"Very good." But Vanessa saw through our charade. She

didn't turn to go and place the order with the kitchen but looked at us with tight eyebrows. "What's up?"

I smiled. "Do you have a minute to sit?"

Vanessa pulled out a chair and sat. "Edwin all right?"

"Oh, yes!" I said. "This has nothing to do with Edwin."

Visibly relieved, she said, "Tell me, then."

"Vanessa, how well do you know your server Jolie?"

"Oh. Not well, but well enough to think she's good at her job. Why? Did she do something?"

"I don't think so, but she used to be married to someone I've recently met, and I'd really like to ask her some questions about that time. It's weird, I know, but I want your permission to talk to her."

Vanessa smiled. "You don't need my permission, but if she doesn't want to talk to you, there's nothing I can do about it. Who was she married to? As far as I was aware, she's happily single."

I told Vanessa about Findlay Sweet. Vanessa knew all the people in my world, including Tom. She was intrigued by the past story of his time as a fisherman and smiled when I told her that Tom had spilled Findlay's misbehaving beans to Jolie— back when she was Jessica.

"I'll grab her. She's here, in the break room, not scheduled to be working for half an hour or so, but I'll see if she agrees to talk to you. Do you really want stew?" Vanessa stood.

"Please."

"I'll have her bring it."

"We'll tip her well," Elias said.

It had been discussed and decided upon; Vanessa wouldn't feed us free of charge. I'd wanted to enjoy the food in her restaurant, but at first she hadn't wanted to charge Edwin's closest friends. We'd decided that it made sense that Edwin ate without paying, but not the rest of us. Vanessa had been agreeable, but I was sure that she still sometimes comped drinks or desserts.

It wasn't long before Jolie was walking toward us, though without our order. She frowned, but not unhappily, just cautiously. Her gray-streaked hair was pulled back neatly, and she was tiny, but with wide shoulders that somehow made her seem young. My mind superimposed the younger picture I'd found on the internet over her present face. She hadn't aged much.

Elias and I stood as we all shook hands.

"You want to talk to me about Findlay?" she said.

"Yes. Is that okay?" I said.

She sat down. "Why?"

I didn't want to tell her everything. I wondered if keeping it simple would work. "I recently married Tom Shannon."

It took her a moment to remember, but then a smile pulled at the corners of her mouth. "A sweet boy, he was. All grown now." She looked at me. "I don't know you, lass, but I get the sense that you and Tom will do well."

"I hope so."

Her eyes unfocused, as if she were thinking back to that time. "He was so nervous to talk to me, but he thought it was the right thing to do. It was, though the task shouldn't have been the responsibility of such a young man. I should have been paying better attention. Anyway, what do you want to know about Findlay? Though I'm not sure I can tell you much."

"You aren't angry that Tom told you about Findlay's behavior?" I said.

Jolie laughed once. "No. I was back then. I was angry at everyone, mostly Findlay. No, that's not exactly true. Ultimately I was angry with myself for not seeing what was right there in front of me." She shrugged. "In fact, it took me another marriage before I realized maybe *I'm* just not meant to be married. I think I pick the wrong ones."

"Did you know that Findlay is a driver for a woman named Shelagh O'Conner?"

Her eyes opened wide with surprise. "The woman who was taken from her home? Really? I had no idea."

"You didn't know he worked for Shelagh?"

"No. And he's not a good driver. He was in a terrible accident."

"I know. Well, I don't really know much, but I knew he was in a car accident. Do you know his brother, Winston? He also works for Shelagh, with her horses. Winston and Findlay are roommates."

"Back when I was married to Findlay, he and his brother weren't speaking. I don't know Winston at all, but as far as I understood, he always worked with horses."

"Did you know the man who was recently killed, Ritchie John? Or did Findlay know him?"

"Not to my knowledge. It was sad to hear about the murder, but the man's name doesn't ring a bell. Should it?"

I shook my head. "No, but maybe Findlay knew him through Winston?"

Jolie sighed. "No, I don't remember knowing him at all, but as I mentioned, Findlay and Winston weren't on good terms back then."

"Do you know why?"

"I think it was just that Findlay was unfaithful and Winston was angry at him because of it. But that could just have been me projecting something. I truly don't know."

I bit my lip. I didn't know what else I wanted to ask. I wanted Findlay to be guilty of something, but that wasn't fair. I'd also wanted to appease my curiosity as to why I was sure I knew the woman in the picture I'd seen on the internet. Talking to her made another puzzle piece fit into place, but it felt like I was working on the wrong puzzle now. Jolie and Findlay hadn't been together in a long time; a lifetime ago it now seemed.

Jolie sat up straighter. "I know Shelagh. Well, I knew her. Maybe eight years ago, she had a big event at her house. At the time I managed a catering company. She hired us. I had to spend a few days with her, going over detail after detail, time and time again. She was—is—very controlling. And strange. You knew about her past—from a long time ago?"

Elias and I nodded.

"Aye, well, I didn't see Findlay anywhere around there back then. If I had, I probably would have declined the job. I'm over that well enough now, but back then I might have been more prickly. I would bet my night's tips that she turns up soon and that she will have been behind her own disappearance. She's a dramatic one, that's for sure. She was probably bored." Jolie shrugged. "I'm going to feel terrible for saying such things if she really is hurt or something. I'm sorry, but I just don't think she's in dire straits. It's just my gut talking, and I hope I'm correct."

"Any guesses as to where she'd hide?" I asked.

"She'd hide in plain sight. If she's putting on an act, it'll be right there in front of everyone. For what it's worth, and I think this is why you're really here, Findlay's not evil really, though maybe a little mean. He was unfaithful, aye, but that was a long time ago. He was never abusive to me." She paused.

"You know, having spent that time with Shelagh, I saw her controlling, dramatic side a few times, but I also saw her philanthropic side. I can understand her hiring someone to be her driver who had gotten into trouble driving. She believes in second chances. You can't blame her, aye? Considering her own need for a second chance or two."

"That makes sense," I said.

"Aye. Can I help ye with something else?" She put her hands on the table.

Another server deposited our bowls of stew in front of us. The scents rising to my nose made me at least temporarily forget about everything but the food.

"Thank you for talking to us," I said to Jolie.

She stood but hesitated and then sat again. "I don't know if you need this, but I think I know where Findlay's living. He was there about three years ago, that I know for sure." She jotted down an address on a paper napkin.

I looked at it and thought it was the same one Hamlet had given me, but I'd double-check. "Thank you."

"Aye. Just so you have it." She said before she quickly turned and got back to work.

"What do ye think?" Elias asked.

"I don't know. She seemed honest. I was really hoping she'd tell us something about Findlay that would somehow lead us to Shelagh, but I'm beginning to think he's not as bad a guy as I might have first thought. I wouldn't be surprised if Shelagh did give Findlay the driving job because of her belief in second chances, though. Are you suspicious of something else?"

"Do ye think she hasnae really seen him over these last ten years, lass? Edinburgh is a big city, aye, but . . . it's just hard tae believe."

I thought that over as I ate my stew. I couldn't figure out why she would lie. I hoped she wouldn't.

"I don't know, Elias, but no matter what, I need to figure out the next clue," I said. "Any ideas?"

"I'll think on it."

We ate the rest of the meal in companionable silence.

TWENTY-THREE

We probably should have just gotten on with our day, Elias going his way and I going mine. But when we didn't figure out the clue, my mind went back to Darcy.

"What do you think, Elias? Do you think she could possibly be the Monster?"

"I don't know," Elias said doubtfully as he started the taxi in the restaurant's parking lot.

"She's so tall," I said.

"Shall we drive back by the Roost?"

"No, that's okay."

"Are ye sure, lass?" Elias was going slowly enough along the parking lot to allow me to change my mind.

"No. We can't very well ask her if she's the Monster. We can't even ask to have a look at her coats and hats."

"Are ye *sure,* lass?"

Elias knew what my eventual answer would be, so he wasn't surprised in the least when I gave in and told him to go ahead and "swing by."

He parked the taxi across the street from the Roost. The snow had started again this late afternoon, and the wind had picked up; it was coming down more heavily now, with bigger flakes.

"Do ye want tae try tae talk with her?" he asked as he had a sip from the takeaway coffee cup Vanessa had handed him as we headed out. She always made sure Elias had extra coffee.

"I don't know yet. Could we just sit here a minute?"

"Aye."

We watched students coming and going. When we'd visited that morning, there hadn't been nearly as much foot traffic. I was intrigued by the students' fashion priorities of comfort and warmth, which was the same as it had been for me when I'd been in college. I smiled at the memory of my time at the University of Kansas. I'd loved school, loved studying, loved research. There had been a time when I wondered if maybe I would be a student or work in a university setting all my life. I was glad for the way things had turned out, but being on a college campus forever didn't sound like a bad duty.

"I think that's her." Elias gestured with his coffee cup.

It took me only a second to spot the tall person amid the other average-size people walking toward the Roost. The snow and some fog on the inside of the windshield distorted my view. I cleared a spot and watched Darcy walk toward the building.

Not only was she in an older coat, but her head was covered in a scarf too, one ragged at the edges. She didn't look destitute, more like a student who'd purchased the coat in a thrift shop. Her style didn't stand out as starkly different from that of the other students around her. Her height did, but not her garb.

I had no sense that this was the same person I'd seen in the parking spot or in Grassmarket. Darcy was tall, yes, but she was thin, with narrow shoulders. There was nothing masculine about her, which I'd been certain the Monster was.

"Lass?" Elias asked.

"I don't think that's who I've seen," I said.

"'Tis good news, I think."

"I think so too. I'm relieved."

I wasn't sure that who I'd seen was the same person who'd been committing the crimes—I wished I'd paid more attention that night by Tom's car. "I don't think it looks like the person on television either. Do you?"

"I dinnae think so."

As Darcy approached the Roost, her head down against the wind, someone coming from the other direction stopped her. There was no doubt in my mind that the person was a man. He wasn't dressed in an old coat, though. His coat was newer and sleeker, but since his back was to us and since he was mostly covered by his clothes, including a hat—the snow messed up our vision—I couldn't make out what he looked like.

"I wonder who she's talking to," I said.

"Doesnae look familiar." Elias had cleared away a spot on his side of the windshield too and deposited his coffee in a cup holder.

They stood outside the Roost as students filed in and out the doors. From our distance and angle, it remained impossible to see the man's face, but I could tell that Darcy seemed to be listening intently to him—he was the one doing most of the talking.

I kept trying to see better, but it wasn't possible. After another few moments, Darcy and the man hugged. Their embrace lasted a beat too long for simple friendship, or so I thought. Again, Hamlet's love life was the least of my worries, but I couldn't help but feel a twinge of regret that Darcy might be in a relationship.

They released the hug and the man turned just as a bus stopped in front of the Roost. We couldn't tell if he boarded, but once the bus was out of our line of vision, we could see Darcy waving at it.

"A boyfriend," I said.

"Aye," Elias said doubtfully.

"What?"

"I dinnae ken the lass, but it didn't seem like that. Perhaps a friend."

"It's good to see someone's there for her."

"Aye."

A moment later Darcy went into the Roost.

"She's not the Monster," I said. "It doesn't feel right."

"I agree," Elias said. "Pleased we looked?"

"Yes. Thank you."

I *was* pleased, but as Elias drove me back to the bookshop, I pondered whether or not to tell Hamlet what we'd seen, and if, in fact, we'd seen anything at all. I felt myself looking for answers in every corner.

At least I was one hundred percent sure Darcy wasn't the Monster. Okay, maybe only ninety-nine.

TWENTY-FOUR

It was just Tom and me. I'd never seen the streets of Edinburgh so quiet. It wasn't because of the weather—it was cold out, but the snow had stopped. It was the Monster. The streets of my new city, the city of my heart, were unusually quiet because of the New Monster.

I hadn't paid much attention to the news today, but apparently it had been filled with authorities cautioning citizens to be careful, be aware. Shelagh O'Conner still hadn't been found; each time she was mentioned, the potential outcome only sounded more dire.

There were discussions of setting a curfew, requiring everyone to be off the streets by seven in the evening. No one wanted that, but from what I could see, not many people wanted to be out either. Whatever was safest was probably the best, but none of this was good.

And I couldn't help but think I knew something that could assist the police in solving all these mysteries. I couldn't decide if I'd been in the orbit of everything or if everything that had happened had nudged itself into my orbit. Either way, I couldn't let go of the sense that I must have missed something, that the events and I were somehow tied together.

Tom's pub was quiet enough that he could take the night off again; the few customers in the place were in Rodger's capable hands.

I'd picked my husband up and asked him if he wanted to go for a walk before we went home, just to show the man (or whoever it was) under the monster costume that we weren't afraid, as well as to pay a visit to someone. Tom had agreed—I probably wouldn't have braved the dark streets by myself if he hadn't.

We walked up Victoria Street toward the Royal Mile, hoping to find the typical crowd there. As we reached the top of the steep road, I was pleased and relieved to see more foot traffic—not as much as normal, but more than in Grassmarket. Although this was the hot tourist spot, it was more than that. It was a thoroughfare, a place brimming with history, an important road for everyone who lived in Edinburgh as well as those who visited.

We strolled downhill toward the sea and Inspector Winters's police station. I wanted to talk to him one more time today, just in case there really was something I knew that could help the police solve the crimes, find Shelagh.

"You think it's something to do with the horses?" Tom asked as we passed in front of the building housing the office that handled the city's business licensing. I'd visited the office a few times recently and currently wondered about the people inside. I hoped all was well with them as Tom and I continued on.

"It's a possibility. I thought about trying to find Findlay and Winston's flat to talk to them, but that felt like stepping way out of my bounds."

"Aye."

A high-pitched voice came from the open door of a gift shop we were walking by. "Look! A monster!"

Tom and I zipped to alert. What was happening? We hurried to the door.

A woman and a little girl, who must have been about seven, were looking at a circular display of key rings dangling on hooks: tartan designs, bagpipes, even swords and dirks. But the little girl had zoned in on one key ring in particular. The charm was in the shape of a hunchbacked man wrapped in an old brown coat.

I went inside, excused myself around the mother and child, and grabbed one. "How in the world did they get this put together so quickly?"

Tom shrugged. "Probably had the charm for something else and just made it work."

"How about that," a man said as he came from the back of the store. "Our very own monster."

Normally I liked the touristy parts of Edinburgh. I liked the small pocket-size souvenir shops. But this sort of marketing left a bad taste in my mouth. I rehung the key ring and nodded at that shopkeeper before Tom and I left the shop. Maybe if I weren't so close to everything that had happened, maybe if I'd never met Shelagh, I'd have distance enough to find it all intriguing.

"The key ring was in poor taste, lass. I'm sorry it bothered you," Tom said.

"I've seen plague masks for sale, and I thought they were fascinating. Maybe it's just what it is. I'm sorry I left so quickly."

"No need to apologize." He grabbed my hand.

The bird-beaked plague masks had been a part of doctors' costumes. The beak in the mask was stuffed with burning herbs and perfumes to fight off the plague, which at one time was thought to have been brought on by foul-smelling air from all the waste that was dumped outside. The costume was also worn so that sick people would know that the person treating them, was in fact a plague doctor.

"You know the plague doctors weren't actually real doctors, real scientists," Tom said.

"I *didn't* know that."

"And those suits—the long coats, the masks—didn't protect most of them very well either. Many of the 'doctors' attending to the patients didn't live long."

"Not surprising."

"Aye. And they could be wicked cruel too. None of them knew what they were doing. Everyone was just trying to figure out how to get rid of the plague. All methods were attempted. Bloodletting, et cetera."

"That's why it's called 'practicing' medicine, huh?" I smiled.

"It's part of our history, I suppose. It was a terrible time, just because of some fleas on rats. Vicious creatures, those fleas."

We'd made it to the bottom of the hill, and Tom reached for the police station's door. The station was in a stone building with a wonderful old short clock tower projecting up from its middle. As I looked around, my eyes landed on the grounds of the Holyroodhouse, the Queen's official residence in Edinburgh. Tonight, though, there was something about it—it rung some sort of bell in my mind. Why did it suddenly seem like something I should pay attention to?

If you tell the truth, you don't have to remember anything.

The bookish voice came from Mark Twain—a voice I had heard before, in recordings of course. It came to me the way I remembered his slow Missouri twang. Why was he talking about lying as I was trying to figure out why the Holyrood-house suddenly seemed pertinent?

"Lass," Tom said.

I looked at him. "Yes, sorry, what?"

Tom smiled knowingly. "That was one of those moments, wasn't it?"

"It was."

"Aye, it's charming."

"Hope you always feel that way."

"Care to tell me what it was about?"

"In my head, I heard a quote about lying as I was looking at the grounds of the Holyroodhouse."

Tom's eyebrows came together. "So, the voices, they're not clear communications?"

"No, not really."

"I wish I could help you."

"Me too." I looked toward Holyrood again and then back at Tom. "Maybe it will come to me. Let's go talk to Inspector Winters."

"Aye. I look forward to seeing how they greet you tonight."

"I do have a reputation."

Tom smiled again. "Nothing wrong with that."

The officer sitting at the front podium did a double take when his eyes landed on me. I hadn't seen him before. He was cute and fresh-faced and younger, I thought, than any officer I'd yet to meet in Scotland.

"Uh-oh," he said as he reached for the phone in front of him. He kept his eyes on us as he pushed some buttons. "She's here, Winters. Yep, that Delaney woman. The redhead from America."

"Delaney woman?" I said to Tom.

The officer hung up the phone. He smiled nervously at me, which was weird. "Winters is on his way up."

"Thank you."

"Delaney and Tom," the inspector said a moment later as he came around a wall that hid a hall that led to offices and interview rooms. He was still in his uniform. "Hello, and welcome. Derek here treat you right?"

"Derek was perfect," I said, making the young man smile in relief.

"Good to hear. Come on back." He turned and started down the hall, but he peered backward at us. "We've debated naming this room after you." He stopped outside the police interview room I'd been inside many times, the first occasion being very shortly after I moved to Edinburgh.

We were there again.

"I feel like I should be able to tell you something that would help," I said after we were all seated around the old dark wooden table.

"How?"

"I don't know, except that I've seen more than anyone has seen, at least collectively. I'd like to just rehash every single thing, just in case," I said. "Talk it out, if that makes sense."

Some police officers or inspectors would roll their eyes and tell me they had everything handled, but Inspector Winters was a friend. Besides, he knew I wasn't exaggerating. He understood what I was feeling.

"Tell me everything," he said.

I went over every detail, from the messenger, to Shelagh's meeting, to her beautiful library, to the clues. Everything I could possibly think of. When I finished, I took a deep breath. I hoped I hadn't forgotten something.

"Have you guys discovered any other reason to talk to Findlay again?" I asked.

"No."

"May I ask why specifically he was arrested?" I said.

Inspector Winters nodded. "We found some of Shelagh's blood in the backseat of the car he drives her in."

"What did he say about that?"

"He said that Shelagh cut her finger the week before, that the two of them tried to clean it up."

"You must have believed him."

"Not at first, but we gained footage of him on errands to the grocery store and the automotive-parts place. His alibis during her abduction were airtight and caught on cameras."

"No one has seen Shelagh anywhere?"

"Not that we know."

"Have you searched all her employees' homes?"

"We have, but thanks for asking."

"Sorry."

"So what about the book? Was the last clue really the Starbar?"

"Yes. The copy of the book we have isn't telling us anything. Hopefully, as with a couple of the other clues, something will just come to one of us. We've visited lots of pubs."

"Tell me which pubs again," Inspector Winters said.

As I listed them, his eyebrows came together. He pulled out his notebook and had me again repeat the names of the pubs so he could write them down. He excused himself and told us not to leave.

He was back a moment later with a copy of a newspaper, the one Brigid worked for.

"Look." He spread the newspaper on the table and pointed

at an article that Brigid had written a couple months back. "This is from a little while ago. We keep old yearly files of copies, and I remembered reading this one, thought it was interesting."

I leaned over and read the headline: EDINBURGH'S MOST HAUNTED PUBS.

There was a list of six, according to Brigid at least. Birk and I had visited five of them. The only one we hadn't been to was called The Banshee Labyrinth.

The article's introduction promised that visits to the six pubs in the article were sure to chill patrons to their bones. Each pub was also described in a separate paragraph or two. The description for The Banshee Labyrinth read:

> This venue proves why Edinburgh is truly a *Jekyll & Hyde* city. Apparently at one time one of the richest and most respected men in Edinburgh lived next door to where the pub is located. At night he brutalized his wife. Some say he was one of the inspirations for Robert Louis Stevenson's *Strange Case of Dr. Jekyll and Mr. Hyde*. It was said that Stevenson knew the violent man and followed his trial closely. Listen with your ears perked and you'll hear yells and screams. It will terrify you, in the best way possible. You'll need a map just to explore all the crannies and crevices. Here's one that will do.

The sketch of a map was underneath.

"I know this story. I read about Eugene Chantrelle," I said. "Shelagh's . . . assistant is . . . That's the part I unintentionally left out! I mean, I don't know if it matters at all, but maybe there's more than one killer with that last name. Or a version thereof, like—"

"Louis Chantrell," Inspector Winters finished.

"His last name is spelled differently, without an *e* at the end, but yes, that's it."

I looked at Tom and then at Inspector Winters and then back at Tom. "I can't believe Brigid hasn't put together that she might have written the article that gave Shelagh the idea of what pubs to use, but I think this is wonderful. Even if Louis's name isn't important, I bet we just figured out another clue in the treasure hunt."

In the history of The Banshee Labyrinth, I bet it had never closed for "routine maintenance." But tonight it was dark and quiet inside, the sign on the door telling us that indeed there was some maintenance going on, even if we couldn't spot anyone doing anything.

"I think the sign is code for 'The owner needed a night off,'" Inspector Winters said. I'd never seen him as aggravated as he'd been when we came upon the pub's locked doors.

"Could you get it open?" Tom asked.

"I could, but I'd like to get a hold of the owner to do it instead. The potential clue isn't really probable cause. I need to get all the officers and inspectors on all the cases here too. And I really do believe this is more about the book than about Shelagh, but what if the book leads us to Shelagh?" He grumbled some curse words and pulled out his phone. "I'm going to try to get in touch with people."

As Inspector Winters worked to reach someone who might open the pub without the need for breaking down doors or windows, Tom and I tried to peer inside the darkness.

"It *is* Tuesday," he said a moment later. "Not a terrible night to be closed."

I glanced at the time. It wasn't that late, only about nine. "I'm going to text Brigid, ask her more about her article."

"All right."

I sent her a text stating that I wanted to talk to her, but there was no sign that she got the text, no dots moving across the screen. I frowned at the phone before I slipped it into my back pocket.

"She'll respond," Tom said.

"At some point." I peered inside the window again.

Inspector Winters rejoined us. "I've got officers working on things. I really don't want to break the door down unless we have to. I'm going to stay here awhile, until I hear from someone. You two can stay as well, but it could be a long night. If we get inside, I'll let you know what we find."

After a few minutes and the arrival of other officers, Tom and I somewhat reluctantly (it really was cold, so not *too* reluctantly) left, catching a bus back to Tom's pub. I kept checking my phone, but Brigid didn't respond.

"Call her," Tom said.

"No, I just want to ask about her article. She'll get back to me. I'll call Birk."

He answered on the first ring, and I told him how we'd put things together to come up with what we hoped was another clue.

"Oh, I hope they find Shelagh," he said. "And figure out who murdered Ritchie John. The book is the least of my worries."

"We can only hope."

"Keep me up to date, lass," Birk said.

"Will do." I ended the call. Brigid still hadn't texted back.

As Tom and I disembarked from the bus on the edge of Grassmarket Square, we looked toward Tom's pub. It wasn't crowded, but the customers inside seemed to be having a good time.

I glanced around the market, fully expecting to see the Monster, for him to jump out and try to scare us. Maybe laugh at us. *Joke's over! There wasn't a murder, and Shelagh gets to go home unharmed. This was all just a setup. None of it's real, just the product of Shelagh's crazy imagination.*

But though it seemed he loomed even more than before, the Monster wasn't there. There were no shabby coats flapping in the breeze, no scary person lurking in the shadows. It was just my wishful thinking.

It was real. The murder was real, and Shelagh was missing. None of this was a setup. It was one tragedy after another.

We remained alert as we stopped by the pub to see if Rodger needed anything. He didn't, so we made our way to Tom's car and went home to our cozy, blue, and hopefully safe house by the sea.

TWENTY-FIVE

"What?" I said as I sat up in bed. "What's going on?"

A noise had awakened me. More conscious now, I heard it again. A knock was sounding on the front door. Tom was sitting up too.

"Stay here, lass, I'll see who's there," he said.

I hopped out of bed and grabbed a sweatshirt to throw over my pajamas. "Nope, I'm going with you. Strength in numbers."

"All right. Stay behind me."

I grabbed my phone and saw it was three in the morning. It was probably the police. I hoped they had some good news. I hoped Shelagh had been found alive and well.

We met Elias and Aggie in the hallway. Elias held a bat. I didn't even know there was a bat in my house, but I was okay with it.

Tom and Elias lead the way, and Aggie and I followed them down the stairs.

"Who's there?" Tom called.

"It's me. Brigid."

The four of us relaxed at once. Elias lowered the bat. "What the 'ell?"

"The lass from the newspaper?" Aggie asked.

"Yes, I sent her a text earlier. She must have wanted to answer it in person." I stepped next to Tom as he opened the door.

"Brigid?" he said.

"I was working, trying to keep a low profile as I spied on some politicians. Can't tell you the details, but I couldn't look at my phone until about twenty minutes ago. I tried to text back," she said as she held her phone toward me. "What's up?"

"It's three in the morning, lass," Elias said as he peered out.

"Well, I know, but I just couldn't wait. I'm sorry." She cocked her head. "Aren't you Delaney's landlord?"

"It's a long story. Come on in, Brigid," I said.

She smiled. "Thank you. And I promise I won't make this awkward."

Tom had told me that he and Brigid had lived together for a short time before they broke up. They'd lived in the blue house. It hadn't bothered me in the least, but her comment made me remember it, now with a little less indifference. I decided I just wouldn't think about it.

"I'll make . . . something," Aggie said before she went into the kitchen.

"I'm going back to bed." Elias, the bat relaxed on his shoulder, made his way upstairs again.

Brigid took a seat on the couch as if it were the spot where she always sat. "What's up, Delaney?"

I sensed Tom gritting his teeth, but he was nothing if not polite. He sat in a chair, and I joined Brigid on the couch—the one that had been hers for a short time. Again I tried not to think about it, hoping my face wasn't involuntarily moving into a cringe.

I explained how it seemed that all the clues led to pubs listed in her article. She looked genuinely surprised.

"I didn't even think about that. It's been months since I wrote that article," she said. "And I never considered it much more than fill, nothing investigative. I think we just needed something, so I threw it together."

"Did Shelagh mention it to you when you were interviewing her?" I asked.

Brigid shook her head slowly. "I don't think so. She said she liked my writing. That's why she approached me to do the article about her and her library. I'm sure she didn't mention that pub article specifically."

Tom and I waited as Brigid fell into thought. She looked up at me a moment later.

"I'm sure she didn't mention it," she confirmed.

"She might not have, simply so you wouldn't be able to help with the treasure hunt she had in mind. Maybe she didn't even know about the treasure hunt at that time." I paused. "Maybe that's it exactly. Something must have happened to cause her to want to set up the hunt. In the first meeting she called us all to, she said that she was healthy but getting old and that it was time to do something with her library. That sort of made sense, but what if it was something else? What if she's ill? Did you get any sense of that?"

Brigid frowned. "She didn't seem sick, Delaney, but she didn't seem completely right either."

"How do you mean?" Tom asked.

Brigid looked at him as if she'd forgotten he was in the room. "Not completely in her right mind, though I have no idea if that's a polite way to say it or not." She turned back to me. "Here's the thing: I really liked her. Before I went to talk to her, I'd researched her history. When I met her, I liked her so much that I couldn't even bring myself to ask her about her past. I know, I know, that doesn't sound like Brigid-go-for-the-jugular reporter, but Shelagh was older, and though she wasn't really ill, I didn't want to contribute to anything that would send her quirky behavior over the edge. It didn't seem necessary for the article I was writing."

Aggie came in, carrying a tray full of cookies and hot chocolate. Momentarily I wondered how she'd managed to get the hot chocolate fixed so quickly.

"Thank you." Brigid reached for the tray. "I'm starving."

"I don't mean to misjudge Shelagh," I said. "And I certainly don't want to make false or irresponsible accusations, but I think it's only fair to have wondered about her mental health all those years ago, and if there are health issues, maybe they could be part of what's happening now."

"Or maybe she's just incredibly creative," Brigid said around a cookie.

"Aren't the two sometimes closely tied together?" Tom said. "Extreme creativity and mental illness?"

"Sometimes." Brigid shrugged. "But"—she paused and thought and chewed—"I really think that if Shelagh is anything, it's . . . energetic and imaginative. And also bored. Well, she used to be. She was an only child growing up in a lonely house. No family other than her horrible parents."

"And her cousins in France," I said.

"Her cousins?" Brigid held a cookie in one hand, a mug of hot chocolate in the other. "What cousins?"

"They live in France. Her second cousin, something removed, is part of the treasure hunt. Jacques."

"I don't understand." Brigid took a bite of cookie and chewed and pondered. "I'm sure there are no cousins. Her parents were also only children."

"Are you sure?" I said.

"Completely."

I thought back to the introductions that first day. Shelagh had presented Jacques as one of her closest relations—no, one of her "closest possible relations." Was the word "closest" meant to modify "possible" or "relations"? There were two distinctly different meanings there. I remembered the look she and Jacques had shared. Was it something familial?

"Goodness," I said to myself. "She could have meant something different from what I thought."

"What's that?" Brigid asked.

I told them about those first moments in that room in the back of Deacon Brodie's Tavern.

"We need to figure out who Jacques is. He still might be a relative, but if not . . . well, if the police don't already have that figured out, they need to," Brigid said.

"I agree." I would tell Inspector Winters first thing—at a reasonable hour.

"Oh, no," Brigid said.

"What?" Tom and I now asked.

Brigid looked at me. "She *wanted* me to get involved."

"In the hunt?" I asked.

"Something. She wanted me involved—or someone involved."

"I don't understand," I said.

"She wanted me somehow involved or she wouldn't have used the pubs I put in that article. I mean, aye, a couple are tied to the *Jekyll and Hyde* story, but not all of them, and all of them are in my article. And she asked me specifically about a bookshop person. I told her about you. She must have wanted me to pay attention."

"Why? For another article?"

Brigid shook her head. "During our interview, our time together, she told me many times how much she enjoyed my writing. She frequently said I could bleed the truth from a stone. She commented on what a valuable trait that was, for a reporter and an officer of the law, she supposed. I bet she was telling me something, and I needed to be on the alert."

I didn't disagree with Brigid completely, but it did seem a little far-fetched.

"That's possible," I said. "But she must have told you more."

"Well, she told me more than once that she had no family left and that was a subject of concern for her."

"Right, we need to figure out who Jacques is."

"Sooner rather than later. What's his full name, and where is he?"

"Last I saw him, he was at Shelagh's house, but he had a room somewhere else too. I didn't ask where. His last name is Underwood. Jacques Underwood."

"Just like the old typewriter in Shelagh's library?"

"Well. Yes, I suppose. I think I remember that it was an Underwood, but I didn't look at it closely."

"How could you not?" Brigid asked. "Typewriters! How could you not want to look at them, touch them, press their keys?"

"Not my thing, I guess."

Brigid made a noise of exasperation. "Let's get over to The Banshee Labyrinth."

Tom and I explained the roadblocks to getting inside The Banshee Labyrinth tonight. Brigid didn't like what we told her, but ultimately she seemed to accept that she wasn't going to get inside that particular pub this evening.

She looked at her watch. "I have an interview with Louis Chantrell in five hours anyway."

"About what?"

"I told him it was about Shelagh, that I wanted to talk to him for another article, one that might help people look harder for her. Truth is, I don't *get* him, and I want to see if I sense he's up to something. That last name is just too weird. I have questions."

"Lass, that could be dangerous," Aggie said as she held the cookie tray out for Brigid.

"I'm a journalist, it's part of the job." She took another cookie.

I didn't agree with her completely, but I didn't argue.

"Anyway"—Brigid looked at me—"want to come along?"

Aggie tsked.

"I do," I said without a moment's hesitation.

"Tom." Aggie nudged Tom's shoulder. "Stop your wife from doing such silliness."

Tom sent a wary smile to Aggie. "I don't think that's the kind of marriage we have, but I will be happy to caution her and ask—*tell*, if that would make you feel better—them both to be careful."

Brigid sent a suspicious glare at my husband and seemed to be waiting for more. When Tom didn't continue, she looked at me again. "All right. I'll pick you up at your bookshop at seven-thirty."

"Sounds good."

Brigid grabbed two more cookies on the way to the door. She told us all goodnight but smiled only at Aggie. Aggie's cookies will do that.

Once she was safe in her car and pulled away from the curb, Tom closed and locked the door.

"You'll be careful, aye?" he said to me.

"Of course."

"You'll text me his address?"

"Barrie!" Aggie said.

We both looked at her.

"Excellent!" she translated.

"I will text you his address," I confirmed.

It must have been Aggie's hot chocolate, because shortly after we said good-bye to our middle-of-the-night visitor, we were all back in bed, sleeping soundly for a few more hours.

TWENTY-SIX

"Lass, I cannae believe you knocked on someone's door in the wee hours," Rosie said as Brigid came into the bookshop.

She cringed. "You know, Rosie, I agree. I feel bad about that." She looked at me. "I really am sorry. I was . . . I don't know, on a roll or something."

"It's okay." I smiled.

Tom had thought the whole thing ridiculous. He harbored no ill will against Brigid, but he thought she should have waited until a decent hour or just texted back and waited for a later reply. He didn't dwell on it, but the fact that she'd come over when she had only highlighted her thoughtlessness.

"Have you heard from Inspector Winters?" Brigid asked me.

"I have. I let him know what we'd discussed about Jacques, and he said he would meet me, us if you want, at The Banshee Labyrinth at noon. The police did get inside last night and confirmed that no one was being held captive anywhere in there, but they didn't look for a book. The owner was out of town or something but is coming back this morning. Winters also told me that Louis Chantrell is not a suspect, though he is a very interesting man."

"Aye?"

"Yes, and left it at that, saying you and I would see soon enough, but he didn't seem concerned about us visiting him."

"What did he say about Jacques?"

"Inspector Winters was aware that Shelagh didn't have any blood relatives. He'd talk to the inspectors on the case, but they probably know too. But the more I think about that first meeting with Shelagh, the more I wonder if Jacques wasn't just a close family friend or something and Shelagh was using a term of endearment. I don't know, I'm just glad the police will double-check."

"Well, I will work on it too." She glanced at her watch. "I have a full day, but we'll see. Let's at least get to the bottom of the somewhat strange and mysterious Louis Chantrell."

Hector whined up at me from where he'd been sitting at my feet. I reached down to pick him up.

"I'll be back. I'll be fine," I assured him.

He wiggled, and I let him kiss my cheek and then reluctantly handed him to Rosie.

"He thinks ye need tae be extra careful around even *some-what* strange and mysterious people," Rosie said.

"I promise I will be."

"I hope so." Rosie sent Brigid some raised eyebrows.

Brigid squirmed as she nodded.

"Och," Rosie said before she and Hector turned and made their way to the back of the shop.

The snow had started again, but the wind wasn't bad. Brigid and I put on hats and, both of us in boots, took off toward the bus stop.

"I didn't want to drive in this weather. Come on," Brigid said.

We boarded the second bus that came along and sat next to

each other. There was no need for small talk, because Brigid was on the phone the entire trip to Louis's house. I caught snippets of her conversations, and at one point I suspected she was speaking to her aunt, Grace, who also happened to be media-relations minister to the city's lord provost. I pricked up my ears, curious to hear about some city business, but she kept her voice low enough and the bus engine was loud enough so that I couldn't make out the details.

Louis Chantrell lived in an old brick house on the edge of one of the rougher neighborhoods. A narrow home, it was two stories and a short attic space high, the first-floor windows almost completely hidden by an overgrown garden. There were no flowers in bloom, and the falling snow was beginning to accumulate on the old, seemingly ignored branches and stems.

"I wonder how this place looks in the summer," Brigid said as we stood on the sidewalk in front of the house, outside the short wrought-iron fence that outlined the property.

From the corner, the view down either bordering street showed older buildings, some covered in the same sort of graffiti I'd seen on the bottom of Darcy's Roost.

"Maybe he cleans up the garden in the spring," I said. "It could be nice."

"*Could* be," Brigid agreed. "I wonder why he lives here, though. I'm sure Shelagh pays him well. This is all odd."

She took a step toward the path that led to the front door. I followed.

Brigid knocked, the sound echoing inside. "If he comes to the door with vampire teeth, we're leaving."

I laughed, but I didn't think she was trying to be funny.

We heard fast footfalls approach, and then the door opened quickly but with a weary creak.

"Ah, hello," Louis said. He blinked at me. "Delaney?"

"Yes," I said. "I really wanted to see your place, and Brigid's a friend."

Brigid shrugged.

Louis smiled. "Ah, don't blame you. Quite the story here. Come in, then. Come in. I'm baking, but I will join you in the drawing room momentarily. Coffee or tea?" He'd already started walking away.

"Coffee, thanks," we both called after him.

"Do you know the story?" I asked Brigid quietly as we went in and shut the door behind us.

"No, but I'm always up for a good one."

The house seemed even narrower from the inside. A steep stairway was close by on our right, its old wooden planks worn shiny and slightly bowed in the spots where feet had stepped.

The same planks made up the flooring. They weren't in terrible shape, but scuffed here and there. Hooks lined the wall to our right. A coat hung from one, a pair of boots on the floor beneath.

I was just about to ask if we should remove our coats when Brigid took the lead and did exactly that. I shrugged out of mine and hung it up too.

"Come on." She set off down the hallway.

She stopped outside what I would call a drawing room, but this one was straight out of the movie *Psycho*. My imagination almost saw it in sepia tones. It was furnished and decorated with antiques. Carved wood framed the couch and chairs around faded pinkish flowered upholstery. This was not an antique revival; the items in this room hadn't been redone, they'd been used and loved, showing their wear.

"Well, this is fabulous," Brigid said quietly.

"I couldn't agree more."

We walked around the skinny but long room, looking at

the multiple items that had been set out on doilies. Lamps, figurines, black-and-white pictures—mostly of people who'd surely been dead a long time. A windup clock ticked so loudly it echoed through the room.

My eyes landed on a familiar picture. A man with mutton-chop facial hair hung in a frame in a prominent spot on the wall.

"I know him," I said quietly as I approached the picture. "Oh, Eugene Chantrelle."

"The murderer?" Brigid hurried up next to me.

"Yes, the one who killed his wife, Elizabeth. Robert Louis Stevenson followed the trial. It might have inspired *Jekyll and Hyde* to some extent." I looked at some of the other framed pictures, noting they all had small plaques or nameplates, and most of them mentioned the last name Chantrelle.

"But Louis's last name is spelled differently," Brigid said.

"I had it changed—legally, of course," Louis said as he came in behind us.

We startled and turned. Louis carried a tray full of more snacks than I'd seen grace any tray in a long time—and I'd seen quite a few trays over the past few days.

"You're a Chantrelle, without an *e*?" I said.

"Well, originally I had the *e*, but with the advent of social media and the internet it all became quite annoying. People would send me bothersome messages and such. It became too much for this man who likes to keep to himself. I had to change it."

"We met when I did the article about Shelagh, but I couldn't find you anywhere on social media," Brigid said. I hadn't either, but I didn't mention it.

"I hope not. I've done the best I can to keep a semi-low pro-file. Even after so much time, people still become fascinated by my ancestor Eugene. Reluctantly, I have posted on social media for this house—it's a museum, and the only way I can keep it is by continuing to show it. But now I can do it by appointment only, infrequently at that. It's amazing the difference one little *e* can make—if my name isn't spelled the way Eugene's was, the connection doesn't get quickly made."

I looked around. "I thought Eugene lived next to where The Banshee Labyrinth is now located."

"He did." Louis set the tray down on a table. "This is a reproduction. My grandfather built it."

"It's fascinating."

"It's old, but it's also home." Louis motioned for us to sit down. Once we had our spots, he continued. "Now, Ms. McBride, you want to talk to me about Shelagh?"

"And about you, Mr. Chantrell."

"Aye? I hope you like biscuits," Louis said.

"I love biscuits." Brigid smiled, and I was beginning to wonder if biscuits—*cookies*—were the only things she ate.

It seemed very chummy, I thought, remembering Elias using the same word when he and I were in a friendly but crowded line at a grocery store. I knew that Brigid wasn't always friendly, and I wondered if she was preparing some sort of attack.

"Very good. May I inquire if, as a journalist, you've heard any news on Shelagh?" Louis asked. "I call the police at least twice a day, but they don't tell me anything."

"I haven't. I'm sorry. You don't have any idea where she might be?" Brigid took a bite of the cookie.

Louis shook his head, and his eyes shadowed. "At first I thought that maybe she'd set this up, but I don't think so anymore."

"Why?" Brigid asked.

"It's gone on too long. If she'd wanted to scare people by disappearing, she would have reappeared shortly thereafter."

"That would be cruel, don't you think? To hide and scare your loved ones into thinking you'd been taken. Blood was found too. Would she go that far?" Brigid asked.

Louis sighed. "She wouldn't think of it as cruel. She'd be so quick about it that we'd all forgive her. But it most definitely has gone on too long now."

"How did you come to work for Shelagh, and when did you begin?" Brigid asked.

"Oh, it was decades ago—goodness, probably sixty years now. I first worked for her parents."

I caluclated that he was probably only five to ten years older than Shelagh, but his bald head still made it difficult to discern his age.

"What did you do?" Brigid asked.

"A wee bit of everything." Louis laughed, but sobered quickly. "I started working for the O'Conners shortly before Shelagh . . . well, lost her way for a wee bit. Until recently her escapades were old news. I look forward to the day they return to being unimportant. Nevertheless, I met the O'Conners back when Shelagh was sixteen. One of my duties was to keep an eye on her. In fact, I'm the one who first gave her *Jekyll and Hyde* to read."

"I suppose that makes sense," I said. "Considering your ancestors."

"Aye. Honestly, I felt guilty about it for a long time, but it wasn't my fault she took things so far. Stevenson's story is brilliant. All I did was introduce her to it. She did the rest." Louis smiled sadly.

Brigid and I shared a quick look. Clearly, Louis would always feel some guilt when it came to Shelagh's behavior.

Though so profound a double-dealer, I was in no sense a hypocrite; both sides of me were in dead earnest; I was no more myself when I laid aside restraint and plunged in shame, than when I laboured, in the eye of the day, at the furtherance of knowledge or the relief of sorrow and suffering.

The bookish voice caught me so offguard that my hand flew to my mouth, hoping to stop any sounds of surprise.

I'd very recently read the words that just played in my head. They were from Dr. Jekyll himself, his final statement in the story. In my head, the deep voice spoke slowly, sadly. Why was the bookish voice talking to me now? Was it simply that I was in this house?

"Delaney?" Brigid asked.

Distantly, I heard her, but I wasn't ready to let go of trying to understand what Jekyll wanted to communicate. What was my intuition keying in on? The words were meant to convey that Hyde was just as real as Jekyll, that both sides existed together, and probably do in most everyone.

"Delaney!" Brigid said as she shook my arm.

"I'm so sorry." I blinked and then nodded at her. I cleared my throat and looked at Louis. Shelagh had said that Louis was her closest advisor, but was there more, and did that matter? "You two are close, then?"

Louis squinted at me. "Are you feeling all right?"

"I'm fine. Sorry." I gathered myself. I'd have to think about the bookish voice later.

"Aye, well, we've never been romantically involved, if that's what you're asking. We are good friends, though. Much love there." His eyes filled with tears, but he blinked them away.

"Would you say you're her closest friend? Confidant?" Brigid turned her focus to taking notes.

"Aye. Some might say I'm her only real friend."

"Really? Why?"

"I've known her the longest, and I don't want anything from

her. She's offered many times to buy me another place to live. This place would sell, but it's falling down brick by brick. It would need a lot of work. Plus, I can't just sell it. It's my history, my family." Louis sighed again. "I've refused to take her help."

"Can you think of someone who has recently requested something of her? Something big and something she said no to?" Brigid asked.

"Oh, lass, I've been trying to remember something—anything that might help the police. Or someone who was angry with her. Nothing unusual has come to mind. I wish it would."

"What about her family?"

"She has no family."

I came to attention even more, but Brigid kept cool. "I thought Jacques was her cousin."

"Oh, that. No, not a blood relation, but I know she had some close friends in France, and she's the type of person to make people into her family."

"Call them cousins?" Brigid said.

Louis squirmed briefly. "Well, she never has before, but she has so much love to give. I can understand why she would say that."

"Did you know Jacques, ever heard of him?"

Louis frowned a moment and said, "No, but that's not necessarily a surprise. Shelagh and I don't share *everything* with each other."

"Were you in on helping her choose the people to be a part of her treasure hunt?" Brigid asked.

"No, in fact I wasn't. Shelagh consults me on many things, though not everything, not that."

"Findlay made sure the messenger delivered the messages?" I interjected.

"Aye. Not everyone was given a handwritten message, however. Just you and Birk."

"Not Tricia? Not Jacques?" Brigid said.

"No, I heard Shelagh and Findlay discussing it. She said she would get a hold of the other two herself, but the messenger was to go to you and Birk."

"Does that seem strange?" I asked, wishing I'd remembered to ask Birk if he'd, in fact, seen a messenger.

"No stranger than anything else."

He had a point.

"He hasn't even been trying to find the book," I added. "If he's out for the library, he's not doing it the right way."

"Maybe he simply doesn't want the library," Louis said. "That seems counterintuitive to Shelagh's inviting him to participate, but maybe he doesn't care about it. Also, he witnessed Shelagh's abduction. He might be traumatized."

"What about Tricia?" Brigid asked. "How did Tricia get invited?"

"Shelagh said she was a great librarian," I said. I turned to Louis. "How would she know that?"

"I wish *I* knew," Louis said. "Well, she's interested in all libraries, all schools with libraries. I'm sure she just came across Tricia along the way."

Brigid nodded.

"Ultimately I was disappointed that she invited Birk Blackburn," Louis said.

"Why?" I asked.

"He wasn't a positive force in her life. They were friends for a time, and he betrayed her."

"Betrayed?" I said.

Brigid sent me and my tone a quick side-eye.

"Aye. He was part of a group that she really enjoyed, some sort of auction group for rich people." He was talking about Fleshmarket. "She broke off the relationship with Birk, and next thing you knew, she was kicked out of the group. It was childish, really."

I hadn't heard the story exactly that way from Birk, but there were always two sides.

"Sounds dicey," Brigid said.

"Aye, but it was a long time ago. I asked her why she invited him to the hunt. She told me that he would do the right thing with the books and that's who she wanted involved." Louis shrugged. "The last time I saw Birk, it was a friendly moment, so I didn't use whatever influence I might have to change her mind."

"When's the last time you saw him?" I asked.

"Just about a month ago or so at his stables. He was hosting an event, and we loaned our horses. It was a fund-raiser for a child in hospital. Lots of money was raised. I saw Birk only briefly, he was in and out—and as I said, it was friendly. Bygones and all."

I sat forward. "Louis, what else happened at that event? Do you remember seeing the murder victim, Ritchie John? Were there any issues—with anyone—that you can remember?"

Louis shook his head slowly. "No, lass, I don't think so. I wasn't there long myself. I just wanted to make sure our people and horses had all gotten there safe and sound. They had."

"Was Shelagh there?" I asked.

"No, no. In fact . . ."

"What?" Brigid said.

"She wouldn't go because she didn't want to see Birk, no matter how good the cause. It's interesting that only a short time later she invited him to a treasure hunt."

"It *is* interesting," I added. "Do you know Darcy John?"

"No, lass, I don't believe I do. Is she related to the victim?"

"His daughter."

"I don't know her."

I couldn't think of another immediately pertinent question.

"Louis, what do you think might have happened to Shelagh?" Brigid said.

Louis sighed. "I have no idea. I miss her terribly, and though I'm trying not to think about it too much, I'm beginning to fear the worst. I would give anything to save her."

"Who do you think is under the monster costume?" Brigid asked.

I thought Louis might brush her off immediately, but he didn't rush his words. His eyes held Brigid's for a long moment.

"I don't know," he finally said.

"No idea?" Brigid said.

"None," Louis said more quickly.

"Well." Brigid seemed to move on to the next subject. "We'd be happy to pay the price of admission, but may we see the rest of the house?"

"Aye. It would be my pleasure. Tickets are free of charge today."

We started with the kitchen. Similar to those in my kitchen, the appliances were old. These were genuinely old, though, not reproductions. An old icebox sat in the corner and was used as a small pantry now. The cooker was the kind that required a handle to pick up the burners so that a fire might be lit underneath.

"I apologize. Usually I have other things set up in here. It was thought that Eugene poisoned Elizabeth, probably with opium, and this is where her body was found. A pot was left boiling on the cooker. Adding one gives the room some atmosphere."

"Did you grow up here? Do you live here?" I asked.

"I did and I do. Things are hidden. There's a small but modernly equipped kitchen through that door. It looks like it leads to a patio or a porch, but it doesn't."

Brigid and I peered out a window, seeing the modernly outfitted small kitchen. It would be fine for just one person.

"How many people were in your family?"

"My grandparents, my mother, and me. My father died when I was a wee bairn. People came and went, but now it's just me. I never married, never had a child of my own. I never even noticed I might be missing something. I have enjoyed this life."

"Always good," Brigid said.

"Aye, now, how about a look at the upstairs and then the basement? The basement is everyone's favorite."

The stairs that took us to the basement were directly underneath the stairs that took us up to the second level. Though we'd become highly intrigued by the mention of the basement, Louis insisted upon showing us the second floor first. I noticed Brigid furtively typing on her phone as we followed Louis. I'd ask her later what she was doing, but I wondered if she was letting someone know where we were. If so, that was a pretty smart move. I thought about doing the same, but I wasn't as dexterous as she was.

The second floor had four bedrooms and a bathroom. Three of the four bedrooms were furnished as the mid-nineteenth-century Chantrelles would have furnished them, but Louis's private room was neat and contemporary. The bathroom was charming vintage.

"They didn't really have a loo back then, so we just kept this one looking old-timey. We didn't even put a shower in," Louis said. "Just a bath. Oddly, even though people know this isn't authentic, they love this little room."

The sink, tub, toilet were white—the tub a claw-foot, the toilet adorned with a pull chain.

"Is that how you flush?" I asked.

Louis stepped inside the bathroom and pulled the chain, proving that was indeed how you flushed.

"It's in great shape," I said.

"It's been well taken care of." Louis looked at the floor. "I haven't been able to match these tiles again, so I dread the day one of them chips or breaks beyond repair."

The floor was tiled with small, white hexagons. I'd seen tiles like them, but there was something slightly different about these. The edges were different.

"My grandmother was an unusual woman. Very clever and full of energy. She was responsible for the decor. The basement, however, will illuminate for you my grandfather's true personality. He was a direct descendant of Eugene, and he knew how to play it up."

"Well, let's go," Brigid said.

Louis led us back down the stairs. When we reached the door to the flight that would take us to the basement, he paused, his hand on an old brass knob.

"These stairs are a wee bit more frightening," he began. "They're reliable, but they appear rickety. Please, if you will, just hold on to the handrail."

Brigid and I nodded together.

It had been a dramatic introduction but didn't even come close to the drama of rest of the basement. If there was anyplace in the world where a Mr. Hyde might show himself, it was there.

TWENTY-SEVEN

It was a laboratory. In my mind I pronounced it "la-*bor-a*-tory," and this one felt much more authentic than the one in the museum basement.

Two tables occupied the middle of one long room. Shelves of jars filled with things from horror movies and nightmares lined every other available space. There were no windows. Nothing felt like a fake or a prop.

"Is that a dead bat?" Brigid asked, pointing at a jar.

Louis peered closely at it. "I do believe it is. Grandfather was particularly intrigued by bats. I don't know if he killed this one or if he found it already dead, but he studied many of them. However, it was my grandmother who dallied with witchcraft for a wee bit. I believe bats were of particular intrigue to her. She wasn't a blood Chantrelle, but again, people love this stuff."

I blinked.

"Of course, there's no such thing as a witch, but she was convinced she had magical powers. My mother once told me that Grandmama wasn't in fact magical—she was just insanely smart. She believed that everything in nature worked with everything else and if we found the right balance, we would all live better, longer, healthier lives. She thought bats held some of those secrets. She herself died at age one hundred and one."

"Other than studying bats, did she claim to know anything about how to live a long life?" Brigid asked.

"She was keen on beets," Louis said. "Bats and beets. I despise them both, and I'm in my late seventies. If I live as long as she and my mother did, we'll have to discount the bats-and-beets theory."

"You think she was crazy?" Brigid asked.

I cringed at the non-PC word, but I was glad to have a better grip on Louis's age.

"A wee bit, but mostly I think she was just smart and bored by the rest of us who simply couldn't keep up with her." Louis shrugged and then smiled. "She ran us all quite ragged."

"How long has she been gone?" I asked.

"Oh, twenty years. My mother just passed last year."

"Your family does live a long time," Brigid said.

"So far."

"Shelagh must love this place," I said.

"She did, when we were all younger and this was a more active museum. We can't remember if I introduced her to the book before this room, but it all made an impression on her. Though she still adores *Jekyll and Hyde,* she hasn't been here for a long time."

"How long?" Brigid asked.

"Gracious, I'm not sure, but it's been years."

I took a general glance around the room.

"Louis, did you know Oliver McCabe?" I asked.

Brigid looked at me with wide eyes that transformed quickly into approval. *Good question.*

"I met the man. Aye," he said.

"Did he get his museum tableau idea from this?" I made a gesture with my hand, but I watched him closely.

"He did," Louis said quickly. "Well, I don't know if he got the idea from it, but he certainly wanted to try to duplicate some of it."

"Did you like him?" I asked.

Louis pursed his lips. "I met him a few times, but I didn't really know him. I wasn't fond of his treatment of Shelagh, if that's what you're asking. She was devastated when he broke things off with her."

"You don't think she killed him, do you?" Brigid asked.

"Of course not!"

"Wasn't he ten or so years older than her?"

"Aye, he was. They were not a good match, but he led her on, I believe, and then broke her heart. But, like Shelagh's behavior, that was a long time ago."

The silence as Brigid and Louis regarded each other stretched a beat too long.

"Yes." I looked at one of the tables. "The liquids in the beakers. Are they just colored water?"

"Good eye, Delaney. In fact, they are more than that. They are potions concocted by my grandmother. However, none have been ingested by anyone. They are scaled for eternity, but I've kept them around."

"I'm glad they haven't been tried."

"I did have one delivered to a local chemist once. He told me that I was 'messing where I shouldn't be messing' and that I should destroy everything in here. I will not do that, willingly at least."

"Good for you," Brigid said.

"Feel free to look around." Louis crossed his arms in front of himself. "It's pretty amazing."

Brigid and I toured the basement lab, stopping to peer more closely at some of the creepy jars—there didn't seem to be any human parts. We also looked at some of the handwritten books. There were three large parchment volumes covered with inked handwriting, most of it illegible to our modern eyes.

"Look at the book on the end there," Louis instructed.

It was open to two filled pages. At the top of the first page were large calligraphic words, "The Monster in the Man." Following that was a list of items and then instructions on what to do with them, a recipe.

I looked at Louis. "May I take a picture?"

"Of course. I've transcribed that one too. I'll give you a copy before you leave, but feel free."

I snapped a picture but looked forward to Louis's transcription; the calligraphy was difficult to decipher, though I did see the word "cyanide." I wouldn't re-create any strange concoctions, but the recipe might be interesting to have.

"This needs to be a museum," Brigid turned to Louis. "I mean, I know this *is* a museum, but I bet you could sell all this stuff to a bigger museum."

"It's now the stuff of an old, melancholy man. I've given it a thought or two, particularly as the years have passed, but I think it's all working fine."

"I'll do a story if you'd like, get more business here first."

Louis's faced blanched briefly, but he recovered. "May I think about it, lass? I hope I still have a job with Shelagh. For now the pace of my life is ideal. I'll let you know, and thank you."

"Of course."

We spent a little longer looking at the strange things in the laboratory, but there was nothing in the house that made me think Louis was hiding Shelagh anywhere. Unless he was the best actor on the planet, he didn't know what had happened to her. If he *was* putting on an act, I hoped the police could sense it better than it seemed Brigid and I were able to do.

"I'm sure you were here to search for Shelagh, but that's fine. I have nothing to hide, and I'm pleased to show you the house," Louis said, keying in on our ulterior motives as we climbed the stairs again.

When we reached the kitchen, Brigid smiled at him. "Well, I'm not sure the three of us are going to be able to figure out what happened to Shelagh. Though that *is* kind of what I was hoping for, some light blinking on, an epiphany of sorts. It's not meant to be, but thank you for welcoming us in."

"I would *welcome* any answers," Louis said.

He walked us to the door, giving us each a folded piece of paper from the drawer of a small cabinet, telling us it was the copy of the transcribed potion. We stuck our copies in our coat pockets.

"Farewell," he said. "Please call me if you hear anything about Shelagh."

"You too," Brigid answered.

"Certainly." Louis closed the door. He was probably glad to have us gone so he could get back to the pace of his life.

"Did you learn what you wanted to learn?" I asked Brigid.

"I don't think so. He's a nice enough guy, but that's one weird place, and people's histories can mess them up sometimes."

"Do you suspect him of something?"

"I don't know. Yet." She paused. "All right, ready to go to The Banshee Labyrinth?"

"Definitely. It's almost time for the next bus. Let's hurry."

TWENTY-EIGHT

The Banshee Labyrinth was one of the craziest places I'd ever seen. Even the sign on the front of the pub advertised the purported ghosts inside.

THE BANSHEE LABYRINTH—
SCOTLAND'S MOST HAUNTED PUB

"*Is* it the most haunted one?" I asked Brigid as we stood out front.

She shrugged. "I see ghosts everywhere."

I opened my mouth to ask her to explain that further, but Birk interrupted.

"Good morning," he said as he got out of his car.

"Birk, I have a question," I said as we came together. "Do you remember seeing Louis Chantrell at the event for the children's hospital?"

Birk hesitated and bit his lip as he thought a moment. "Oh. I do. I was just walking through, and he said hello. He behaved as if we knew each other, so I did too, I think. It had been years since I'd seen him. Even the other day at Deacon Brodie's, I didn't put it all together. Goodness, it *has* been years, but I feel terrible for forgetting."

"You had some of Shelagh's horses there. You didn't remember he worked for Shelagh when you saw him there?"

"I'm still trying to wrap my head around the idea that Ritchie John worked for me. I didn't know until this moment that Shelagh's horses were part of the event. I only stopped by to write a check for the cause. I didn't organize any part of it. My people run things just fine without me."

"Years back, when you and Shelagh were close, how did Louis treat you?"

"He was fine." Birk frowned. "Until we broke up. He was none too pleased. He told me as much, but it was only a brief moment of vitriol."

"You broke it off with Shelagh?"

"No, lass, but it was I who had to ask her to leave a group we were a part of. Mutually, we ended our relationship. I suppose that could be twisted around some though."

"I do too, I guess."

Birk shook his head. "It's been a long time, Delaney."

"Right."

Brigid had been listening to Birk and me with focused attention. She didn't say anything, but I was sure she processed every word.

"Shall we?" Birk reached for the door and pulled it open.

It was a tunneled, undergroundish establishment; it sure seemed a likely place for ghosts. Whoever oversaw the furnishings had done a great job of playing up the reputation. Since it was daytime, I was sure we didn't get the full effect of the lighting, but the purple-painted and naked lightbulbs probably filled the place with an eerie glow at night.

There was a tunnel where scary or B movies could be

watched, a pocket of space that reminded me of a stark church with concrete pews. A pool table took up another tunnel, and old jailhouse bars filled the entrance to another; I couldn't determine if there were more tunnels to discover farther along. Throughout the pub there were several skeletons, enjoying a dance or a drink or a meal, or just poised to observe the still-living crowd. I shivered, at either the sights or the distinct chill in the air.

Inspector Winters greeted us and filled us in. The police were long done with their search for any sign of Shelagh in the pub. They didn't think the owner, Krew Gilbert, had anything at all to do with her disappearance.

"Mr. Gilbert has been waiting for you," he said. "Poor man. He needs to get home, but when he found out you were the treasure hunters, he insisted upon staying. He shut down for the day because he's low on staff and just couldn't find the energy to work."

The three of us nodded, and we all walked toward the sick man sitting on a stool at the end of the bar, a box of tissues at the ready. We would have to work to avoid his violent sneezes.

"Are ye here because of the hunt?" he said as we approached.

"We are," Birk, Brigid, and I said together.

Birk and I looked at Brigid; she shrugged.

"I just need tae know one thing: What book did you get at the last clue's location?" Krew asked.

"*The Strange Case of Dr. Jekyll and Mr. Hyde,*" I said.

His eyes rolled up to the sky briefly. "Thank the heavens. I can get rid of this burden now."

Krew scooted off the stool and walked toward the other end of the bar.

"It's in my safe. Come on, everyone, I'm sure you'll all want to see this, and I don't want to be accused of doing something behind the police's back."

The three of us and Inspector Winters followed Krew into his tiny office. He closed the door and then tugged the chain on a desk lamp, filling the room with yellow light. He faced the wall behind his desk as the four of us remained on the other side. An old painting of a bowl of apples hung on the wall, and I wondered if Krew had been the artist. Our host pulled one side of the painting away from the wall to expose a safe. Out of the corner of my eye, I thought I saw Inspector Winters shake his head a tiny bit. I didn't say anything aloud, but I agreed with what he was probably thinking—the cliché of the safe's hiding place made its security less than ideal.

"I will be so glad to get rid of this," Krew repeated. "It's been stressful just to have it under my roof."

Krew turned the safe's dial back and forth and then cranked the handle. He reached in and ever so gently drew out a wrapped package. He turned and handed it to me.

"Take it and never bring it back here again. It's very valuable, apparently."

"Okay, Mr. Gilbert, I need to understand the circumstances of how you came to be in possession of this," Inspector Winters asked.

"There's a note in the package. A woman in a hat and with a scarf around her face—so I have no idea what she looked like—brought that package in to me, but all the previous negotiations were done over the phone."

"Negotiations?"

"How much money they would give me to keep it in my safe. The amount is ten thousand pounds, and I've already deposited it. I'm not giving it back, so don't bother asking. The rest of the story is on that note. I'm keeping the money. Make yourself at home in here while you look."

Krew walked around the rest of us and out of the office.

Inspector Winters sighed. "Let's have a look."

I did everything carefully. Opened the bag, peered inside, reached in, grabbed the book, and took it out. It was wrapped in two pieces of fabric, both of them made of white cotton. I would have preferred seeing something more hermetic, something made specifically to protect these sorts of artifacts, but now wasn't the time to be critical.

After I unwrapped the book, I knew immediately that it was an extremely valuable copy of *Jekyll & Hyde*.

Made with a simple red hardback cover, there wasn't much to it. However, this one was spotless. I could imagine it in the secret room in Shelagh's library.

"This must be it," I said.

Brigid, Birk, and Inspector Winters looked at the book and then at me. Birk was the only one whose eyes held any reverence. He knew the wonder of this object; Brigid and Inspector Winters just saw another old book.

I lifted the cover and turned to the title page. The title and the publisher—"Longmans, Green, and Co."—were listed, as well as "Price One Shilling." And yes, the copyright date had been scribbled and then written over. The 6 in 1886 was not in the original print. The book might have been one of the most terrifyingly beautiful things I'd ever seen.

"Aye, that's it," Birk said.

"Where's the note?" Inspector Winters asked.

I knew he was anxious, we all were, but I took the time to rewrap the book before I reached back into the bag and removed the note. I unfolded it and handed it to Brigid. Shelagh hadn't invited her to the hunt, but I was beyond caring who was involved and ready to use any of Brigid's contacts to get to the bottom of where Shelagh had gone. I hoped this maneuver made her feel welcomed to the team.

She read aloud:

"'Congratulations! This is the book. You've done it. Make sure you sign this paper and ask the proprietor, Mr. Gilbert, to sign it too. I will use this to confirm that you are the winner of my library, this book and my other most prized treasures. Oh, I can't wait to hear what you'll do with everything. See you soon. Shelagh.'"

"You know what this tells me?" Brigid said as she looked at Inspector Winters. "Other than the obvious, I mean."

"What?" he said.

"That she had nothing to do with her disappearance. She wouldn't have written the letter this way if she had. She's truly been taken." Brigid handed me the note.

"Aye," Inspector Winters said. "We *are* operating as if her disappearance is real."

I looked at the short, handwritten paragraph. I understood why Brigid's mind went in that direction, but something else had started niggling at me, somewhere in the back of my brain. What was it?

It came at me with such force I had to sit down on Mr. Gilbert's chair. In fact, my knees wobbled on the verge of buckling. A few moments earlier I'd been imagining the book in Shelagh's secret room. The full force of that vision hit me hard.

"Delaney!" Brigid said as she came around Inspector Winters and took my arm.

"What is it?" Inspector Winters asked.

Pictures flashed through my mind. Shelagh in her library, Edwin and I standing at her front door, the mess in the library after she was gone, and then the blood.

"Did you confirm if the blood on the doorframe was Shelagh's?" I asked Inspector Winters.

"I have no idea, lass," he said. "Why?"

Poor Inspector Winters. This wasn't even his case. I'd called him. I'd taken him from his other investigations just so he could help me with . . . well, with mine, as strange as that was.

"I just thought of something that I should have considered a long time ago," I said.

"What?" Inspector Winters asked, impatience now marking his tone.

"Did the police search the secret hiding place in Shelagh's library?"

"Again, I don't have any idea." Inspector Winters took out his phone. "I don't know about any secret hiding place. I don't know what the officers know."

I swallowed hard, not understanding why I hadn't thought to mention it to them before. "We should *let* them know."

"Right away." Inspector Winters moved to right outside the office.

"Did you know about the secret room?" I asked Brigid.

"No, Delaney. She never said a word."

I looked at Birk.

"I never even thought to mention it to anyone. I thought everyone knew," he said.

"I bet she wasn't taken from her library that day. I bet she was hidden. That's why we didn't see her. . . . It somehow makes more sense." My voice was pitching too high. "What if she's still there?"

"Holy moly," Brigid said.

"Holy something," I said as we heard Inspector Winters start issuing instructions into his phone.

TWENTY-NINE

I felt stupid. Beyond stupid. I didn't understand why I hadn't mentioned the secret room to the police. It wasn't that I was trying to keep the secret.

"You were upset," Birk said. "No one else mentioned it to them, and we all knew about it. She showed us all."

"But Edwin and I were there the moment she was taken. No one else understood the circumstances."

Brigid and I had climbed into Birk's car. We followed Inspector Winters toward Shelagh's estate. The police inspectors in charge of the case were going to meet us there.

It felt like we were moving in slow motion. I wanted to be inside that library, opening that secret door, and finding Shelagh. I just knew that's where she was. It was the only thing that made sense. It was the only way there could've been no trace of her leaving, other than the bloody handprint. Why the timing had been so swift.

"Now I wonder about the handprint," I said. "As I look back on it, it seems weirdly unreal, like it was drawn there or blotted perfectly. There were no smudges to it. I didn't process that until right now."

"But it was blood, Delaney. It came from someone," Brigid said.

"Was it really, though?"

"We'll see."

When we finally got there, Birk parked his car next to Inspector Winters's, whom we followed inside to the library. The other officers were already there, waiting unhappily.

I walked around everyone toward the shelves in the back of the room. I found the right book immediately and pushed on it. The door clicked and swung open. The police inspectors moved me out of the way as they entered, but I followed them into the small space. Brigid craned her neck to look from the entry.

Perhaps the biggest surprise of the day was that Shelagh wasn't there. No one was. However, there was clear evidence that someone *had* been. Things were in there that Shelagh wouldn't have allowed: an empty water bottle and discarded biscuit wrappers littered the floor. There was no obvious blood, but someone had been inside this space, drinking water and eating cookies. It could have been anyone who knew about the room and had access to her house.

I held tight to the fact that there was no sign that anyone had been hurt, no visible blood.

"She could have done this herself," one of the inspectors said.

"Or maybe not," Inspector Winters said.

A voice sounded from the outer room of the library.

"Qu'est-ce que c'est?"

"Jacques," I said as I looked at Inspector Winters.

We all exited the secret room and saw Jacques. He was dressed in jeans and a sweater, but he looked unkempt, as if he'd just awakened.

"What's going on?" Jacques swept his bed-head hair back with his hand. "Did you all just let yourselves in?"

"We need to talk to you in a minute," one of the official inspectors said. "Everyone wait right outside the door, except for Ms. Nichols." He looked at me. "We'd like a word with you first. Please sit over there."

I was told to call them Boyd and Harris, and they were mightily suspicious of me, even after I told them I was the one who'd brought the secret room to light. They thought my timing of doing such a *noble* thing, when no one was inside it anymore, seemed odd. It was hard to blame them; it was their job to be suspicious of everyone.

"We'd like to know when exactly Shelagh O'Conner showed you the room," Boyd said, his mouth in a serious, inquisitorial line.

I told them the details. I told them I thought the other participants in the hunt had seen it too, including Jacques. They told me they'd talk to Jacques, as well as Birk and Tricia, all about it, but I couldn't stop kicking myself. How had I not remembered the room until now?

"Can you explain why you didn't mention this room to us before?" Boyd asked.

I sighed. "I really don't know. I can only chalk it up to the trauma or something, but I didn't even think about that room until today, probably because I saw a book that was kept in there. You know about the treasure hunt?"

"We do," Boyd said.

"We've found the prize." I nodded toward the hallway. "My friend Birk has it. Seeing it must have made me remember the room, because that's where Shelagh said the book had been kept. She told me it was a secret room. Maybe my subconscious decided to keep the secret."

As explanations went, it was pretty weak, but it was the best I could do.

They stared at me a long moment, hoping I'd say more. I thought about calling my attorney, but I really just wanted them to find Shelagh and solve the murder of Ritchie John. I'd answer whatever questions they asked even if I made myself look bad—though hopefully not guilty—along the way.

"Do you think she staged it?" I asked them.

They weren't there to answer my questions.

"Tell us about your relationship with Ms. O'Conner," Boyd said.

"There wasn't one. I'd just met her."

After a few more times of being asked the same sorts of questions, I decided that the police truly didn't think I'd done anything criminal. I wished I could eavesdrop on their conversation with Jacques, but it wasn't to be. They dismissed me and motioned me to leave the room, then asked Jacques to join them.

However, I turned around and walked back to them.

"Do you know for sure the handprint was blood?" I asked.

They looked at me but still weren't in the mood to answer any of my questions.

"I mean, maybe double-check if you haven't determined that yet. And maybe it wasn't Shelagh's. Just saying," I added, because I couldn't help myself.

"Thank you, Ms. Nichols. You may go now," Boyd said.

Other than Jacques, no one had waited in the hallway, but I was glad to see that Brigid, Birk, and Inspector Winters were out front. It was cold outside but the sky was bright blue, currently not a cloud in sight.

"Glad they didn't arrest you." Brigid bounced herself away from Birk's car.

I shook my head. "I think they just wanted a little clarification."

"Makes sense," Inspector Winters said.

I looked at the house and then back at Inspector Winters. "Do you think this will help find Shelagh or Ritchie's killer?"

"I don't know, Delaney. I hope so. The other inspectors spoke to me briefly. I also told them about the charity event."

"Happy to welcome them to my stables," Birk said.

"What will you do with the book?" Inspector Winters asked me.

"Birk is going to put it in his safe," I said.

"I am," Birk added. "However, I will make it available to the police if they want it."

"Aye."

Brigid moved to my side. "Now what?"

"They'll want to talk to Birk, but I'm going back to the bookshop."

"I'll take you," Inspector Winters said.

"I'll get to work too," Brigid said.

"I'll take you too."

Before we left Birk, though, Inspector Winters faced us all. "Be careful, everyone. I mean it, maybe more than I ever have. Remember, the Monster hasn't been caught. The killer hasn't been caught. I have no idea if all this is tied together, but each of you is a part of . . . something, and now you have a priceless book in your possession."

"I'll give it to the inspectors if you think that would be better," Birk said.

"Ask them. But, again I want you all to be careful."

We nodded and assured him we would.

THIRTY

It was impossible not to wonder how everything might be connected. I'd been trying so hard to put it all together that my brain hurt. After Birk dropped me off, I went directly to the warehouse just so I could be alone, with the hope that something good would come from some quiet pondering. So far nothing had.

"Why in the world was Ritchie John killed?" I asked aloud, to no one except ghosts who might be hanging out in the warehouse with me.

Ritchie John worked with horses as well as behind a bar. He'd worked for Birk, but I still didn't know the reasons he'd left except that he seemed scared and in a hurry to go. No one at Birk's stables could understand why, but there had been a cashbox incident. The money had been returned. Other than that righted infraction, nothing else seemed to have gone sideways the day Shelagh's horses and people had been at Birk's stables.

Winston had been in trouble with Shelagh the day I'd met him. I didn't know anything at all about Winston other than that Shelagh was worried about his alleged drinking and he was Findlay Sweet's brother.

Despite all the new pieces of the possible puzzle, my mind kept going back to Findlay Sweet. He and Winston were also roommates. Were they up to something together? Louis seemed to like Findlay well enough, but that might not mean anything.

Everyone at the bookshop had gone home. I was the last one there. Rosie and Hector had walked over to let me know they were leaving and that Hamlet had left an hour earlier. An hour or so ago, I'd glanced up at the dark widows along the top of the wall, thinking I should head home too. But I hadn't. I'd spent more time lost in those brain-cramping thoughts.

I hadn't visited Findlay and Winston's flat. I knew where Findlay and Winston lived. Both addresses I'd been given for Findlay—from Hamlet and Jolie—were the same. I'd wanted to visit them, but other things had distracted me, and the police had told me they'd visited all of Shelagh's employees' homes. Still, I was curious.

It was as I was looking at both notes again that I remembered something. Hadn't Jacques mentioned to me that Findlay and Winston's flat was by Holyrood Palace? I was pretty sure he had. The identical address that Hamlet and Jolie had given me was nowhere near Holyrood. I was suddenly sure that's why my intuition was nagging me as Tom and I were walking into the police station, pulling my attention toward the palace.

I walked over to the light side, double-checking all the door locks behind me. The lights had been turned off, except for a small lamp on the back table Hamlet had left on. As I came to the bottom of the stairs on the light side, I glanced out the front windows and gasped.

I was living in a real-life snow globe again.

The snow was falling; big, fluffy flakes whispering their way down from the clouds. The Grassmarket lamps and the bustling crowd made me think that Dickens must have somehow seen this particular sight too.

"How in the world did I get here?" I said to myself as I walked toward the window. I could have watched it for hours, but I had other things to do.

I called Tom, but he didn't answer. I glanced up toward his pub, and though there wasn't a line out the door, it was obvious by the shadows from the window that there were lots of people inside.

I dialed Birk, Edwin, and then Elias, but none of my rides seemed to be answering. Everyone must be busy.

I wasn't going to knock on Findlay and Winston's door without someone else with me, but I still wanted to see it, have a quick look, make sure it really wasn't by Holyrood. I would look inside the bus, and then just ride back to the bookshop or home, depending on timing.

I texted Tom what I was doing, but there was no indication that he was able to read the text immediately. I texted Elias too, just to be safe.

I bundled up and stepped out into the snow-globe world. As luck would have it, it wasn't too cold. I was once again glad for my new boots, though.

The bus showed up a few minutes later. I boarded and checked my phone. No response from anyone yet.

Last year the snow had caused a disruption in cell-phone coverage, which had led to some further trouble. I didn't think that would be the case tonight, and I wasn't doing anything dangerous anyway, so I wasn't too worried.

The bus took a route toward Louis's house, not anywhere near Holyrood. The falling snow softened the building's sinister edges, but it still seemed run-down. Once we were farther into the neighborhood, it didn't appear so charming. I tried not to be judgmental, but the obvious signs of drug activity were there.

We traveled through the worst parts quickly and came out to an area on the other side that felt safer, if not completely safe.

Conveniently, the bus drew to a stop right outside the building where I presumed Findlay and Winston lived. Their flat number was 315. I looked out the bus's window, up to the third floor. Lights were on in the middle of three wide windows. Unless I climbed the stairs inside, I couldn't know if that was their flat. I looked up for a long moment, comfortably warm and confident that the bus would be heading back toward the bookshop any minute and that I'd seen what I'd come to see. If someone had been with me, I would have knocked on the door, but not now.

Then I saw something that changed everything. I gasped as I stood for a better view. There was a face in the building's third-floor window, and I was pretty sure it belonged to Shelagh O'Conner.

The bus started to pull away from the stop.

"Stop!" I yelled. "I mean, this is my stop. Sorry."

Thankfully, the bus driver braked again. I hurried down the aisle toward the door, catching the driver's impatient glance as I exited. Once I was off the bus, he closed the door and pulled away again. I reached into my pocket for my phone.

It wasn't there.

I checked other pockets. It wasn't in any of them. I'd just had it, hadn't I?

Of course I had. I'd been looking at it on the bus, waiting for someone to either call or text me back. In a flurry of panic when I'd seen the face, I must have dropped it, either on the seat or to the floor.

I looked in the direction the bus had gone. Its taillights were still in view, but there was no way I'd be able to catch it.

"Oh, no," I muttered. It was the understatement of all understatements.

I looked around. Just a street ago, there'd been people out and about—yes, some were homeless and some were dealing drugs, but I'd have asked anyone to borrow their phone for a minute.

But now everyone had disappeared, gone to seek shelter from the storm. I didn't see any pedestrians, nor pubs or restaurants. Only buildings made into apartments, flats. I could knock on doors and ask for help, or I could travel back a block to a pub. I was pretty sure I'd seen one a moment ago. And I was just a few streets away from Louis's house. I could try to run over the slushy sidewalks—I did have my new boots on.

I stepped sideways a bit and looked up at the window. It was still lit, but there were no faces in it anymore. No one standing there. Had I really seen what I thought I had?

I needed to call the police. Just one call to the police—999, that's all I needed to do. Okay, I'd walk a block or so in the direction I'd come from and make a call at the first phone I found. It would be fine. If I had seen Shelagh, it seemed she hadn't been in any huge distress. People used to function just fine without cell phones. I could figure this out.

I set out at the quickest pace I could manage given the weather. The snow was quiet now, drowned out by my breathing and the heartbeat in my ears.

I told myself to calm down. It was all going to be just fine.

But a moment later I knew it wasn't going to be fine. It was going to be something else entirely.

I'd been walking past a close, not giving it a second glance. Before I could register much of anything, a figure rushed out of it—I saw it out the corner of my eye—in a shabby coat and hat. I didn't get the chance to fully take in what this person looked like before a hand was over my mouth, an arm around my neck, from behind.

"Hush now," a harsh voice said in my ear. "If you make a noise, I will kill you."

My heartbeat got even louder in my ears, but I did exactly as the New Monster said. I stayed silent as I was snatched back into the close.

THIRTY-ONE

The Monster dragged me through the dark, narrow alleyway and then through the apartment building's back door. Along with the sensation of steel-strength arms around me, I thought I smelled horses.

"I'm taking you upstairs. You are going to be quiet. Do you understand?"

With one hand over my mouth and one around my neck, I still managed a nod. I willed my mind to clear, push away the fear so I could think of how to free myself. Maybe I could kick with my heel, use my elbow, something.

But I wasn't coordinated enough to do much of anything except keep my feet moving as I was pulled along. I should have let myself be killed before being dragged indoors. This sort of thing never ended well. But it was all going so fast. My thoughts couldn't quite catch up.

I held on to the idea that there was a chance I would find Shelagh and that since she'd seemed okay when I saw her in the window, I'd be okay too.

We climbed three flights of stairs, seeing no one. What

would have happened if we'd come upon someone? Would the Monster have hurt them?

I could hear and feel heavy breathing by the time we made it to the third floor, but the grip around me hadn't loosened. One of the Monster's hands reached into a coat pocket as the other remained over my mouth. If I angled my eyes, I could see a hand pull a set of keys from a pocket; they were hanging from a ring adorned with a macramé strip. I'd seen that macramé somewhere. Where? The stables! When Winston was locking the storage cabinet.

Had I not been distracted by trying to remember where I'd seen the key ring, I might have used the opportunity to try an escape maneuver. I told myself that I wouldn't miss another chance if it presented itself.

Was it Winston who had me? Was the seemingly quiet, mild-mannered horseman the New Monster?

Once the door was open, the Monster shoved me inside, sending me tumbling toward the back side of a couch that was facing the window I'd been watching.

There was a person sitting there—she turned and gasped when she saw me.

"Delancy?" Shelagh said as she reached over to me, her hand landing on my shoulder. "What's going on?"

I righted myself and took a couple of breaths; my body craved the deep pulls of oxygen. A few seconds later, I looked at Shelagh.

"You're not hurt?" I asked, my voice gravelly.

"I'm okay," she said, but her eyes told me she was afraid.

I gave my full attention to the Monster, who was removing a hat.

It wasn't Winston but someone else I'd seen in the stables, with the horses.

"Jacques?" I said.

"Not quite Jacques," Shelagh said.

I looked at her and then back at him. "Who are you?"

He only smirked.

"His name is Jack, not Jacques. Jack John and he's behind all of this, Delaney," Shelagh said.

"Shut up, Shelagh," Jack said, with no sign of a French accent and only a slight Scottish brogue.

"Related to Ritchie John?" I asked.

"His son," Shelagh said.

"Shut. Up. Shelagh," Jack said.

I'd been so interested in the fact that Darcy was Ritchie John's daughter, that Hamlet knew her, that I'd never thought about her having siblings.

"What do you want?" I asked him.

"He wants to ruin me, leave me penniless and on the streets, my reputation irreparable." Shelagh's words came out fast.

Jack's eyes simmered as they looked at Shelagh. I wondered if he might hurt her.

"I don't get it," I said, hopefully redirecting his violent thoughts. "What's going on?"

"Enough," Jack said. "Both of you stop talking. I need silence. Get over on the other side of the couch and sit down, Delaney. I told Shelagh I wouldn't tie her up if she cooperated. The same applies to you. I'm not going to hurt you, not unless you do something stupid. Do you understand? But I can tie you up, I *can* hurt you, don't think I won't."

I nodded as I stood. Adrenaline was coursing through me, keeping my frightened limbs from crumbling and sending me back to the ground.

"Give me your mobile," he said as he extended his hand.

"I left it on the bus." In a weird but involuntary gesture, I lifted my arms in the air, stick-'em-up style.

"Right." He sent me a wry frown.

"Truly. You can search me. I was looking up and was so surprised to see Shelagh in the window that I hurried off the bus. I dropped my phone somewhere."

"Yeah, you aren't good at sneaky. Peering up in the window, your red hair, those big curious eyes. If you'd just minded your own business or stayed on the bus . . ."

I bit back some reactive words. I also acknowledged to myself that he was correct. If I'd just stayed on the bus . . . I could have simply called the police, but when I'd seen what I thought was Shelagh's face, I felt I had to somehow stay close by.

Jack patted me down quickly and then took my backpack. He rifled through it, and when he was done he threw it on the small kitchen counter next to a square white sink.

It was an old but cozy place, comfortable, with a wide living space attached to a small kitchen. I assumed that bedrooms and the loo were down a hallway off the left side of the kitchen, but it was impossible to see down that way from the couch.

Though sparsely decorated, there *were* a few things that could be used as a weapon: lamps, a glass bowl.

"Just sit down. Both of you," Jack said, interrupting my visual inventory.

"I thought this was Findlay and Winston's place," I said, turning to Shelagh. "Are they in on this together?"

"I own this building," Shelagh said quietly as she looked at me. "Findlay and Winston used to live in this flat, but it's been empty for a while. Jack found that it was in my name. This is where he brought me."

"Shelagh, enough talking!" Jack said.

I was glad she hadn't been hurt. She seemed fine, if scared. There was that at least.

I had texted Tom and Elias. Eventually they would figure out where I was, and we'd be okay. Shelagh and I just needed to remain quiet until they arrived. Plus, the bus driver would know at which stop I'd disembarked, if he was asked. I'd made a small scene. In my mind I was ticking off all the good things; there were a lot of good things. We'd be found, if Jack didn't hurt or move us first.

A phone rang. Jack reached into his pocket and glanced at the screen. "Damn." He looked at us. "Don't make a sound or even think of going anywhere. I promise it will end badly."

Shelagh and I nodded.

"Allô," Jack said, the French accent returning as he answered the phone. "No, no, I'll be there soon. An hour or so—will that work? I understand. Of course you're welcome back. The horses need to be cared for. All right, see you then." He ended the call.

Shelagh and I looked at Jack as he bit his bottom lip, staring at his phone as if it were going to help him answer a burning question.

He regarded us sharply a moment later. "Don't move from that couch."

Jack turned and locked the door from the inside and then glared at us as he moved down the hallway off the kitchen. The second we heard a door shut from down there, I scooted closer to Shelagh.

"He will leave at some point." I whispered aloud.

"I think so."

"We'll get out of here," I said.

She shook her head. "We can't. We have to stay here. He

has people watching us from outside." She nodded toward the window and then the door. "The door is rigged. If we break it, it will set off a bomb and not only kill us but everyone else in the surrounding area. We have to stay right where we are."

I looked at her. I could hear noises coming from down the hallway, and I knew Jack would be back in a minute.

"No, Shelagh. Unless you've seen someone else, he's working alone. I promise. We'll get out of here. There's no bomb."

"You're wrong." Her eyes grew big.

I didn't know what was going on. Had she been convinced by words, threats he'd made? There was no doubt in my mind that there was no bomb on the door. As for people watching us—I didn't believe that either. I also didn't care. Let them watch us escape.

I told myself I'd take care of things once Jack was gone. I scooted back to my side of the couch just as he emerged from the hallway.

He looked at me. "You are being watched from out there. If you try to escape through the windows, you'll be killed. I'm going to lock the door and re-rig a bomb wired to the door. If you try to break it down, you'll explode the bomb and kill not only yourselves but lots of others too. Do you understand?"

"Absolutely," I said. "What do you want from us, Jack?"

"I'll tell you that when I'm good and ready."

I nodded but I'd heard the uncertainty in his voice, maybe even some fear. That was good, but I didn't want him to know I might have keyed in on some of his weaknesses, on the fact that his plan seemed unstable.

A moment later he was out the apartment door, locking it from the other side.

I scooted toward Shelagh again. "There's no bomb, Shelagh. I promise you. No one else is watching us. We can get out of here. We'll just give it a second or two so Jack's far enough from the area."

Her big eyes got bigger. "No! Delaney, we will die, and we will kill others."

She was speaking what she believed was the truth. I knew it would take hours, as well as a therapist or two, to convince her that her thoughts or imagination had been manipulated.

Or that's what I hoped. There was a tiny instant when I wondered if she was right. No. No, she couldn't be. I shook my head, pushing away the unwelcome intrusion of fear.

But we still needed to wait a few more seconds.

"I don't understand what's going on, Shelagh. Why is he doing this?"

"He took some money, a cashbox from an event at Birk's stables. He saw Louis there, thought maybe Louis saw him, so he'd planned to confront him. But when he learned that Louis worked for me, he came to me instead."

"To have you pay back the theft?"

"If it were only that simple. No, Delaney, once he learned who I was, about my past, and how much money I had, he began to blackmail me."

"Blackmail?"

"Aye, he threatened to become the Monster again, but do more harm—steal, maybe even murder."

"Which is what happened. He's the New Monster, right?"

She nodded. "I wouldn't play along. I thought he needed to be taught a lesson. I'd been planning the treasure hunt. I told him I would give him money, but he had to do it my way." Tears filled her eyes. "I should have just given him the money."

"When you didn't, he dressed as the Monster and robbed people. Did he kill Ritchie?"

Shelagh's eyes filled with tears. "Yes. His own father!"

"Why?"

Shelagh shook her head. "The best I can understand is that Jack has a sister who was at the event too. She told her father that she'd seen Jack take the money. Ritchie knew his son was up to something so he'd been following him. He followed him into Deacon Brodie's Tavern that day, inserted himself behind the bar. No one questioned him because he'd worked there before. Later, when Ritchie confronted his son about what he thought he was up to, told him to stop, Jack killed him."

"That's so horrible," I said. "Shelagh, the money was paid back the day after it was stolen."

"Oh, Delaney, it wasn't even about that, really. When Jack learned who I was it became about *my* money."

"Why did you get Birk and me involved?"

"I'd been working on the treasure hunt. I was going to invite you and Birk anyway. I couldn't go to the police—Jack had threatened that he would cause even more damage if I did, kill me or people I cared about. I needed help. I thought between the two of you you'd figure it out. Birk is so smart, and Brigid said you were smart too. I called him Jacques Underwood. Remember how I showed you the typewriter? The Underwood?"

"Yes."

"That was a clue. I wanted your help. I was going to tell you more, but the police came for me, and it got so much more complicated after that."

She was scared. She was old. She had a lively imagination, and perhaps she'd even been bored, but though she hadn't committed burglary or murder herself, she was responsible for everything that the New Monster had done. I wasn't going to tell her that, but if she'd only just told the police when they brought her in the first time . . . Still, Jack had killed his father—he was surely capable of killing again. She was terrified for her own life.

"Why did he bring you here?"

"I think he figured out I was trying to find another way to expose him. Truly, I don't think he has any idea what to do with me. I don't think he knows what to do with you either. Though he's clever and sly, I don't think he's thought through anything. He just wanted my money. I'd already come to the conclusion that he was going to have to kill me at some point. I don't know what he'll do now."

"Oh, Shelagh, this really isn't your fault," I said, feeling like it was a necessary lie.

"I'm afraid it is."

I wasn't going to be able to change her mind right now, and it was time to get going.

I stood. "Come on. We're getting out of here."

Shelagh grabbed my arm. "No! The bomb!"

I wrenched my arm out of her grasp. She was just going to have to be scared. I wasn't going to wait for Tom or Elias. I didn't want to risk one more moment with someone as unhinged as Jack.

I grabbed the brass lamp from the side table, ripped off the dingy white shade, and quickly unscrewed the bulb. I hurried to the door. There was a chance I could pick the lock if I wanted to spend the time trying, but I had another idea. Shelagh yelled at me to stop as I lifted the lamp. I didn't stop but swung it at the knob. It took two tries, but the knob finally fell clanking to the floor.

I dropped the lamp and used my finger in the now-exposed mechanism to undo the bolt. I opened the door and looked back at Shelagh. "No bomb."

She was still sitting on the couch, her eyes even wider and more scared now. Something was wrong. She hadn't gotten off the couch.

"What's wrong?"

"I hurt my ankle when he threw me into my secret room," she said. "I still can't walk well. Go, go get help."

There was no way I was leaving her there. I hurried to the couch and hoisted her to her feet.

"I can't walk," she repeated.

"Lean on me. We are getting out of here." Her arm went across my shoulder as I grabbed her around the waist and pulled her along.

It wasn't easy, and I could tell she was in pain, but we were getting out of that flat, even if I had to drag her the whole way.

THIRTY-TWO

"My ankle can't do this, Delaney," Shelagh said as we reached the top of the stairway.

No one seemed to have heard the destruction of the doorknob. At least no one was coming to our aid.

"Is anyone else in this building?"

"No, I own the whole thing, but I kicked everyone out a few months ago. I didn't think people were taking care of it. I might tend to overreact sometimes, Delaney."

Another understatement, but again I was going to leave that for a therapist to handle.

"Hop onto my back if you need to. We are out of here, Shelagh."

"I'll hang on tight." She gritted her teeth.

She stayed upright, though just barely. I sighed with relief when we reached the bottom of the stairs.

But I hadn't considered the other player. I should have. I hadn't even thought to ask Shelagh about the fourth member of our hunting group.

As we reached the bottom of the stairs, Tricia came through

the door that Jack had brought me through less than an hour earlier.

For an instant I was glad to see her, but then I realized I shouldn't be.

"Tricia?" I said, hoping the question in my voice would be answered with something positive.

It wasn't. In fact, just the opposite. She pulled a knife from her pocket and pointed it at us. It wasn't a big knife, but it wasn't a butter knife either. It could kill.

"Tricia and Jack are together, a couple," Shelagh said, her voice tired from the effort of making it down the stairs. She nodded upward. "I tried to tell you that you were wrong about no one else being involved."

"Get back up there. You didn't believe someone was watching, did you?" Tricia said.

Nope, sure didn't. But I didn't say that out loud.

I have found both freedom and safety in my madness; the freedom of loneliness and the safety from being understood, for those who understand us enslave something in us.

The bookish voice was from *The Madman* by Kahlil Gibran. I had no idea what it was trying to tell me, but no matter—it seemed appropriate. I didn't want to give up my freedom again.

"All right, all right, we'll go," Shelagh said as she started to pull backward.

I still held on to her tightly. The door was right behind Tricia. We were that close to our escape. I wasn't going upstairs again. I didn't want to get hurt and I didn't want to hurt Shelagh, but I wasn't going back up there.

With a speed that seemed both fast and in slow motion, I turned, let Shelagh fall the short distance to lean on the stair railing, and then kicked at the knife in Tricia's hand.

I hit my mark, and the knife went flying and then clattered to the floor. I kicked again, at Tricia's stomach, sending her to the floor too, in the other direction from the knife. I grabbed Shelagh and propelled us out the door. We still had to run out of that close, we had to get where Tricia wouldn't be able to hurt us—hopefully someone would help.

But the close was no longer empty. Two of the most beautiful people I'd ever seen were there; one was a huge man with lots of tattoos over his bare arms and the other was a skinny woman, more appropriately dressed with a winter coat but seemingly struggling with . . . everything.

We'd come upon a drug transaction. It was a most joyful moment.

"Help us," I said. "There's a woman with a knife coming after us."

The heavily tattooed man blinked, seemed to display some regret with his eyes, but then walked away from his customer and walked toward us.

"You okay?" he asked.

I nodded. "Can you call the police?"

"I'd rather not. Hang on a sec." He took a step around us just as Tricia burst out of the building, the knife in her hand again.

"Aye?" the man said as he reached into his back waistband and pulled out a bigger knife.

"Out of my way," Tricia said.

Tattooed man just chuckled once.

"Don't let her run," I said.

From behind I could see the tattooed man's shoulders rise and fall with a heavy sigh. Then, in the flash of an instant, his meaty fist came up and punched away Tricia's knife. A second later he had her hands zip-tied behind her back. Briefly I wondered where he'd gotten a zip tie, but I didn't really want to know.

"Good work, young man!" Shelagh cried.

"You're welcome." He rubbed his fist and then pulled a mobile from a back pocket, handing it to me. "Not my phone. Use this to call the police, then destroy it."

"I can do that." I took the phone and dialed—all kinds of numbers.

The tattooed man and his customer were gone in a flash, and after I'd called everyone, I did exactly as I was instructed: I destroyed the phone.

THIRTY-THREE

The police arrived quickly. Tom, Elias, and Aggie did too. Tom and Elias hadn't checked their phones for a while. They'd both missed my texts. They answered my calls now, though they hadn't recognized the number. I was glad everyone's intuition was back in working order. Tom might never let me out of his sight again.

A paramedic attended to Shelagh, who did have a sprained ankle—as she said, she'd received it the day Jack shoved her into her secret room in her library. Neither of them had had any idea that Edwin and I were at the front door. Jack had put her in the secret room and gagged her before he made the library look as if an abducation and assault had taken place inside it. He was going to call the police himself, but when he spied Edwin and me in the back, he had to redirect. He hit himself in his head and propelled himself out for us to "rescue."

Still, that part of his plan had mostly worked. It was after Tricia picked him up from the hospital that they went back to Shelagh's, finding her still gagged and tied in the room. They gave her water and some food before transporting her to the apartment.

The blood on the doorframe was fake blood, from a costume store. The police hadn't shared that with the public, but of course they'd figured it out quickly. I wished Inspector Winters had told me, but he couldn't share that much with a civilian, even one who'd become a friend. According to Shelagh, Jack was shocked that I'd neglected to tell the police about the secret room. He'd thought he was done for. But I *had* forgotten about it, and I might never forgive myself.

Findlay and Winston did now live over by Holyrood Palace. They'd been there a few months. Hamlet had come upon an old address; the same one where Jolie had thought her long-ago ex still lived. My gut was right about it being a little weird that Jack mentioned that the men lived over by Holyrood, but I couldn't have understood why my intuition was trying to get my attention.

Winston and Findlay had been nothing but sober and co-operative whenever they talked to the police, according to Inspector Winters. I wondered if the drinking issue I'd heard about was really a problem or just another figment of Shelagh's imagination.

We were in Inspector Winters's station now, all of us, in a common room big enough to hold a crowd but private enough to allow the police to question us without unwelcome ears listening. I'd never been in this part of the station, but I didn't point that out to anyone. I did wonder how much more there was to see.

Inspector Winters and I had already talked a long time; I was grateful that he tried to answer some of the questions I still had. After Jack and Tricia were arrested, officers had gone over to speak to Darcy. Yes, she'd seen what she thought was her brother taking money from the event at Birk's stables. Yes, she'd told her father—and clammed up when he and Mort had come upon her at the event. She was afraid they were about to ask her if her brother was a thief. The police were one hundred percent sure Darcy didn't know that her brother was the New Monster or the person who'd killed their father. Inspector Winters learned that it had been Darcy and Jack in Ritchie John's flat the day Mort overheard angry voices. Darcy was angry that Jack had caused their father to quit his job, and she wanted her brother to just return the money, but he told her he had other plans, that it was all going to be okay.

Jack had told his sister he was leaving town for a bit, told the police when they'd tracked him down on his phone that he wasn't in town. The police had known him as Jacques. They would have figured out eventually that they were the same man, but they hadn't yet.

When we'd witnessed Darcy embracing a man outside her Roost, the weather had been too much in our way for us to know it was Jack, having returned to take care of Darcy, or that's what he told her at the time. The betrayal she must have felt hurt my heart.

None of them had known the money had been returned. And no one was admitting to doing so. It was being assumed that Ritchie had done it, but that didn't ring so true to me. When Inspector Winters told me that part, I'd said, "If Ritchie returned the money, why would he still think Jack was up to something? Why would he follow him?"

Inspector Winters shrugged. "We will never know, I'm afraid."

I looked at Shelagh over my mug of hot chocolate. We were both wrapped in blankets and had been attended to with cocoa and cookies. Tom sat on one side of me, and Elias and Aggie were on the other, in between me and Shelagh.

"Shelagh," I said. "The next-to-last clue. The *Jekyll and*

Hyde that wasn't valuable. That came from The Cracked Spine, didn't it?"

"Aye, Delaney, it did." Shelagh smiled. "Louis bought it a few months ago. It was, in fact, that book that gave me the initial spark for the hunt. Before I thought about who to include, long before Jack and Tricia."

Shelagh was fine. My hair was wild and frizzy; I looked like the one who'd been held captive for several days. Shelagh's hair had been smoothed back at some point. Her sprained ankle was propped up on a chair as ice was being applied. Though her official statement had been taken, she continued to tell the story to anyone who wanted to hear it; many officers seemed interested.

Again, she began to explain what had happened, how Jack had first approached her. Tricia had joined him after Shelagh told him about the treasure hunt. Shelagh then put the hunt in motion quickly, inviting me and Birk before Jack and Tricia could do much more than go along with it. In a way, it was brilliant, in other ways it was stupid and poorly thought out on Shelagh's part.

Jack and Tricia had both been arrested only moments after I'd made the calls with the drug dealer's phone. No one had asked me about the phone I'd used. I was glad; I would never tell on Shelagh's and my unexpected angels.

Inspector Winters also told me that the only reason Tricia stopped by Tom's pub was because she thought we'd seen her with the Monster, and she just wanted us to think she happened to be in the area. In fact, we'd only seen the flap of a coat. She'd confessed to being with him near The Cracked Spine too, when I'd joined Birk in his car and thought I'd heard a growl. Apparently, Tom was correct, Jack and Tricia were following me, in a way, at least when they weren't with Shelagh.

Inspector Winters told me that Jack and Tricia were pretty sure I was either onto them or about to be. They were trying to divert my "nosiness." It almost worked because I'd almost played right into their hands.

Tricia wasn't a librarian anywhere, but she had gone to Firrhill High School. A quick call to the school would have exposed her lie, but I didn't even think about making such a call. I wondered why she didn't just come along with Birk and me on the hunt if she wanted to keep an eye on me, but she truly was spending a lot of her time watching Shelagh; maybe going with us wouldn't have fit with her other duties.

Her being the one to bring up Shelagh's past during the first meeting at Deacon Brodie's made much more sense now. She thought she was helping Jack set things up.

After he'd forced me into the flat, Jack had gone back to Shelagh's house to give Winston the keys. That key ring opened many doors in Shelagh's world, including all the cabinets inside the stable—cabinets that held grooming supplies, medications, even feed. Initially Jack had told Winston to take some time off, that he'd take care of the horses. It was just another way to try to take control of Shelagh's life, but taking care of horses is a lot of work, much more than Jack had bargained for. He was ready to give the duty and the keys back to Winston—thankfully, we'd had those moments to escape.

Of course, Jack and Tricia were in big trouble. Jack *had* murdered Ritchie, and that was by far the worst of their crimes. But they'd committed many other offenses too and had almost gotten away with them.

"What was Jack going to do with you?" Aggie asked Shelagh.

I didn't think Shelagh remembered Aggie yet, but I'd eventually remind her of their past if Aggie didn't.

"I don't know. I really don't think he *wanted* to hurt me, or Delaney—and he wouldn't have grabbed Delaney if she hadn't gotten off the bus. I think he was trying to figure out what to do next and I'm afraid his choices would have all led to more murder."

"As I think back to the first meeting in Deacon Brodie's pub, I realize I mistook your shared smile with Jack as loving, friendly. Now, with what I know, you were icy with each other," I said.

"He wasn't happy about the turn of events, and he thought I'd gotten his father there. I hadn't. I wasn't responsible for that part at all. Ritchie was there of his own accord, wanting to let his son know he knew he was up to something."

"Shelagh!" Louis came through the common room's doors. Brigid followed close behind.

Louis hurried to Shelagh, but Brigid stayed by the doorway. She nodded for me to join her.

No one seemed to notice or care that I stood and moved away from the crowd.

"You okay?" Brigid asked.

"I am. It's quite a story. I'll share it all with you." It was the least I could do.

"I think I know most of it by now, but thank you," she said doubtfully as she looked toward Shelagh and Louis.

"What?"

"Have you seen the picture from all those years ago? The one that got Shelagh in trouble?"

"No. Why?"

"Want to?"

"Of course."

She reached into her pocket.

As she retrieved a photocopy of the picture from her pocket, another piece of paper came out too and floated to the ground.

She handed me the copy of the picture, and then she reached to the ground for the other paper. She kept it folded, her attention on me as if waiting for a reaction.

I inspected the picture. It was much more disturbing than I could have imagined. Oliver McCabe's body was facedown in front of the museum. I would have recognized those stairs anywhere.

Surrounding him was a crowd of people.

"Is this Shelagh?" I pointed at a smallish woman in a shabby coat and hat.

"Aye."

"I can't see her face well, but she seems . . . shocked."

"Aye. Keep looking."

My eyes scanned the rest of the people in the crowd. At first I didn't see anything, but a second time over, I did.

Behind Shelagh a bit, hunched over with a dirty face and a terrifying expression was someone else I was pretty sure I recognized. He'd been bald even when he was younger.

"Louis?" I whispered to her.

"I can't get confirmation, but I'm working on it. Look at him. Look how he's dressed, the evil in his eyes."

I looked again. Everything she said was true.

Together we looked toward Shelagh and Louis. They were speaking to each other, holding each other's hands.

"You think he killed Ollie?" I said, thinking about the word Birk had used when he mentioned his conversation with Louis after Shelagh and he had broken up. *Vitriol.*

"I don't know, but I'm going to try to find out."

"Back then he worked for Shelagh's family but the connection might not have been made."

"Aye." Brigid opened the piece of paper that had fallen to the ground. "It's the potion he gave us at the museum."

I glanced at the paper, but there was more than the potion on the page, there were other words along the bottom.

"What else does it say?" I asked as Brigid read aloud.

" 'Though so profound a double-dealer, I was in no sense a hypocrite; both sides of me were in dead earnest; I was no more myself when I laid aside restraint and plunged in shame, than when I laboured, in the eye of the day, at the furtherance of knowledge or the relief of sorrow and suffering.' "

She looked at me. "What in the heck?"

"It's Dr. Jekyll," I said. "From his final statement in the story."

They were the words, via a bookish voice, that he'd spoken to me inside Louis's basement. I rubbed at the hair that had risen on my arm.

"Aye, it's creepy," Brigid said.

She had no idea.

"Come with me," I said.

Brigid followed me back to the crowd.

When there was a lull in all the conversations, I said, "Louis, you did see Jack take the money from Birk's event, didn't you? You're the one who returned it the next day."

At first he was going to deny it, but even he knew it was time to be honest; well, about most things.

"Aye, lass, it seemed like the right thing to do."

"Anonymously?" Inspector Winters interjected.

"Aye. At the time, I didn't know what trouble the lad would bring, couldn't have known what he would eventually do. I thought he must have needed the money. I didn't think much about it. Just slipped the money back into the office at the stables the next day. No one saw me."

"You are the best man on the planet," Shelagh said to him as she took his hand again. "The absolute best. You always save the day."

Both sides of me were in dead earnest.

I heard the good doctor's voice as clearly as if he really were in the room. I looked at Louis.

Maybe he was.

Shelagh turned to me. "You found the book?"

I pulled myself back to the moment. "Yes. Birk, Brigid, and I did. At The Banshee Labyrinth."

"It's quite the place, isn't it?"

"It is, and considering the legend associated with it, we should have probably tried there first," I said.

Shelagh shrugged. "You had to follow the clues."

As Shelagh turned back to Louis and everyone fell back into conversations, Elias moved in between me and Tom.

"Ye ken, people do forget that Jekyll and Hyde were the same person. It's my humble opinion that, ultimately, Hyde was just an excuse for Jekyll tae behave badly without any consequence. It wasnae two different creatures—it was one."

I looked at Louis, then lowered my voice to match Elias's. "Are you saying we aren't getting the full story?"

Elias thought a moment before he answered. "Lass, I dinnae think we will ever get the full story."

"Aye, ye have a point," Tom said.

"Yes."

Ritchie John's killer had been caught and arrested, Shelagh's ankle would heal. The New Monster was gone. Or so we all hoped. I agreed with Elias, that we never really knew everyone's full story. The best we could hope for was that all the monsters were gone for good, but that didn't mean we shouldn't stay aware.

We'd all be more careful now, at least for a little while. I looked at my husband and hoped with every fiber of my being there wasn't a Mr. Hyde in there somewhere. I was pretty sure there wasn't.

But what about me? Though I'd named the side of the bookshop with the warehouse the dark side because of the lighting, there was still a connotation there. No, we never did know the whole story, and bad usually did come right along with the good.

I squeezed Tom's hand again, and he squeezed back, smiling at me, his cobalt eyes telling me how much he loved me, how worried he'd been.

I leaned close to his ear and said, "Let's always be the Jekylls to each other's Hydes. Or something like that."

Tom smiled and winked. "Aye, lass, I'll drink to that."

We were going to be just fine.

ACKNOWLEDGMENTS

Many thanks to my agent, Jessica Faust, and my editor, Hannah O'Grady.

As always, thanks to my husband, Charlie, and my son, Tyler. Thanks too to Lauren—I'm so excited about the future.

I wanted to go back to Edinburgh to visit all the pubs I talk about in this story but it wasn't meant to be. Thankfully the internet was very helpful. Any mistakes I made are on me—but I still hope to go back again soon and see what I got wrong, and what I got right.

Take care, dear readers.